Josh leaned down to look into her eyes, searching for answers in those blue depths.

"I can't help you." She stared back at him, unblinking.

"We don't have to be on opposite sides here, Dr. Gannon." He leaned closer to her. He couldn't help it.

"I hope you're right about that," she said, lifting her chin.

Their lips were so close, it took almost nothing to brush his mouth against hers, to caress the softness of that full lower lip with his own. It was only a brush and only for a second, but fire raced through Josh's veins. He pulled back and searched her face. Her cheeks were flushed, her eyes wide. Her breath came in short pants, smelling of cinnamon. That one brief taste of her had been intoxicating, but he needed more. He leaned back in.

She stopped him with her hand on his chest.

More praise for

HOLD BACK THE DARK

"Eileen Carr blends smooth romance and fine observation with an intriguingly twisted plot for romantic suspense with a kick."

— Virginia Kantra, *New York Times* bestselling author of *Sea Fever*

"Fueled with a turbo-charged narrative drive, a strong plot, psychological complexity, and a sympathetic couple navigating their mutual attraction through troubled waters, Eileen Carr's *Hold Back the Dark* is a definite winner in the romantic thriller category. Carr is a writer to watch."

— John Lescroart, *New York Times* bestselling author of *Betrayal.*

"Gripping suspense, taut characterization, and a heart-pounder of a plot establish Eileen Carr as an unforgettable new voice in romantic suspense."

— Roxanne St. Claire, national bestselling author of *Now You Die*

EILEEN CARR

HOLD BACK THE DARK

POCKET BOOKS

NEW YORK LONDON TORONTO SYDNEY

Pocket Books
A Division of Simon & Schuster, Inc.
1230 Avenue of the Americas
New York, NY 10020

This book is a work of fiction. Names, characters, places, and incidents either are products of the author's imagination or are used fictitiously. Any resemblance to actual events or locales or persons, living or dead, is entirely coincidental.

Copyright © 2009 by Eileen Rendahl

First Pocket Books paperback edition March 2009

POCKET and colophon are registered trademarks of Simon & Schuster, Inc.

For information about special discounts for bulk purchases, please contact Simon & Schuster Special Sales at 1-800-456-6798 or business@simonandschuster.com

Designed by Julie Schroeder

Front cover, step back design, and montage by Boy Design.

Manufactured in the United States of America

10 9 8 7 6 5 4 3 2 1

ISBN-13: 978-1-4165-8794-1
ISBN-10: 1-4165-8794-2

To Carol.
For starting me on this path,
walking me through the middle,
and dancing with me
at the end.

ACKNOWLEDGMENTS

Thank you, first and foremost, to Carol, Andy, and Spring. Without you, I would not have had the courage to even begin this project, much less finish it.

Huge thanks to Carol Kirshnit for her endless patience while discussing my imaginary friends. Any details that I've gotten wrong are the result of my faulty understanding and not her excellent tutelage. Thank you to Sergeant Matt Young of the Sacramento Police Department for the fascinating tour, to Adam Weintraub for knowing the answer to every question I ask, to Antoinette O'Neill for her great eye for detail, and to Allison Brennan for her help and encouragement.

Last, but certainly not least, thank you to Pamela Ahearn and Micki Nuding for believing in me and in this book. You guys are the best.

CHAPTER
1

Phone calls at two a.m. were never good news. So when Aimee Gannon's cell phone rang, vibrating its way across the bedside table early Tuesday morning, she woke with a knot in her chest.

She'd been swimming at the edge of a nightmare, getting caught in its current and then fighting her way clear, never quite waking but not resting, either. It was almost a relief to be woken by the call. She groped for the phone as she struggled upright, then flipped the phone open. "This is Dr. Gannon."

"Dr. Gannon, this is Detective Josh Wolf of the Sacramento Police Department."

The *police*? "What can I do for you, Detective?" Aimee swung her feet over the side of the bed onto the cool wood floor. Why the hell were the cops calling her in the middle of the night? She stretched her shoulders, trying to unkink her neck and readying herself to find out who was in trouble and why.

"I think I have one of your patients in custody and I was hoping you could come help us with her. She's . . . uncooperative at present," the man said, his deep voice crackling over the cellular connection.

Uncooperative plus custody definitely equaled trouble. Janelle, maybe? She was an angry drunk, and altercations at bars often led to police custody. Or maybe Gary, her sex addict, had been picked up in a prostitution sting? Wait—the detective said "she." "Who are you talking about, Detective?" Aimee rubbed some of the sleep from her eyes.

"The girl's name is Taylor Dawkin," Wolf said.

Aimee sat upright. "Taylor? In custody?" Crap. Taylor had plenty of problems, but Aimee felt they were making progress. Big progress.

"Can you come?" Wolf asked, ignoring her question. "She's at Mercy General."

"Why is she at the hospital? Has she been hurt?" Aimee tucked the phone against her shoulder and grabbed a pair of jeans out of the dresser.

"I'd prefer to explain things in person," Wolf said, his staticky voice hard to read.

Shit. This guy was going to give her zero information. "Are her parents already there? Can I speak to them?" Taylor was only seventeen. Her relationship with Orrin and Stacey was everything ugly that a teenage girl's could be, but they would certainly be at the hospital with her.

There was a pause at the other end. "That's not an option at the moment. I can send a squad car for you. Someone could be there in ten minutes."

Aimee froze for a second. Not an option—what the hell did that mean? "Has Taylor done something? Is she under arrest?"

Another pause. "I'd really prefer to explain in person." Wolf's impatience was clear despite the bad connection. "Shall I have an officer pick you up?"

"I can get myself there, Detective," Aimee said curtly, fishing a tank top from a drawer. Impatience was a two-way street. "Give me thirty-five minutes." She snapped the phone shut.

The bright bathroom lights hurt her eyes when she snapped them on and their faint electronic hum made the muscles of her neck tense up. She pulled her hair back into a ponytail, quickly brushed her teeth, then threw a jean jacket on over her tank top and hoodie. It had been in the sixties that afternoon, but the night would be cool and the hospital would be freezing.

Aimee took a deep breath at her front door. She hated the anxiety that formed in the pit of her stomach at the thought of walking through the parking garage alone in the middle of the night, but Taylor needed her. *Push through it. You're bigger than the fear.*

She locked the condo and took the elevator down to the parking garage. Even wearing sneakers, her footsteps echoed in the deserted garage. The harsh lights cast stark shadows that seemed to leap out, and the low ceiling felt like it was pressing down on her. Checking behind her, she pressed the keyless entry and her Subaru gave a welcoming double beep. She got in and locked the door as fast as she could, then stopped and made herself breathe. The locked, secure garage was part of why she'd bought the condo after she and Danny had split up. She was safe here.

Still, as she drove up 18th Street to J and then headed east, she shivered as she drove past all the darkened houses. She reminded herself that her problems were much smaller than whatever had landed an already traumatized teenaged girl in the hospital with no one but the police looking after her.

Aimee pushed the gas pedal a little harder toward the floor.

Detective Josh Wolf closed his cell. The shrink didn't sound delighted at being woken up in the middle of the night, but at least she was coming. It was a straw to grasp at, and he didn't have much else. Who could have done this? And why?

He stared down at the two bodies that lay on the floor, hands duct-taped behind their backs and more duct tape covering their mouths. The back of the man's head had been bashed in, most likely with the blood-covered lamp lying next to him. The woman had clearly been strangled. He didn't know what had been used to choke the life out of the slightly overweight blonde with the gray roots; the murderer hadn't left that behind. A souvenir, or something incriminating? He ran his hand over his face. It was going to be a very long night.

Camera flashes strobed the living room, making it even more macabre as the crime scene technicians and photographers tried to find anything and everything that could possibly point to who had done this. The place was covered with fingerprints and blood. The driveway was a road map of tire tracks. An empty wine bottle had been smashed. A pile of cigarette butts was mounded in the bushes outside the front door, a puddle of vomit nearby. Footprints abounded. Sorting through and tracking down the possible leads could keep him and Elise busy for weeks. His best lead was the girl, and she was in no shape to lead anywhere.

"Nice place." Elise Jacobs, Josh's partner, looked around the large living room.

She was right. Even with the bottom falling out of California real estate, this place would be worth a pile of dough. Great neighborhood in the Pocket, the little U-shaped section of Sacramento that jutted out into the river from the west side of I-5. A well-tended half-Tudor on a big lot with a pool in back. The kitchen was all stainless steel and granite, and an entire family could live in one of the bathrooms. They didn't build places like this anymore. Josh had a cousin who was a contractor, and he knew this place must have cost a mint.

"Call me crazy, but I'm not sure I like what they've done with the place." Josh gave Elise a wry smile. Not many other people appreciated his gallows humor.

"I know what you mean," she replied and they both turned to look at the smears of blood covering the living room walls. "Someone spent some time on that, but it is *so* not a good thing."

"True that," Josh replied. A series of geometric figures covered the walls, the same pattern again and again: a long, low rectangle divided in three, a circle, then another long, low rectangle divided in three.

"Any idea what it means?" Elise stepped closer on her plastic-covered feet.

"Not a damn clue." Josh moved up to peer more closely at the blood-smeared walls. Was it a message? From the killer? It wouldn't be the first time that a killer had left messages to taunt the police. Josh had seen *Zodiac*, and that was based on a real case and one pretty close to home.

Elise shook her head and turned away from the wall as if to dismiss it from her mind. "They figure out what to do with the girl yet?"

"They've got her at the ER at Mercy with a guard. They already had two gunshot wounds at the ER at UC-Davis, and she didn't need a level one trauma center. At least I didn't think so. Hard to tell."

Until they figured out whether the girl they'd found covered with blood, mumbling incoherently, and rocking herself violently needed a victim's advocate or a lawyer. Or both.

"I called the shrink," Josh said.

"Good." Elise nodded. "Sometimes it's easier to get what we need with honey than vinegar."

Josh squatted next to the bodies, killed where they lay. The way the blood had pooled beneath them when their hearts stopped circulating it and the spatter of blood and brain matter on the carpet and furniture and walls told him that. Whoever had done this would be none too clean, either. There was no way you could bash a man's brain in that way and not end up getting some on you. Was someone wandering around Sacramento right now with another man's blood on his clothes?

Josh stood. "Meanwhile, whoever did this is getting a little extra time to clean up."

Elise held up her hands. "The shrink's worth a try and we need to try something. By the way, no forced entry at any of the doors and windows. Whoever did this waltzed right in." She sighed, looking around at the crime scene.

Josh looked, too. It was littered with potential evidence. The problem was going to be figuring out what was evidence and what was only the detritus of an ordinary family leading their ordinary lives until someone interrupted them with unthinkable violence.

Unless that someone already lived here or had invited whoever had done it in. Then it was going to be even harder to figure it out what was what.

Hence the phone call to the shrink.

Josh had been half-ready to shake some sense into the girl, but Elise had suggested that contacting the shrink might be the kinder, gentler way of getting what he wanted, and wouldn't that be nice for a change?

He was willing to try anything to get the girl to talk to them. It was hard to figure out what to do until he knew if the girl, covered in blood at the scene of her parents' murder, was another victim, a witness, or his prime suspect.

"The girl wouldn't have had to force entry," he said. "She lives here. She had a key."

Elise smoothed her hair back into her already smooth ponytail. "I'd like to think a child could never do this to its parents."

"We both know better." Their eyes met. They did indeed know better. He wished they didn't. Josh didn't know if it made him feel better or worse to see the same hopeless hardening in Elise's eyes that he knew was in his own.

"It seems awfully brutal, though," Elise observed.

"She's not that big. I doubt she's much over five foot four and she's pretty scrawny. Hard to believe she could get them bound up like that, bash her father's head in, and choke her mother. It would take someone big, someone strong."

"Or someone armed. Or she could have let someone else in to do the dirty work. Whoever did it didn't feel bad about it." The murderer had left them splayed on the floor like discarded rag dolls. Killers hit with remorse made attempts to cover the bodies or arrange them in a way that wouldn't embarrass them. This murderer had dropped them like pieces of garbage when he or she was done with them.

"No sign of restitution attempts; you're right." Elise nodded. "Don't you think a daughter would feel bad?"

"Maybe. Maybe not." Josh shrugged. "No telling what's going on inside with that one."

That was an understatement. The girl had just sat there and rocked herself, making little whimpering noises. She didn't respond to anyone except to try to slap away the paramedics when they were putting her on the gurney.

Josh glanced at his watch. "The shrink should be at Mercy in about thirty minutes. We should leave here in fifteen to beat her there."

"It'll be good to know what she was seeing the kid for." Elise tapped her pen against her pad.

Absolutely—it could be a place to start to build his case. That and the fact that she was found covered with blood at the murder scene. Josh shook his head. Did a brutal double homicide become okay if the murderer had a rotten childhood?

Not in his book. No way.

"I found the roll of duct tape," said one of the techs, a young Latino with a pierced eyebrow. "Over this way."

The detectives followed the tech down the hallway to a craft room. A sewing machine with a swatch of fabric still pinned by the machine's foot stood in the corner. A basket of yarn with knitting needles sat by a recliner. Shit. Had Stacey Dawkin been fucking knitting when someone came in and murdered her? Josh's mother knitted.

A small TV mounted on the wall was still on. Loud. "Make a note of the channel and the volume and turn that crap off."

A roll of duct tape sat on the credenza next to the chair. "Bag it and tag it," Josh told the tech. Elise shot him a look. "Please," he added.

There was no mark on the credenza from where the tape had sat. "It hasn't been there long," Elise observed.

"Check this out," the tech said. "These marks in the carpet."

Starting a few feet from the chair, there were long indentations in the carpet. "Drag marks?" Josh asked.

"Not long enough," said the tech.

"We should go," Elise said, glancing at her watch.

Josh nodded and they headed out. As they passed the brutally murdered bodies of the Dawkins, he took in once more the brutality of what had been done to them and let the outrage rise up in his chest.

Outside, the glare of TV camera lights engulfed them. Beyond the circle of their glare, Josh saw a small crowd of neighbors in bathrobes and sweatshirts, probably curious and frightened. He didn't have time to reassure them now. He wasn't even sure if he could. He took a deep breath of the cool night air and tried to clear his head, girding himself for the long night to come.

Mercy General blazed like a beacon among the bungalows and mock colonials that made up the rest of the neighborhood. Aimee parked as close as she could and jogged up to the entrance, willing the automatic doors to open faster.

The lobby was half full. A young Latina with dark circles under her eyes and smeared makeup sat in one of the cheap padded chairs and rocked a toddler sprawled in her arms. A skinny white girl with spiked bleached blond hair and tattoos that she'd regret before she turned forty clutched her stomach. A scared-looking middle-aged woman whose hair had been dyed way too many times pretended to read a six-month-old issue of *People* over in the corner. The small room behind the glass window marked TRIAGE was empty. Aimee pressed the button for service and waited.

A stocky woman in scrubs with short, bristling reddish hair and a stethoscope around her neck bustled into the room. She looked Aimee up and down, clearly searching for an injury. "Can I help you?"

"I'm looking for Taylor Dawkin," Aimee said into the round metal grate on the window.

The woman's face slammed shut. "I'll send someone out," she said and turned on her squeaky rubber-soled heel.

Aimee closed her eyes, let her head fall back, and shrugged her shoulders, trying to release the tension that knotted them.

"Dr. Gannon?" the deep voice she recognized from the telephone said.

She opened her eyes. "Yes."

Talk about tall, dark, and armed. He had to lean down to speak into the microphone in the triage room, braced on muscled forearms visible under the rolled-up cuffs of the shirt. His tie hung askew across his broad chest. His dark hair was a little too long; it curled a bit over the collar of his faded blue shirt and fell forward over his forehead. Everything from his broad shoulders down screamed *man*.

Something completely female in Aimee fluttered in response, even as she checked out the gun and badge on his belt.

His gaze traveled up and down, assessing her with deep brown eyes, intense and unblinking. Aimee stared right back. He'd need more than Intimidation 101 to make her step back.

"I'm Detective Wolf." He hit the buzzer to unlock the door. "Thank you for coming," he said, extending his hand but keeping his hip cocked back. His gun hip, Aimee realized. Lord save her from big men with guns.

"May I see Taylor?" Aimee asked. His palm was hard and dry, his handshake businesslike and strong.

"Sure." He turned and walked out of the little room, leaving Aimee to follow.

They walked past the chaos of the nurses' station and a series of curtained enclosures. All around, Aimee heard moans and sobs, gasps and whispered reassurances. Even on a Tuesday night, the ER was brutal emotional territory. She drew her denim jacket tighter around herself.

At the end of the hall a uniformed officer sat on a plastic and metal chair, chatting with a woman wearing a dark navy suit and white lace shell. Her skin was the color of a New Orleans café au lait and her dark, curling hair was pulled into a ponytail at the nape of her neck. "You the doc?" she asked as they approached.

Aimee smiled. "Licensed clinical psychologist. I'm the Ph.D. kind of doc, not the M.D. kind."

"Good enough for me. Plenty of the M.D. kind around here and they haven't made much progress." The woman held out her hand. "Elise Jacobs. I'm Detective Wolf's partner."

Aimee shook her hand. "Is Taylor okay?" she asked. "Is she in trouble? Did she do something?"

"We're still trying to figure that out ourselves." Wolf pushed aside the curtain. "She's in here."

Taylor Dawkin sat curled up on the floor in a corner. Her left wrist was handcuffed to the gurney, her arm twisted up above her head while the other wrapped around her knees. She had curled herself into a ball and was soundlessly rocking herself, eyes squeezed tight shut. Her arms and legs were scored with deep, sharp cuts that still oozed through the glistening antibiotic ointment. Her fingers were black with ink.

A cry escaped Aimee's lips and she started toward the girl, but the world spun around her. She put her hands out to steady herself, but there was nothing to grab. She felt a hand at the small of her back, steadying her. She registered its strength and size and warmth and leaned into it. The heat of it traveled through her entire body. Then she realized the hand belonged to Wolf. She took a deep breath and tried to still the racing of her heart as she pulled away. "What happened to her?" she whispered.

"We're trying to figure that out," Detective Wolf said from behind her. "She's not talking to us. She's not talking to anyone."

"She's not talking, period," Elise said, coming to stand next to Aimee.

"Where did you find her?" Aimee turned to look at the detectives.

"At home." Wolf's brown eyes watched her face, his gaze impossible to read.

"Home? Like this? Did someone break in?" Aimee turned back to look at Taylor and her gut clenched. Taylor had been cutting herself, but nothing remotely like this. The tentative cuts had been more for show than destruction. Aimee had interpreted them as a cry for help, an outward sign of the pain that the girl was feeling inside. This looked like Taylor had crashed through a plate glass window going ninety miles an hour.

"We don't know yet," Wolf replied.

"What about her parents? Were they attacked as well? Who did this to them?" Aimee's mind raced through horrid possibilities.

Detective Wolf tilted his head at the uniformed officer in a silent command. The officer immediately stood and Wolf offered the chair to Aimee. "I think you'd better sit down to hear the rest of this."

Aimee looked from one shuttered face to the other. She didn't want to sit. She wanted to shake someone; she wanted to scream. But Taylor needed her, and to help Taylor, Aimee needed information. She sat, ready to spring up. "Please tell me what's happening."

Detective Wolf grabbed a chair from the other side of the hallway, turned it around, and straddled it. "We received a nine-one-one call from the Dawkin home at approximately ten thirty-five tonight. The father of one of Taylor's friends had become concerned. Taylor had walked home from the Norchesters' house after studying for a test with their daughter, and was supposed to call to let them know she'd arrived safely. When they didn't hear from her and no one answered the Dawkins' phone, Mr. Norchester drove there and found Taylor much as you see her now—sitting between her parents' corpses."

CHAPTER
2

The shrink's face went white. Her eyes looked huge in her face, wide and staring.

Her low, mellow voice on the phone had led him to expect someone older than the teenybopper outfit and the ponytail indicated. The harsh fluorescent lights showed the start of lines around her eyes, but hospital lights made newborns look wrinkly. Her eyes were startlingly blue in the frame of her dark hair, highly visible even behind the narrow black-framed glasses. The pull he felt low in his gut was totally unexpected; he hadn't felt that in quite a while—not since Holly.

Elise tapped the back of his chair with her foot and Josh realized he'd been staring. He cleared his throat. "Taylor won't speak to us. She's covered with cuts, but it looks like she might have inflicted those herself. There was a lot of broken glass at the scene. We can't tell if someone's tried to hurt her, or . . ."

"Or what, Detective Wolf?" Dr. Gannon clasped her ringless hands in front of her. She looked calm, but Josh could see her fingers trembling.

"Or if she might have done some of the hurting herself," Elise said behind him.

The comment was well put. They weren't sure if Taylor had inflicted those cuts on herself, nor were they certain whether or not she had had something to do with killing her parents. Elise's words left the question of whose wounds they were discussing ambiguous. How the shrink interpreted Elise's remark could be just as informative as the answer itself.

Gannon took a deep breath, then rubbed her forehead. "Taylor has never been violent toward anyone. Her problems run more toward self-destructive behavior, but nothing anywhere near this level." Gannon glanced over her shoulder into the curtained cubicle again. "Nowhere near," she murmured.

So she could have made those cuts on herself. It wasn't exactly a Sherlock Holmes–worthy deduction, what with the bloody broken glass that had littered the floor around her. The question in Josh's mind was what kind of response that was to her parents' murder. Guilt? Or had shock and grief made her attack herself? Violence touched different people in different ways.

Or was it something else? Something that he couldn't possibly guess without help from someone who knew Taylor inside and out? Like her therapist.

If Taylor had stumbled on that scene, lost it, and needed help, he wanted her to get that help, and fast.

"How was Taylor's relationship with her parents?" Josh asked.

Gannon sighed. "What seventeen-year-old girl gets along with her parents? It's a difficult age. I certainly didn't get along with my parents when I was seventeen, did you, Detective?" Her hands dropped back in her lap and the trembling lessened.

"So no more anger than a typical adolescent might

have?" Elise asked. That honey-sweet voice and serene face fooled a lot of people into not noticing the razor-sharp mind beneath.

Gannon's brow furrowed. "I wouldn't say that, either. In fact, I'm not quite sure what I can and can't say. There are confidentiality issues here."

"There's also a double homicide here," Elise said icily. "Two people are dead. Murdered in their own home."

"I realize that as well." Gannon's voice shook a bit and Josh thought he saw more there than shock. What precisely was Aimee Gannon afraid of? "And I want to help. There's an aunt in Redding who's close with Taylor. I'm not sure if she's the legal guardian now, but there's a good chance she is. If we could contact her and get permission to release my files . . ."

Wolf flipped open his notebook and scanned through his notes. "Marian Phillips? Of 2752 Hummingbird Lane?"

"Quite possibly," Gannon said. "I can check my files."

"Not necessary," he answered. "We've already called. She'll be here in the morning."

Gannon nodded and twisted her hands in front of her again. "All right, then. Contact me when she gets here and we can talk more about why I was seeing Taylor." She hesitated. "May I to speak to Taylor?"

Josh exchanged a look with Elise, who gave an imperceptible nod. If she could get the girl to do something besides make little animal noises, maybe they could get some information out of her. It was entirely possible that this girl held the key to the case. If she hadn't done it, she may well have seen something that could break the thing wide open. "Of course, be my guest."

The uniformed officer pulled the curtain aside again and Gannon stepped through.

"Taylor," she said, her low voice quiet. "Taylor, it's me, Dr. Gannon."

If Taylor heard her, she gave no sign. She continued rocking and making the whimpering noises she'd been making since she'd been found.

Gannon knelt beside the girl, placing her hand lightly on her back. "Taylor, it's all right. You're safe now," she murmured.

Taylor rocked faster.

"No one here is going to hurt you," Gannon said.

Taylor kept rocking.

"Can you tell me what happened? What happened to your parents? To you, Taylor? Can you tell me what happened to you?" Gannon's voice was nearly a whisper, as if her throat had constricted.

Taylor didn't even look at her.

Gannon turned the force of her blue eyes onto Josh, who now leaned against the counter that ran along the side of the cubicle, arms folded across his chest, legs crossed at the ankle in front of him. Fatigue dragged at him like cement boots. He'd been on duty for eighteen hours, and everything that happened in these first few hours of the investigation was crucial. Mess up now, and he could find himself in the kind of quagmire that never got fully resolved and would leave a stain on his record.

He'd push through it. It wasn't like he hadn't done it before.

People expected homicides to be cleared up fast. People especially expected to have homicides involving upstanding citizens who were knitting in their homes when they were bound and strangled to be cleared up lightning fast.

"She's in shock," Gannon said.

"Really," Wolf said. Did she think he was an idiot? He was hoping for some way to bring Taylor out of shock that didn't involve a slap across the face. "I'd never have guessed."

Gannon's eyes narrowed and her lips pursed. "Do you have a plan to deal with that?"

She was cute when she was mad, especially with those hot librarian glasses. Not that he was noticing or anything. "Calling you pretty much *was* my plan."

She sighed and sat back on her heels, her hand never leaving Taylor's back. "She's freezing. She needs a blanket and someplace to sit besides the floor."

"She wouldn't stay on the gurney," Smitty, the uniformed cop, volunteered. "She kept climbing down onto the floor. After a while, I figured it was easier to let her stay there."

Gannon's head turned toward him with a laser-beam stare. "Easier for whom?"

Smitty blushed.

"And why is she handcuffed?" Gannon's voice rose a bit.

Smitty glanced over at Josh, and Gannon's gaze

followed. Josh felt that tug in the pit of his belly again.

"Because we didn't—don't—know what we're dealing with here," he said.

"Meaning what?" Gannon asked, rising to a standing position.

"Meaning that I don't know if Taylor had something to do with her parents' murder or not." Josh shoved himself off the counter to stand up straight.

"Is Taylor a suspect?" Gannon's feet were spread, her hands fisted on her hips. Her eyes narrowed into slits.

He liked that she challenged him about it. He also liked that she was almost tall enough to look him in the eye. "Yes, as far as I'm concerned, she's still a suspect here, Dr. Gannon. She's lucky I'm not putting her under arrest and sending her over to the correctional medical facility."

"Taylor didn't do this. She couldn't have." Her chin jutted out.

"Can you alibi her? You have something that proves she didn't do it?" If the shrink knew something more solid than namby-pamby feelings, he needed to know it now.

The blue eyes shuttered closed. "No," she said on an exhale. "No. I don't have anything like that." Her head dropped.

Josh felt disappointed, and he wasn't sure if it was because she didn't have any info to further his case or if it was because he wasn't looking into the deep blue lakes of her eyes anymore.

"Could we at least uncuff her and get her some more blankets?" Gannon's head rose back, challenge in her voice.

"Sure." He was willing to give a little, especially if it might get him something. He glanced over at Smitty, who came over and uncuffed Taylor's arm. The girl wrapped the freed arm tightly around her knees and rocked a little faster.

"I'll see about more blankets," Elise said, heading down the hall toward the nurses' station. Most of the staff were too busy for requests for things like blankets.

"Where will you keep Taylor until her aunt gets here?" Gannon asked.

Josh held aside the curtain and motioned with his head for her to follow him. Once they were outside, he said, "Right here. Her wounds aren't deep enough to admit her, according to the doc. We're lucky they'll let us have this space. She won't be alone. We'll keep a guard on her."

There was no pysch ward at Mercy. He looked around the understaffed ER. Keeping her here on the floors would mean restraining her physically or chemically. Gannon was probably more aware of that than him.

"Here?" Gannon didn't sound pleased.

"You got another suggestion? I could 5150 her, but then she'd be in the system for days. Juvie doesn't seem like the place for her right now, either."

The doctor's hands unclenched and she nodded thoughtfully. "This way the aunt can get her out of here tomorrow. I suppose it's the best we can do for now. I'm not crazy about it, though." She pulled her jacket closed and rubbed at her arms as if to warm herself.

Elise returned with two thin blankets. "This is the best I could do."

Gannon took the blankets from Elise. "Thanks. I'd like to wait with Taylor until she's more settled."

"Of course. Any idea what could have made her act like this?" Josh asked.

"I'm guessing that finding your parents' murdered bodies would send anyone into shock," Gannon answered. Sarcasm tinged her reply.

"Sure. Being in that house upset *me* tonight, and I'm used to it. But shocked into being totally nonverbal? Not so much." He crossed his arms across his chest. "Anything I should know about this girl?"

The blue eyes narrowed for a moment as if she was considering, then she took a deep breath. "I'd prefer to wait until the aunt gets here and gives me formal permission to discuss Taylor's case with you."

Damn, he'd thought he had her on his side. Maybe he could still eke a little more information from the good doctor. "The first twenty-four to forty-eight hours of a case are crucial. If there's information that could lead to arresting her parents' killer and I don't have it when I need it, I doubt anyone's going to congratulate you on what a great job you did of protecting client confidentiality by withholding information from the police."

She bit her lip, and Josh could see the indecision on her face. Then she took a deep breath and said, "Taylor's parents brought her to me because her behavior changed about six months ago. She'd started cutting herself, although nothing like what I saw tonight. Her grades had dropped. She'd become uncommunicative. We've been getting closer in our therapy to her revealing what had happened to start all this, but we haven't gotten there yet. I suspect it was something quite traumatic, something that she's been repressing. Being close to remembering something like that puts a person in a very emotionally fragile state. And finding your parents dead on your living room floor would affect a fragile person more than one who was emotionally stronger."

"What kind of traumatic event?" Josh pressed.

Gannon bit her lip and leaned toward him. He caught the floral scent of her shampoo and swallowed hard. She straightened again and shook her head. "I don't know anything for sure."

Josh leaned forward. "But you suspect something?"

"Nothing definitive."

Josh uncrossed his arms, his face impassive. "That's all you're willing to say?"

She massaged the wrinkle that had formed between her brows, and Josh's pulse quickened. He was wearing her down. Screw waiting for the aunt. He wanted whatever information Dr. Gannon had *now*.

Then his cell phone buzzed in his pocket. He sighed and pulled it out. Miss one step in these delicate dances of negotiation, and you never got back in the rhythm. He flipped the phone open. "Wolf here."

"We've got some preliminary fingerprint information you'll want to see," Clyde said on the other end. "And the PIO wants to see you and Jacobs pronto. All the morning news shows are going to lead with this thing. He needs to know what you've got."

"We'll be there in twenty." He snapped the phone shut, then looked at the shrink. "Detective Jacobs and I are going to have to leave."

Aimee settled Taylor as comfortably as she could on the bed with a few blankets tucked around her. Her skin was no longer ice cold to the touch and the rocking had almost stopped. She lay on the thin mattress and stared at the wall, her dyed black hair limp against the hospital pillow. The room smelled like antiseptic. Not exactly where Aimee wanted to see her traumatized patient warehoused for the rest of the night. She wanted to wrap her in soft quilts and make her feel safe again, but neither was remotely possible at the moment.

The police would never let her take Taylor home with her, even if she dared to do it. She continued patting Taylor's back, one of the few places not covered with scores of cuts. How much pain had she endured? How much pain was it masking? And was there anything Aimee could do to make it stop?

For months, they'd been circling the issue that had sent Taylor into the self-mutilating, substance-abusing tailspin that had prompted the Dawkins to bring her to Aimee. In the past few sessions Aimee had become convinced that they were about to come in for a very bumpy landing, but a landing that could be the beginning of the healing for Taylor.

Aimee couldn't begin to imagine how far back Taylor's therapy had just been set. As if any of that mattered now.

Hot tears filled her eyes. Her relationship with Orrin and Stacey had been strictly professional, especially with Orrin, who had always struck her as chilly and distant. Still, they were gone, irrevocably and completely erased from the world. It wasn't right. How could this have happened? And now that it had, what would happen to Taylor?

Josh made sure Smitty was stationed outside Taylor's bay with orders to call if the girl started to talk, and headed out of the hospital with Elise. He was relieved that there were no TV crews waiting for a glimpse of Taylor or to ambush Elise and him with questions, but he knew that wouldn't last long. There'd already been at least two crews at the Dawkin house. Two upright citizens killed in their nice house in the Pocket? Blood smeared on the walls? A catatonic teenager? The news crews would be on this like white on rice and twice as sticky. He probably should have warned Dr. Gannon about it. Speaking of which . . .

"What's your take on the shrink?" Josh asked. Elise had great instincts; he'd learned to trust her judgment of people long ago.

"Mmm mmm mmm," Elise cooed as they reached the parking lot. "She's a looker, all right. I'd sure like to have that swing in my backyard."

Josh snorted. "Don't try to talk girls with me, Jacobs. Where'd you hear that, anyway? A construction site?"

She laughed. "Just tryin' to be a full-service partner, big guy. She is most definitely your type, right down to those 'Hot for Teacher' glasses."

"I don't have a type." Those quiet, smart ones weren't his style at all. Holly hadn't been anything like that, except for the graduate student thing.

"And I'm Paris Hilton," Elise said, unlocking their sedan and getting behind the wheel.

Josh snorted again as he got in. "Not unless Paris gets one heck of a tan."

"Disparaging remarks about my ethnic background? I'm wounded!"

Josh looked at his watch—almost four a.m. "Well, Paris, don't you think you should be getting back to your penthouse suite?"

"As soon as Clyde gives us the down-low on whatever he's found." She headed toward Broadway.

"You want me to talk to the PIO?" The public information officer would need the basics to give to the press soon, and Josh didn't mind talking to Mark Elder. The guy was ambitious, but he wasn't an ass.

"Okay by me," Elise said.

Josh's eyes were starting to droop by the time they turned into the parking lot for the coroner's office and forensic lab sandwiched between the DMV and the UC-Davis Med Center's Broadway building. They walked past the metal sculpture that Josh always thought looked like an elongated surfboard stuck into a rock, and buzzed to be let in.

Clyde was waiting for them on the second floor, practically dancing from foot to foot.

"Calm down, buddy," Elise said, dropping into a chair. "You don't want to burst something."

"You'll never guess!" the lab tech said. "You won't believe it."

Josh leaned against a desk. "We won't bother trying, then. What's up?"

"All that stuff on the walls? All those rectangles and circles?" Clyde looked from one to the other. "The girl did it. She painted that wall with her own blood."

CHAPTER
3

D awn began to streak the sky as Aimee drove down the alley behind her building and pulled up to the grated gate on her garage. She pressed the button and let her head fall back against the seat while the gate creaked its way upward. Exhaustion was catching up with her.

She pulled through the gate, parked in her assigned slot, and took the key from the ignition, her movements slow, like someone moving underwater. She felt as if she were drowning, this nightmare of a night dragging her down.

Aimee locked the car and went to the elevator, her hand never far from the canister of pepper spray in her purse. Her thoughts whirled back to the first time she'd met the Dawkins. Stacey's fear and revulsion about her daughter's behavior had been clear.

"She's cutting herself with a razor blade," Mrs. Dawkin had said, her voice trembling, looking almost nauseated. "On purpose."

"Deep cuts?" Aimee had asked. She needed to differentiate between the kind of cutting that signified a failed suicide attempt and the shallower cutting that seemed nearly pandemic among teenage girls these days.

"Not deep. Just enough to make herself bleed.

Please, Dr. Gannon, tell me why my baby is hurting herself this way," Mrs. Dawkin had pleaded with her.

If only it were that simple.

If only half the time, the parents didn't already have all the information they needed to understand why their baby was hurting herself.

Was there even more to it than Aimee had thought? Had Stacey Dawkin known more than Aimee realized? Had that gotten her killed?

The elevator doors slid open and with a quick glance to make sure the car was empty, Aimee stepped inside. She pushed the button for the third floor and leaned against the wall while the elevator rose.

Besides cutting, Taylor had been experimenting with alcohol and marijuana, skipping class, and generally isolating herself from the friends she had treasured only a few months before, hanging with a new crowd that wasn't a stellar influence. Actually, everything had started to fall apart for Taylor.

At first Taylor's parents had thought that it was just a phase, something Taylor would grow out of, like Pretty Ponies and the Backstreet Boys. Then Stacey had walked in on her daughter in the bathroom, seen the cuts on Taylor's thighs and breasts, and panicked.

Orrin Dawkin had been concerned but had remained calm, possibly even a little bit detached. It was hard for some fathers to stay connected with their teenaged daughters. All those hormones, all that burgeoning sexuality. It changed everything.

The elevator doors opened and Aimee glanced up and down the hallway as she stepped out. Empty. No surprise there, at five-thirty in the morning. She walked to her apartment, where she clicked the lock shut behind her and put on the security chain. Her tight shoulders and neck relaxed and she sagged against the door, glad to be back safe in her cocoon.

It would be pointless to go back to bed now. She wouldn't sleep, even though she was exhausted. She set her keys on the table by the door and headed to the kitchen. Acid churned in her stomach, and the thought of coffee made her a little queasy. Toast, she decided. A little comfort food. One of her clients, a middle-aged woman coping with the stresses of being trapped in the sandwich generation with elderly parents and dependent children, had described eating more than a dozen English muffins at one sitting as a way to deal with having to take her mother to the cancer center one more time. She'd talked about melted butter the way Aimee had heard junkies talk about heroin.

Aimee didn't get a butter-high, but the toast did help settle her stomach. She put the coffee on.

A knock at the door made her jump. She looked through the peephole. Damn, she'd forgotten to call Simone. There was no way she was going running this morning.

Aimee undid the chain and the deadbolt and let her friend in.

"You're not dressed," Simone said, clearly dismayed. She had on running tights and a tank top and was bouncing on the toes of her running shoes. "Well, I mean, you are dressed. Just in the wrong stuff."

Aimee smiled. "Do you want some coffee?"

"Are the novels of Cormac McCarthy pretentious and misogynistic?" Simone replied, following Aimee into the kitchen.

"You are *so* going to have to get over him winning the Pulitzer." Aimee grabbed two mugs from the cabinet.

"No, I don't. It's a bone I'll be able to gnaw on for the rest of my natural life." Simone sighed as she sat at the granite counter and looked around at the open loft. "Your place is always so clean. I want my house to be this neat and restful."

"You should probably have thought about that before you had the three kids and adopted the two dogs." Aimee poured two cups of coffee and pulled the half-and-half out of the refrigerator.

"I also wish I had your metabolism, and could have half-and-half and not gain weight." Simone poured a liberal amount of cream in her coffee anyway. She was two inches shorter than Aimee and about ten pounds heavier, but she carried it in all the right places.

"I gain plenty of weight." Aimee sat down at the counter, braced her elbows on it, and covered her eyes, which suddenly felt scratchy.

"Rough night?" Simone asked.

"You could say that," Aimee replied from behind her hands. "A two a.m. phone call about a client."

Simone's nose wrinkled. "Bummer. Say what you will about the sorrows of writing copy for the biology department's newsletter, they never have middle-of-the-night emergencies. Was it bad?"

Aimee nodded. "And probably going to get worse."

Simone patted Aimee on the back. "Sorry." She'd

learned not to ask for particulars about Aimee's clients; she just listened to whatever Aimee could share and offered sympathy. She was worth her weight in gold. "Will it at least be over soon?"

"I'm guessing I'll be out of it by tomorrow. She needs to be institutionalized—at least for a while. And once a patient is committed, the psychologist who had the case isn't generally wanted anymore." The new doctor would want to make his or her own diagnosis and treatment plan.

Whoever took over the case was going to be starting from square one without any of the background and history Aimee had with Taylor. On the other hand, maybe someone looking at it with fresh eyes could be of more assistance. Things were very different now for Taylor than they had been twenty-four hours ago.

"There's no way I'm running this morning. Why don't you go ahead, and I'll join you tomorrow morning. Okay?"

Simone hopped up and gave Aimee a quick squeeze. "Sure. Let me know if you need anything. I'll call tonight and check on you."

Aimee locked and chained the door after her. Great—Simone would call and check on her. She didn't like being treated like a piece of fine china; she wasn't that fragile anymore. She hated feeling like an item on someone's to-do list. Defrost chicken for dinner. Check on Aimee. Pick up dry cleaning.

She refilled her coffee mug. She might as well take a look at Taylor's file before she handed her off to her new doctor. Maybe there was something there that could help with the investigation. Something whose significance she'd missed before.

Josh and Elise had given the PIO enough for the *Sacramento Bee* to run a two-paragraph teaser about the murders on the second page of the Metro section, and the morning TV news shows would have a few facts to go along with the footage they'd taken at the house. The press would want more soon, but Elder thought he could hold them off for a while. Good thing; there wasn't much to give them yet.

The chief, however, had made it clear that there better be something sooner rather than later. Josh had expected to get heat from up top; he just hadn't expected it this fast.

After meeting with the chief, they'd each headed home briefly. Josh had showered, changed, and dropped a few crickets into the cage of his gecko, Dean. The lizard was pretty much the only pet that could withstand his sudden and prolonged absences. Dean didn't exactly greet him at the door, but he did hiss and then slurp up a cricket. If that wasn't love, what was? He was all the company Josh needed most nights; Dean might be a little grouchy, but he never talked during the game or drank the last of the beer.

When they returned to headquarters on Freeport, the M.E. had left a message that he already had preliminary autopsy results on the Dawkins. He must have put a hell of a rush on it; the screws were clearly being turned on the M.E. as well.

Josh and Elise climbed into their city-issued white

sedan and headed up Freeport toward the morgue, past the strip malls filled with check cashing stores and nail salons and the occasional fast food restaurant.

"It'll be faster if you cut over on Sutterville and tack over on King," Elise said.

"Do I kibbitz when you drive?" Josh shot her a look.

"No, but you sigh a lot."

"Fine. I'll go up King." He hung a right and then a left.

At the morgue, they flashed their badges and were buzzed through. The forensic pathologist was waiting for them in the autopsy bay.

"Whatcha got for us, doc?" Elise asked, popping her gum like a teenager.

Dr. Halpern smiled his too toothy and whitened grin. "What might make you consider spending a little more quality time here?"

Josh shook his head. Halpern had had a little crush on Elise ever since she was a cadet, and he flirted with her whenever they came in. Elise either didn't mind, or had decided it was worth it to get autopsy results faster.

Elise fluttered her eyelashes. "Well, a cause of death on that double that came in last night might soften my heart a little."

Josh rolled his eyes.

Halpern waved his hand in the air. "You're setting the bar far too low, m'dear. You're worth so much more."

"I'm all ears," Elise said, perching on the stool next to Halpern's desk.

"Well, your forty-seven-year-old male died between

eight and ten p.m. last night from a cerebral hemorrhage caused by blunt force trauma. The lamp found at the scene is undoubtedly your weapon. I found flakes of the copper plate finish from the lamp base in the head wound."

Josh nodded. No surprise there.

"Your female vic had a slightly different story to tell."

Josh settled down in the chair across from Halpern, braced his elbows on the arms, and steepled his fingers. "Do tell."

"She was strangled. I'm guessing with some kind of electrical cord, probably the cord from the lamp used to kill her husband. It was missing, you know." Halpern smiled and leaned back in his chair.

Elise looked over at Josh, brows slightly raised. Josh raised his, too, and shook his head. Why take the cord? What made it necessary to take it? Or worth potentially being caught with it?

"Here's the interesting part, though. The male vic was killed wham bam thank you, ma'am. The female? He took his time with her." Halpern stood up and motioned them over to where Stacey Dawkin's body lay on the cold metal gurney. "See how there are multiple ligature marks around her neck? I think he toyed with her. Choked her almost unconscious, released the cord and let her think she might still have a chance, then choked her some more. Based on what I'm seeing here, he went through that cycle three or four times."

Josh was known for his iron stomach; he was used to walking out of these autopsy bays and then going to order a gyro. But what the doc had just said made him a little sick.

"She fought," Halpern said. "She's got something under her fingernails. We're sending it on for analysis. Clyde'll have more details for you later."

Josh had been a homicide cop long enough to understand how a person could be driven to take another's life. But to savor it? To prolong it and enjoy it like that? "Sadistic son of a bitch," he muttered.

"Absolutely." Halpern lifted the lower part of the sheet that covered Mrs. Dawkin. "Look at her knees."

They were red and rough.

"Rug burn," he explained. "I think the bastard made her crawl, after he bound her hands and covered her mouth with the duct tape."

"He made her crawl?" Anger rose in Elise's voice. Then a connection dawned on her face. "The marks in the carpet—the ones too short to be drag marks. The bastard made her crawl to her own death."

"We don't know it's a he yet, Elise," Josh said, keeping his voice even. He understood her anger, but feeding it would get them nowhere.

Elise threw him a caustic glance. "Strangulation is a man's crime. And that kind of freaky control and power game? You *know* that's a guy thing. Any sign of sexual assault? On the male or the female?"

Josh knew why she was asking. Sexual assault was rarely about lust. It was about being in charge, giving and taking away; it was about control. The way choking someone until they were almost unconscious and then letting them live for a few moments longer, over and over again, was about control. Whoever had done the choking probably had the right mind-set to also be a sexual predator.

"Nope. Nothing like that at all," Halpern said.

Elise shook her head. "There's no way that little girl back in that hospital did this, Josh."

"Little girl?" Halpern asked.

"The victims' daughter," Josh replied. "We found her at the scene. She's totally shut down and we can't get her to talk."

"I should know more about the height of your perp once I figure out all the angles here. I wouldn't rule anybody out yet, though," Halpern said. "But she'd have to be an awfully angry little girl. And I agree with Elise on this one. Choking is a man's crime."

Josh sighed in relief. Neither of them had wanted to think the kid was the murderer. The only thing worse than kid criminals were the kid victims. The look in their eyes never left him. The betrayal. The hurt. The confusion. The pain. Nothing would ever be the same for them again. They'd never trust easily again, never be able to erase the marks left on them by violence. Those were the ones who broke his heart.

"By the way, the male vic's got rug burns on his knees, too," Halpern continued. "He may have been killed more quickly than his wife, but our perpetrator made him crawl to his death, too."

"So why kill the male vic fast and easy, and torture the female vic?" Elise asked, clearly still disgruntled.

"A male is more of a physical threat," Josh said as he buckled his seatbelt. "He or she could be more sure of physically dominating Mrs. Dawkin than her husband. Best to get him out of the way quickly and then take his or her time with her."

"Stinking sadistic asshole," Elise muttered.

"Absolutely," Josh agreed. "Maybe killing the husband was way more of a rush than he expected, and he decided to draw out the pleasure with the missus."

"Sick twisted bastard," Elise muttered, starting the car.

"True that," Josh said.

Elise gave him a dirty look before backing the car out of its space. "Stop humoring me."

Josh raised his hands in the air. "You're driving. I'm just trying to get out of this alive."

As she threw the car into drive and edged into traffic, Josh's cell phone buzzed in his pocket. "Wolf here."

"Hey, Wolf, it's Reed." Reed had taken over for Smitty at the hospital at about seven this morning. "I thought you'd want to know her aunt is here."

"Thanks. We'll be right there." Josh hung up and told Elise, "Marian Phillips is at the hospital."

"Someone should call the shrink and tell her. You know, so she can get permission to release those files to us." Elise didn't look over at Josh, but he saw the shadow of a smile on her face.

"You go right ahead," he said.

"But it wouldn't be safe to talk on the phone while I was driving," Elise answered, her tone sickly sweet.

"I've seen you talk on the phone, switch CDs in the player, and drink coffee while you drive. You're telling me you're suddenly against multitasking?"

Elise smiled wider. "I read an article about that the other day. Multitasking is bad for your brain. I have seen the error of my ways, and I'm striving to be a better person. I think you should call the doc while I drive, to help me on my road to self-improvement. It's the least you can do, as my friend and partner."

"You are a sarcastic bitch. You know that, don't you?" Josh pulled up the list of his most recent calls.

"Just one of the many reasons you love me," Elise replied.

He laughed in spite of himself. She was right. "So tell me why you're so hot to see me hook up with the headshrinker. You thinking I could get some free services that would set me right?"

"I have a good feeling about her."

"A good feeling? That's it?"

"That's it."

"You want me to call her because you have a good feeling," he repeated. "That's so girly, Jacobs. I can't believe you said that."

"I *am* actually a girl, you know," Elise answered. "So call her."

"Fine," Josh grumbled. "But I'm calling the station first to check in."

"Assert your manhood however you see fit." Elise moved into the left-hand lane. "By the way, does Dr. Gannon seem familiar to you? I keep thinking I've seen her or heard about her somewhere before."

"No," Josh said, dialing his phone. "I'm pretty sure I'd have remembered her."

Elise grinned. "So you think she's cute."

Cute wasn't the right word for Dr. Aimee Gannon. Cute generally didn't do it for him. And Dr. Gannon? She definitely did something for him. He just wished she'd cut it the hell out. He didn't need distractions right now.

Elise's phone buzzed in her pocket. "Jacobs here," she said and listened for a moment. "We'll be there as soon as we can." She snapped her phone shut and grinned at Josh. "After we deal with the aunt and the shrink, we'll go look at what Maribel in the computer lab found on Taylor Dawkin's laptop."

Sean's father broke the news to him first, before calling the rest of the office staff of Dawkin-Walter Web Consultants, Inc., the company that Carl Walter had cofounded with Orrin Dawkin almost a decade ago, into the conference room. Carl said he wanted to give Sean time to adjust before all hell broke loose. As if it hadn't already.

Sean wished like hell it hadn't given him a rush of pride that his father had confided in him first. It had both warmed him and worried him a little, too. Sean scrutinized his father's face. Did he know more than he was letting on?

His father *always* knew more than he was letting on. Carl always knew every secret, every shame, every misstep. Why would this be any different?

"What about Taylor?" Sean kept his voice even, which wasn't easy while his heart thudded in his chest like a bass drum. He knew how he should sound. Concerned. Compassionate. He had taught himself to make the right sounds and to have his face be right. Furrow the brow slightly. Tilt the head just so. He had watched other people and worked at duplicating it in the mirror, practicing for hours.

Carl's brow creased, and it was almost like looking in the mirror. The same furrow in the forehead. The same tilt to the head. The same head of thick sandy brown hair. He wondered if his father practiced in front of the mirror like he had.

"Marian said the girl's still in shock. She's not speaking. She's probably going to have to be institutionalized, at least for a while."

The relief was so intense, Sean just nodded, not trusting himself to speak. Then, as always, the shame flooded in.

The worries rushed in behind the shame. Would Taylor start to talk? When? What would she say?

Sean followed his father into the conference room where the Dawkin-Walter staff had assembled, watching Carl's every move. He was so slick. Sean felt another surge of pride as his father hit the absolutely right notes while he delivered the horrible news of Orrin's murder to the staff. He analyzed the deft way Carl deflected questions about the future of the company without appearing not to answer. And the way he comforted Orrin's assistant, who collapsed in tears, was masterful. There was a lot Sean could still learn from him.

Maybe there'd be time. Maybe everything could stay the same—but Sean doubted it. Secrets had a way of working themselves into the open, and he knew that once his secrets were out, nothing would ever be the same.

CHAPTER

4

Aimee flipped through her initial notes about Taylor and her family.

The first thing she'd asked Taylor was if she knew why she was in her office. Taylor had looked up from her inspection of the fluorescent skull and bones pattern on her fingerless gloves and fixed Aimee with a look that expressed terminal boredom. "How should I know? It's not like it was my idea."

Fabulous. Defiance and angst all wrapped up in one goth-flavored package. "So you don't see a problem with any of your behavior? There's nothing that you're doing that could indicate that you're feeling overwhelmed? Or angry? Or sad?" Aimee had asked.

"Overwhelmed by what? School?" Taylor had slumped back in her chair, her lank dyed-black hair accentuating the pallor of her face.

"Okay, that's one option. Are you feeling overwhelmed by school?" It wasn't going to be that easy. It never was.

Taylor had shaken her head and twisted a lock of hair around her finger. "School's a joke."

"Really? Then why are your grades dropping? If it's such a joke, it shouldn't be that difficult."

"It's stupid and boring and pointless. Why should I bother?" Taylor had said, inspecting her split ends.

Aimee was sure Taylor had heard more than enough about getting into a good college and succeeding in life, so why not go directly to the real issue? "Taylor, do you cut yourself?"

Taylor sat bolt upright and stared at Aimee, her blue eyes suddenly moist. Had no one spoken to Taylor matter-of-factly about her self-mutilation? It was definitely a possibility. Stacey had reacted with alarm and revulsion. Orrin had shied away. Of course, that was part of what Taylor wanted, on some level. She wanted the attention. She wanted the horror. She wanted the drama.

She also couldn't talk to anyone who reacted that way to her cutting. Taylor needed someone who could hear what she had to say without having their own brand of hysterics. Aimee could be that person. More important, Taylor needed her to be that person.

"Do you, Taylor?" Aimee pressed.

Taylor nodded. She swallowed hard once, then again. She held her body tense, every muscle clenched.

"Would you show me your arms, Taylor?" Aimee had leaned forward.

Without taking her eyes off Aimee, Taylor had slowly peeled down the sleeves of her fingerless gloves to reveal a patchwork of old scars and fresh cuts going up the inside of her arms—and then she'd begun to cry.

Aimee shut the file. If there was something useful here, she couldn't figure it out yet. What she saw in her notes was a scared little girl who was holding herself together with a coping mechanism that was terribly flawed.

Aimee had her suspicions about what exactly Taylor was trying to cope with, but she needed concrete information. It wasn't the kind of thing anyone should guess about; lives were changed forever with those kinds of accusations.

She leaned her head back against her chair, too keyed up to sleep and too exhausted to move. She was grateful when her cell phone rang to shake her out of her doldrums.

She fished it out of her purse. "Dr. Aimee Gannon."

"Dr. Gannon, this is Josh Wolf of the Sacramento PD again."

How many Josh Wolfs did he think she met in a day? "Hi. What's happening?"

"I wanted to let you know that Taylor's aunt is here in Sacramento."

"Great." She rubbed at her face. "That will help in so many ways." They could get Taylor out of the emergency room and into someplace comfortable; maybe a place where she felt safe enough to come out of the shell she'd encased herself in. Aimee had never met Marian Phillips, but Taylor loved her. She'd spoken of her in almost the same tone she used when she talked about Good Charlotte, and that was saying something.

"She's at the hospital now. She was hoping you'd come down and help her figure out what to do with Taylor."

"I'd love to. I'll be there in half an hour." At last there

was something concrete she could do. She dropped the file on the desk and headed for the door.

The drive to Mercy General was a hell of a lot different in the daylight. McKinley Park lost its menace and looked like a nice place to eat a sack lunch. The hospital no longer loomed out of the residential area like a tower of doom. It just looked like a hospital, brick and glass and cement. She needed to rein in her imagination.

Aimee was soon walking down the hallway to where she'd left Taylor earlier that morning. Detectives Wolf and Jacobs stood outside the curtain next to another uniformed police officer sitting outside the curtain, giving Taylor and her aunt a little privacy. This officer was a woman, a squat blonde with her hair pulled back into two skinny French braids with bangs dusting across her forehead. She stood as Aimee approached.

"It's okay, Reed," Wolf said, dropping his large hand onto the woman's shoulder. "She's the doc the aunt has been waiting for."

Reed gave Aimee a quick once-over and then a curt nod. Everybody but Aimee seemed to have a gun.

"Good morning," Aimee said to everyone and then let herself behind the curtain.

It looked as though Taylor hadn't moved since Aimee had left. She still lay on her side, facing the wall. Her eyes were closed, but Aimee couldn't tell if she was sleeping or just trying to shut everything out.

The woman who sat with Taylor was in her early fifties. Silver strands of hair twined in among the dark brunette ones, and laugh lines crinkled around her red, puffy eyes. She wore creased white capris that looked like she'd driven down in them and a black V-necked sweater. She looked up from Taylor, whose back she was patting as Aimee entered.

"Dr. Gannon?" she said, her voice quavering.

"Mrs. Phillips?" Aimee said, putting out her hand.

"Call me Marian, please." She took both of Aimee's hands in hers. "Thank you so much for coming. I don't know what to do for poor Taylor, and there's so much to figure out. I can't believe any of this is even happening." Tears welled in her hazel eyes as she spoke, and her chin began to tremble.

"It is unbelievable," Aimee said, drawing a chair up next to Marian's so they could sit down.

"How could this happen?" Marian said, the tears spilling over and rolling down her cheeks. "Who would do this to Orrin and Stacey? They didn't have any enemies. Who would dream of doing such a thing?"

"I don't know, Marian. I can't begin to imagine. It really is horrible—but let's talk now about what we can do for Taylor to get her out of the emergency room."

"At first I thought I'd take her home with me," Marian whispered, as if that would keep Taylor from hearing. "But the police don't want me taking her out of the city."

Not to mention that keeping her under suicide watch required trained professionals. But there wasn't any point in telling Marian that and upsetting her further. She'd just lost a sister and a brother-in-law and was already in shock. "I think there are some good options here in Sacramento," Aimee said. "Places that will be able to offer her some therapy to get her through this time, and keep her safe, too."

"Oh." Marian pressed the wadded-up tissue in her hand to her mouth and her eyes grew wide. "Do you think she's in danger? Do you think whoever did this will come after her now?"

"It's hard to say," Aimee answered. *Was* Taylor in danger? If she'd seen something at her parents' house, could the murderer come after her as well? Regardless of the answers, Taylor was certainly a danger to herself right now. "I think it's better to play it safe, don't you?"

Marian nodded. "Yes, I do. I just don't have the first clue how to do that."

"It's okay," Aimee said, putting her hand on Marian's arm. "I do."

MyChemicalGirl42: That was close.
HardasRock: Yeah. RU sure she didn't see me?
MyChemicalGirl42: Yeah. I'm sure. Otherwise I'd be grounded 4ever. LOL. Stupid cow.
HardasRock: ROFLMAO. 2morrow night?
MyChemicalGirl42: I'll be here.

Josh rubbed his hand over his face as he read through the instant messages and e-mails between HardasRock and MyChemicalGirl42. MyChemical-Girl42 was Taylor. Maribel Butera, the forensic computer specialist who was combing through Taylor's hard drive like a prospector searching for gold, was sure of that. HardasRock's identity was another story. Maribel knew that he was male, involved with Taylor, and not a favorite of her parents. Other than that, they didn't have many clues. Or they had too many. Josh wasn't sure anymore. It was starting to give him a headache.

"I'm not even sure what half this stuff means. It's all letters and numbers," he complained. It was like getting e-mails from his niece. When he told her to write in English, she just rolled her eyes. He needed a translator who was fluent in teenagerese.

"You're not supposed to know what it means," Maribel said. She was thirty-two and had a computer science degree from Sac State. She also had such smooth, unlined skin that she could still do undercover work in the high schools when the department needed it. If anybody in the department spoke teenagerese, it was Maribel.

"It's supposed to be confusing for adults. That's part of the point. It's like the cell phone tones that we can't hear. They're putting one over on us without hardly trying." Maribel leaned over the computer and her dark hair swung forward over her face.

"There are cell phone tones I can't hear?" he asked.

Maribel looked up at him, then over at Elise, and rolled her eyes. "Yes, grandpa. There are cell phone tones that you can't hear and the kids can. They use them at school. That way they can text message each other without the teachers catching them."

"Great." One more thing to make him feel old and out of the loop. He gestured at the e-mails on the computer. "So what are we supposed to do with these?"

Maribel shrugged. "I'm not sure. I read through a

lot of it before I called you. You want a rundown, or you want to wade through it yourself?"

"A rundown would be great," Elise said. "I don't need all the details. Yet."

"Okay, then," Maribel said, shooing Josh out of her chair and sitting down in front of the monitor. "This HardasRock dude is clearly Taylor's boyfriend. I'm pretty sure she's been sneaking him into her house at night. Was her bedroom on the first floor?"

"Yeah," Josh said. "Her room was off the living room on the other side of the house from her parents. She could probably have snuck the whole Russian army in without them knowing."

Maribel shrugged. "It wasn't the Russian army, but he definitely was an invader. It looks like he was sneaking in there two, three nights a week and they weren't playing pattycake."

Josh's eyebrows went up. "What were they doing?"

"The usual. Smoking a little weed. Fooling around. There's a couple comments that make me think they were dropping some X."

"Yeah? Why do you think that?" Josh asked.

Maribel scrolled down. "There's a part in here where he says something about their friend Adam dropping by. It's another term for X."

"That's some pretty heady stuff," Elise said.

"Can be," Maribel confirmed. "It's also just about everywhere. The kids like it because they don't have to inject it or smoke it. It's just a little pill. Plus, if they were having sex—you know about X and sex, right?"

He did. Why the hell would kids need something to jazz up their sex lives? At seventeen, you were nothing but a walking erogenous zone anyway. "So who is this HardasRock kid? Where can we find him?"

"I'm trying to track down who he is, but it takes time and I may not ever be able to get any results. These things are made to be anonymous."

"Well, that's a big help," Josh said.

Maribel threw him a dirty look. "I know that he's seeing her without her parents' permission. In fact, from what I can tell, they forbade her to see him."

"Oh, super. Why not slap a big ole 'Forbidden Fruit' sign on him and spray him down with pheromones?" Elise said.

That was true. Was there any way to make a boy more attractive to a teenage girl than letting her know her parents hated him? Josh was pretty sure he'd made it to third base with Trisha Jakowski in tenth grade based solely on Trisha's mother's loathing for him. He was grateful then and he was grateful now. It had been a life-changing experience for him.

"Somebody's got to know who he is, though. Have you talked to her friends?" Maribel asked.

Josh looked at Elise. "We haven't interviewed the study buddy yet."

"No, we haven't. I think it's time we gave little Jenna Norchester a call, don't you?"

Elise sat down at her desk. Josh was in his cube calling the Norchester home to set up a time to chat with their daughter, who was one of the last people to see Taylor before she went all freaky. Elise hoped Josh didn't piss off the girl's parents before they even got there. He certainly was in a mood today.

The case was obviously getting to him. It was a righteous response. What had happened in that house was nasty business. If it didn't get to them a little, they probably shouldn't be cops anymore. It was a fine line to walk. If you didn't harden your heart to some of the things you saw, you'd self-destruct. Yet if you didn't care anymore, then why were you still wearing the badge?

But there was something more going on with Josh. Something besides a hunger for justice for people who could no longer speak for themselves. Something besides a need to try to set things right when they'd been knocked so terribly, terribly wrong.

Elise wondered if it had anything to do with Aimee Gannon. She'd certainly made him sit up and take notice. No one else had since Holly had broken his foolish heart. Elise had thought Josh was going to fall right out of his chair at the hospital the night before, or go all silent and drooly like Taylor. Now he was all moody and grumpy—which wasn't entirely out of the norm.

Remembering that she'd meant to run Dr. Gannon's familiar name through the computer, Elise typed in some searches and started to scroll through the results.

She switched the screen to a report as she heard Josh hang up the phone. He stood up and leaned over the cubicle wall. "We can see Jenna this afternoon. With her dad."

Elise made a face. "We'll get more if she's by herself."

"We'll get nothing if we don't let Daddy sit in. He made that clear." Josh stretched. "Looks like Gannon and Phillips want to go get some stuff for Taylor over at the house. I'll take them, unless you want to."

"Be my guest," Elise said.

Josh nodded and headed downstairs, where the staff social worker had been talking to the aunt and the shrink. Elise gnawed on the end of her pencil and considered the fact that the kid had needed a shrink.

So Taylor had already been mentally unstable. Aimee Gannon could call her fragile or any other euphemism she wanted; it meant the same thing. The kid was a few tacos shy of a full combination plate. But was she unstable enough to fly into the kind of rage necessary to bash in her father's head and strangle her mother?

It didn't feel right to her. Especially the strangulation. She'd told Josh it was a man's crime and Doc Halpern had agreed with her, but now they knew that Taylor had a boyfriend and a drug habit. Teenagers revved up on hormones and rebellion and drugs had committed murder before.

Yet something about the girl screamed "victim" to Elise. Not perpetrator. Not instigator. With any luck, she'd start talking soon. She'd responded to the aunt a little bit. She'd reached for her hand and stopped rocking for a while. Supposedly that was great progress. Elise had asked Gannon how long she thought it would be until Taylor spoke again, and Gannon had been less than committal.

"Later this afternoon, or not for a month. I wish I could be more specific, but there's really no way to predict how long it will take Taylor to feel safe enough to speak again," she'd said in that smooth contralto.

Elise didn't want her fellow cops to know how often she used hunches to decide whether or not to trust someone. Cops didn't want to hear about someone's aura. They wanted facts, evidence. Things that can be presented in court. Bad mojo pouring off someone like poisoned syrup? Not a thing the district attorney could do with that in front of a judge. But her gift served Elise well from time to time, and she'd gotten a reputation as a cop with good instincts. That carried some weight with her fellow officers. Go figure. How exactly were good instincts different from the energy she felt emanating off of people? She guessed presentation was always half the battle.

Elise's instincts told her that Aimee Gannon was okay. There was some private pain under that smooth, calm surface that Elise could sense. She had a hunch that Josh would have more luck in that department. It would take a little heat to melt that icy veneer, but she had faith in her partner. She was pretty sure he could bring the heat when he wanted to.

And she was pretty sure he wanted to. It wasn't like Josh to be willing to take a babysitting run. He could have sent a uniform with Aimee and Marian to the Dawkin home.

The phone on her desk rang. "Hey, Elise," Clyde Owen said.

"Yeah?" she answered the crime lab tech. "What you got?"

"The duct tape on your victims? It's all contiguous."

Another un-surprise. Most murderers didn't stop to patch up the air-conditioning unit between binding up their victims. "Thanks, Clyde." She started to hang up.

"Here's the interesting part, though," Clyde said. "The first piece of tape off the roll matches a piece that was used to patch the desk chair in the victim's study."

Elise stopped. "Really?"

"Yeah. So I figure the duct tape must have already been in the study, and the murderer used what was handy. Same way he used the lamp and the cord. They were there, right? He didn't bring the lamp with him."

"So you're saying it was spontaneous. He didn't plan it." Was it possible that whoever had done this hadn't thought it out first? That something or some-one had suddenly enraged them enough to suddenly turn unspeakably violent? What could possibly do that? Money and sex were generally the first two answers on the list. What had been going on in that house under its placid suburban exterior?

"But that doesn't fit with the glove thing," Clyde continued.

"I didn't realize there was a glove thing." Elise waited for Clyde to finish processing his thoughts. It didn't pay to rush him. With Clyde, it was best to let the choo-choo train go all the way around the track without interrupting its journey.

"Yeah. There were no fingerprints on the tape, except for the victim's fingerprints on the tape that patched his chair. Whoever taped those people up like that had to have been wearing gloves. Halpern told me that the stuff he found under the female vic's fingernails was latex. It could be consistent with her trying to get away from someone wearing latex gloves. Not much of a lead—you can buy those things in any drugstore in town."

"You never know what might help. Thanks, Clyde." Elise hung up and pondered that particular conundrum. If the murderer came to the house not intending to do any harm, why did he have gloves handy? Maybe it was somebody with some weird germ phobia? It definitely was something that they should keep in mind.

Elise stared at the photos of Stacey Dawkin lying facedown on her living room floor. Whoever had killed her hadn't come to her house planning on murder. That seemed pretty certain. But from those multiple ligature marks on Stacey's throat, Elise was pretty sure that the murderer had started to enjoy it.

She hoped they found the bastard before he decided to throw himself another little party where the guests would never go home.

CHAPTER
5

Josh parked in front of the Dawkins' house. The television crews had trampled the hell out of the lawn, but except for that and the yellow crime scene tape across the front door, it looked like all of the other single-family homes in the neighborhood—big, solid, and costly. He got out and Marian Phillips and Aimee Gannon stepped onto the curb next to him.

Gannon's dark hair was down today, lying thick around her shoulders. Her eyes, no longer shielded by the black-framed glasses, looked as weary as they had the night before. Josh doubted that she'd slept much. She had on a pair of trousers that had Josh wondering just how long her legs were, and a white blouse with a camisole damnably shielding her cleavage. He couldn't say what Marian Phillips was wearing. He could hardly tear his eyes off Aimee long enough to watch the road while he was driving.

"I have to ask you ladies to touch as few things as possible," Josh said.

Marian Phillips nodded, her mouth pressed into a tight thin line. Dr. Gannon placed her hand gently on Marian's back and asked, "Are you okay with this? Do you want to wait outside?"

"I'd love to wait outside, but I need to do this for

Taylor." Her voice caught. "I need to do this for my sister."

Gannon put her arm around the smaller woman's shoulders. "Okay, then. Let's go in."

Josh opened the front door and stood aside to let them in. He saw Gannon flinch at the vomit by the bushes near the front door, and wondered what her reaction would be to the scene inside. He knew it was harsh, but he wanted to see her response unfiltered by any warning.

Marian walked in and stopped short. Her hands flew to her mouth; her shoulders hunched as if she might be physically ill. Behind her, Gannon put an arm around Marian and steadied her. Then she looked around and gasped at the blood-covered walls.

Her face drained of color and she swayed on her feet. He couldn't blame her. He'd been repulsed even before he found out that Taylor had used the broken shards of a wine bottle to cut herself, then used her own blood to paint the walls with those weird geometric shapes. And it wasn't as if this was his first homicide.

Aimee felt her gorge rise. "What does that mean?" she asked, unable to look away from the blood-smeared walls.

"We're not sure," Wolf said behind her. "I was hoping you might know."

"Why would I know?" Aimee turned to look up at him. His dark eyes were trained on her face and gave her the disturbing impression that he saw way more than what was on the surface.

"Because you know Taylor better than we do," he said, looking from Aimee to Marian.

"You think Taylor did this?" she asked.

"They're pretty sure about that." Wolf gestured to the wall with his chin. "It's her blood and her fingerprints all over the walls."

"Her own blood?" Aimee echoed. Of course—the cuts all over Taylor's body. The room wavered around her, graying at the edges.

"You okay, doc?" Wolf reached out a hand and placed it on her arm to steady her.

She focused on the warmth of his hand, big and strong on her arm. The rest of her felt so cold. "Fine," she said. "It's just shocking."

Wolf rubbed a hand over his face. "True that."

Apparently it hadn't been easy for him to see this room, either.

"Any idea what it means? Why she would paint that same symbol over and over again?" Wolf asked.

Aimee steeled herself and looked back at the wall. "I have no idea."

She looked over at Marian, who stood stock still, her hand over her mouth with tears coursing down her cheeks. Realization dawned on Aimee and a fire sparked in her belly. Josh Wolf had known what they were walking into. He'd known precisely what they were going to see, and he had brought them in here unprepared so he could watch them like bugs under a microscope.

She shook his hand off and put her arms around Marian, turning her away from the gory scene. "You don't have to look. You don't have to think about it."

Marian began to sob. "Oh, my poor sister. Who would do such a thing? Who could even think of it?"

Aimee patted Marian's back and glared at Detective Wolf. "I don't know, Marian. There's no telling what goes on in some people's minds."

It took nearly a half hour to calm Marian Phillips down. It didn't help that under the calm Aimee was trying to project, she was seething at Detective Wolf. Could he *be* more callous and insensitive? He might be tall and hot, but that didn't mean he was on the side of the angels.

How could she have forgotten everything she'd learned about dealing with cops? Their goals were not her goals. Their methods weren't hers, either.

Aimee distracted Marian by asking questions about the framed photographs lining the hallway that led to the bedrooms. There were several of Orrin Dawkin and a handsome taller man with thick, sandy blond hair. In one photo, they were wearing jumpsuits and parachutes. In a second one, they wore scuba gear. A third showed the two men halfway up a cliff face.

"Who is the man with Orrin in these photos? Is it his brother?" Aimee asked.

Marian shook her head and smiled a little, although fresh tears pooled in her eyes. "No. Not his brother. Although he might as well have been, as close as those two were. That's Carl Walter, Orrin's business partner."

"Quite the adventurers, aren't they?" Aimee said, then winced. Orrin would no longer be an adventurer. His opportunities had been crushed along with the back of his skull.

"That's how they met," Marian said. "On some desert adventure trip. Orrin used to take them alone. Stacey was never one for much risk-taking, but Orrin got a real thrill from it. That whole opposites attract thing really worked for them. Anyway, he met Carl and the two hit it off. They came up with a way to go into business together about a year after that."

"How old was Taylor in this photo?" A grinning pigtailed Taylor stood on top of a picnic bench, mugging for the camera. It was hard to imagine her little black cloud of a client in the denim shorts and tie-dyed T-shirt she wore in the photo.

"Let's see. That was the summer we all went up to Lassen together." Marian closed her eyes for a moment. "They had just moved here. Taylor was maybe seven? Eight?"

There was a light in little Taylor's eyes that Aimee had never seen while she'd been treating her. "She looks happy."

Marian smiled. "She was then. Things didn't change until later."

"How much later?"

It was always interesting to get another perspective. People lied to their therapists, as counterproductive as that seemed. More often, they lied to themselves. Even if they didn't lie outright, they reframed things in different contexts to make them more palatable; to make themselves seem better, truer, more heroic. One more person's viewpoint meant one more possibility of seeing the truth—or as close to the truth as anyone could ever come.

"Not all that long," Marian murmured, a crease furrowing her forehead. "Maybe a year later."

Aimee's head snapped up. She'd expected to hear about recent problems, not a behavior change at seven or eight. None of the Dawkins had mentioned that. "Really. What happened then?"

Marian shook her head. "I never did figure that out. Maybe it was the move. That can be hard on a kid."

"But it sounds like it didn't start until well after the move." Aimee turned back to the picture, the wheels turning in her head. "How exactly did she change?"

Marian chewed her lip. "It was like she turned inward. Suddenly she went all clingy. Never wanted to let go of Stacey's legs. Even wet the bed a few times." Marian blushed, clearly feeling that she was violating a confidence. "Stacey didn't like to talk about it too much. She worried, but I think she thought if she acted like everything was okay, it would be okay. Orrin wasn't too sympathetic about people being weak. He was such a strong man. So definite. He didn't always understand when other people couldn't be the same way."

The hairs on the back of Aimee's neck rose a little. There weren't many clearer signs that a child had been traumatized than that. Regressing to the behavior of a younger child was a classic symptom. She'd have to go back to her notes and see if there was anything else that would point to something that might have happened when Taylor was seven or eight. "And you have no idea what happened, what might have brought this on?"

"I always figured it was something at school. Kids

can be so cruel." Marian turned away from the photo, tears spilling down her cheeks again.

True that, as Detective Wolf would say. Aimee glanced over her shoulder. He was standing in the kitchen, but she had a feeling that everything they said was being analyzed.

Aimee looked back at the photo, at the joyful, laughing child so sure of herself and her place in the world. It was nearly impossible to connect this image with the blood-covered, wordless girl in the emergency room. Her heart sped up a bit. Knowing when whatever had happened to Taylor had occurred was a first step in figuring out *what* had happened.

Then Aimee's heart sank. She wouldn't have the opportunity to try. By the end of the day, Taylor would be safely ensconced in the Whispering Pines Center and Aimee's services would no longer be necessary.

Aimee looked again at the carefree little girl in the photo, wishing she could ask that sweet, open face who had hurt her. When, and how? There would be no answer to why; there never really was. At least not enough of a reason to rob someone of their innocence, of their trust.

"I'm sure it was nothing at home," Marian went on. "My sister . . . my sister was a wonderful mother. Orrin was a wonderful provider. He always wanted the very best of everything for Stacey and Taylor." Her voice shook. "Top of the line for his girls. Nothing less. Ever." She wiped her eyes. "Taylor's room is this way."

Aimee followed her down the hallway, Detective Wolf at their heels. Aimee ignored him.

Taylor's bedroom was a testament to how recently her personality had changed and how desperately someone—most likely her mother—had been clinging to whom she had been before. The centerpiece of the room was a confection of a canopy bed, the top still covered with a flowered and eyeleted flounce of fabric. The desk was white and pink and the dressers were candy-colored, too. The light lavender walls with the orchid stencil motif around the ceiling, however, had been covered with posters of bands. My Chemical Romance. Death Cab for Cutie. AFI. Aimee recognized most of the names. Taylor had often come to therapy with her arms covered with elaborate ballpoint pen drawings with the names of those bands as the centerpiece. Stacey had actually been relieved when she had started writing on herself instead of cutting; she had felt it was great progress.

The rumpled bedspread on the unmade bed and the curtains were clearly new additions. The bedspread was red satin with a black velvet lining. The curtains were lacey with a spider motif worked into them. The bookshelf had books with titles like *Everything That Creeps* and *Amphigorey*, although the book on the nightstand was *Be Your Own Best Friend*. Another book, a graphic novel about Buffy the Vampire Slayer, sat on the dresser. Aimee picked it up. There was a yellow Post-it note attached to it that read, "Thought you might enjoy this. Sean."

"Very goth," Aimee said, looking around.

"More emo, actually," Marian said.

Aimee raised her eyebrows in a question.

"My Margot is five years older than Taylor. That's

what she said when Taylor started acting this way. She said she'd gone emo. You know, emotional rock. Sort of like punk but with more feeling." Marian was already opening drawers and taking out clothing.

Detective Wolf, standing in the doorway, nodded toward the posters. "Those bands are all emo bands." When Aimee turned to him, he shrugged. "I've got nieces and nephews."

Marian tried to smooth the bedspread out to stack the clothing and encountered a lump under the covers. She fished underneath and pulled out a battered stuffed dog. "Oh," she said, sinking down on the bed. "It's Sammy."

Aimee sat down next to her. "Is Sammy special to Taylor?"

Marian hugged the dog to herself. "He went everywhere with Taylor for years. I had no idea she still had him, much less slept with him." She frowned. "I'm pretty sure she didn't have him with her when she came up to stay with us last summer. Maybe she just kept him here on her bed. Do you think I should take him with me?"

"I think anything that might comfort Taylor right now is a good idea," Aimee said.

Wolf's phone buzzed in his pocket. "Wolf here."

He listened for a moment. Something about the change in his posture—a new alertness, tension—made Aimee watch him intently.

"Good," he said and shrugged his big shoulders a little. "I think we're almost done here. I should be back soon." He snapped the phone shut, then said, "We have a lead, ladies. Can we wrap this up quickly?"

"I got a hit off one of the fingerprints from the Dawkin place." Clyde motioned Josh and Elise over to the computer. Josh had dropped Marian and Aimee off with the staff social worker at police headquarters to do the rest of the paperwork to release Taylor, and picked up Elise. He'd hoped to glean some information from eavesdropping on them in Taylor's room, but that hadn't gone as he'd planned. He kept getting distracted every time Aimee Gannon leaned over the bed, imagining her spread on top of it, imagining those long legs wrapped around him, his lips against hers.

Imagining was all that was going to happen with that. Dr. Gannon had been pretty pissed off at him after they'd walked into the Dawkin home.

Clyde, bless his nerdy soul, had some actual evidence. He clicked a few buttons on his computer and a mug shot came up.

"Lois Bradley," Elise read off the screen. "Identity theft. Check fraud."

"I'll call Ed in financials and have him start checking the money trail. See if there's anything hinky going on." Josh pulled his cell phone from his pocket.

Ed was his favorite detective in the financial division. He was a paperwork ninja. He could cut through huge amounts of bullshit armed with nothing but a calculator and a spreadsheet. Josh could keep his checkbook balanced and had a rough idea of what was in his pension fund, but walking into Ed's office with its piles of paper and folders and ledgers made his skin itch. Anyone who could plow through all that paperwork and find something that would hold up in court was a hero in Josh's book. After all, Al Capone had been put away for tax evasion in the end.

"Any idea what connection she might have had with the Dawkins?" he asked.

Clyde scrolled down the computer screen. "Last known job was with a cleaning company. Maybe she was their housekeeper."

"I thought those people had to be bonded. What kind of idiot would give an identity thief access to their home and all their records?" Elise asked.

"The kind of idiot who gets ripped off," Josh suggested. "The kind who might get angry when he finds out what's happened and confront that person."

"And get himself killed for his trouble? Like that professor over in Davis who confronted his yard guy about a stolen check and ended up dead?" Elise shook her head. "I don't know, Josh. This looked personal. It looked deeply angry."

Josh peered at Lois Bradley's record. She'd just come off a year at county. She'd done six months two years before. "It would be her third strike. What's more personal than someone threatening to send you away for the rest of your life?"

"But what would this have to do with that stuff on the walls? That has to mean something."

He gave the only answer he had: a shrug.

Elise sighed. "Fine. What's her last known address? We'll go pay Ms. Bradley a visit."

"Right after we see Jenna Norchester," Josh agreed.

CHAPTER
6

"I really don't know how to thank you." Marian Phillips had a tight grip with both hands around Aimee's hand an hour later. The lobby shared between the police department and the fire department was nearly empty, and her voice echoed in the huge atrium. "You've been so kind and so generous with your time. I really appreciate everything you've done for me and for Taylor."

A stab of guilt hit Aimee. She was beginning to feel like she hadn't done much for the girl at all. It was hard to feel successful when your patient's main form of communication was scrawling cryptic symbols in her own blood and then rocking herself. "I wish I could do more."

"All the driving back and forth, and getting us settled at Whispering Pines? I don't know what more anyone could do. Nothing will bring my sister back to me. Or my brother-in-law. I wish you could have known them." She stopped sniffing and looked up. "Then again, I suppose you did."

"Not in any real way," Aimee said, patting Marian's hand. As a therapist she was privy to things that people wouldn't tell their closest relative or their most trusted friends, sometimes in much more graphic and lurid detail than she wanted or needed to know—but that didn't mean she really knew those people. She didn't know what it was like to sit and watch a movie with them or share a meal. She didn't know what books they liked to read or how they liked their coffee. Mostly she knew what they were afraid to let anyone else know, even themselves.

Marian threw her arms around Aimee. "You're a sweet girl."

Aimee smiled into Marian's hair. "It's been nice to meet you, too," she said, thankful that someone with this much compassion would now be looking after Taylor. "I wish it had been under different circumstances."

Marian released Aimee from her hug and blew her nose. "You'll come and visit Taylor, won't you?"

"Her new doctor may not want that, Marian. I'll do what I can, but I don't want to antagonize her new doctor. That's not in Taylor's best interests."

"Why would your visiting antagonize anyone?" Marian's brow furrowed.

"The new doctors will want to draw their own conclusions about Taylor's behavior and draw up their own treatment plan. They won't want anything to interfere with that, and visits from a previous therapist could be viewed as interference," Aimee explained. It galled her, though. It was hard to let Taylor out of her protective hands.

Marian nodded slowly. "I suppose I can see their point. I don't necessarily agree with it, though."

"I'd like to keep in touch," Aimee said, pulling one of her cards from her purse. She wrote her home phone on the back. "Here are all my numbers. Call me anytime you want, and please keep me informed of Taylor's progress."

"Of course I will," Marian said, and gave Aimee a last hug good-bye.

Aimee walked past the glassed-in booth where the desk sergeant sat and out to the parking lot, feeling like she was leaving an awful lot of unfinished business behind.

"But I promised not to tell," Jenna Norchester whispered.

Josh rubbed his hand over his face, took a deep breath, and counted to ten. Again. Another teenaged girl that he'd like to shake until her teeth rattled. Did this one have a hot shrink who could distract him, too? That would make it all into just the most perfect clusterfuck ever.

"I'm sure that Taylor would understand if you broke your promise to her," he said. "Things have changed a lot since you made that promise to her. A whole lot."

Jenna's lower lip quivered, and she let her straight brown hair fall in front of her slightly horsey face. "I know that. My dad told me. All the kids at school are talking about it and it's been on the news and everything. It's so awful."

"That's right," Elise said softly. "Everyone's talking about it anyway, so it'll be okay if you tell us what really happened. Jenna, if you know anything that might help us catch who did this, you know it's right to tell us."

Josh couldn't tell if Elise wanted to smack the girl as much as he did. She had a knack for looking all concerned and sympathetic; then when you least expected it, *POW*! The tough broad inside nailed you. It was damn effective.

Jenna looked up at her dad, who stood behind her at the kitchen table. "It's just that Taylor and I have been friends for years. Absolute years," Jenna wailed, which was pretty much the way she talked about everything. She wailed. She shrieked. Josh had a distaste for drama.

"They went to kindergarten together," Charles Norchester said. "They walked to school together when they were old enough to cross the street by themselves."

"But lately . . ." Jenna's voice trailed off and she started with the lower lip quiver again.

Josh was sure that the quiver thing melted her daddy's heart, but it had been tried on him too many times by too many perps and too many girlfriends for it to affect him anymore. "Lately what?" he asked.

"She started hanging with a different group of kids. She never wants to come over and hang out anymore. I had like this whole *O.C.* party where we wore bikinis and everything and watched the DVDs, and she wouldn't even come. She said it was lame. All she wants to do is lie around and talk about . . ."

Josh wanted to bang his head on the table when Jenna trailed off again.

"Talk about what?" he asked, apparently a shade too quickly or a touch too sharply, since Elise kicked the back of his chair.

Mr. Norchester crouched down next to Jenna's chair. "It's okay, honey. I know you want to honor the promise that you made your friend, but sometimes breaking your word is the right thing to do. I know it's confusing and hard."

Josh wanted to gag. What was this, a freakin' after-school special?

"But she'll never ever talk to me again. She said she wouldn't if I told, and I don't think she really cares if she does or not, anyway." Jenna was crying now.

"So you and Taylor had a falling-out?" Elise asked. "What was it about?"

Jenna took a deep, quavery breath. "It wasn't really about anything. Taylor just . . . changed."

Oh, great, Josh thought. Another discourse on Taylor's mood changes.

Elise put her hand on his shoulder and kept talking. "But she came over the other night. To study, right?" Her voice was a soft melody of concern and understanding.

Jenna Norchester burst into tears again. Josh rolled his eyes and shoved the tissue box across the kitchen table. How could someone possibly think a promise made to a friend was more important than a homicide investigation?

"We just said that—about the studying. We weren't, really. I mean, there really was a test in World Civ and I studied for it. Really, Dad, I did." She looked up at her father, who patted her again and assured her that he knew she had.

"But Taylor didn't study for the World Civ exam," Elise said.

Jenna shook her head. "No, she didn't."

"What did Taylor do instead?" Josh asked.

"She snuck out to see him. She made me promise not to tell," Jenna whispered.

Elise and Josh exchanged looks. So Taylor had not been here the entire evening, and she'd been with someone. Things were starting to get interesting. "Who did she sneak out to see, Jenna?" Elise asked.

"Flick," she mumbled.

"Flick? Is that someone's real name?" Josh had met enough Rainbows and Cedars and Sunshines to know how deeply the hippie movement had sent down its roots here, but Flick?

"I don't know his real name. Everybody calls him Flick," Jenna said.

"You don't know it, or won't tell it?" Josh asked.

Jenna lifted her head high. "I don't know it. I'm telling you, everybody calls him Flick."

Josh rose out of his seat. He'd had enough. If he had to take this little brat down to the station and lock her up for a while to get the information he needed, that was precisely what he was going to do.

Elise put a hand on his arm. "When did she leave? Do you remember what time?"

Jenna gnawed on her lower lip. "We waited until Dad was watching *The Daily Show* rerun. That's at like eight o'clock. So it was after that."

"And when did she come back?" Josh pressed. They knew she had; Norchester had told them he'd watched her walk out the door.

"Around nine-thirty. I was getting really nervous. *The Colbert Report* was over and my dad could have checked on us any minute. He does that just randomly. Walks in to see what I'm doing." She glanced at her dad again. This time the glance didn't seem quite as loving.

Josh looked over at Mr. Norchester, too. Apparently there was at least one parent who was keeping track of his kid. He wondered how much longer he would be able to do that. "She just snuck out and left you here? That doesn't seem like something a friend would do. Why didn't she take you with her?"

Jenna's eyes grew wide. "Do you have any idea what my dad would do to me if he caught me sneaking out? I'd be grounded until I was like thirty, and Mom promised to take me shopping on Saturday! I wouldn't have gone with Taylor if she had begged me. Besides, I don't like Flick. I think he's mean."

Norchester suddenly slumped down into a chair and put his head in his hands. Josh supposed it could be pretty overwhelming to suddenly realize that the only reason your daughter wasn't going to be a suspect in a murder investigation was because she was afraid she wouldn't get to go to the mall.

"What did Taylor do while she was gone?" Elise asked. "Did she tell you?"

"I don't know." Jenna's face went pink.

"Jenna," Elise said, her voice making it clear that she didn't believe her. "What did Taylor do?"

"She had a bottle of wine that somebody gave her dad. Her and that boy were going to go to the park and drink it and make out. Her parents wouldn't let her see him, so she had to find ways to sneak out to see him. Her mom had figured out she was sneaking him in at

night, so she'd locked Taylor's windows and was checking on her all the time, and making her take drug tests
and stuff. She said they were like the Gestapo."

Josh looked over at Elise. They weren't going to get
anything else from Jenna.

Elise had clearly reached the same conclusion; she
stood up from the table. "Thank you, Jenna," she said
gravely. "We appreciate your help."

Jenna slumped down in her chair. "I hope so. Taylor will never forgive me." Then the waterworks started
again. Mr. Norchester patted his daughter's back while
she sobbed onto his shoulder that she should have tried
to stop Taylor, but she hadn't known how, and nobody
knew how mean Taylor could be now.

Josh followed Elise out the front door. Forgiving
Jenna was going to be the least of Taylor's problems.
Her alibi had just been blown, and she'd just been
put back in the running as a suspect in her parents'
murder.

He fingered the lamp cord in his pocket. All around him,
his life went on as normal. Everyone doing everything
the way they did it every day—the fools. Nothing was
as it had been. Food tasted more savory. The spring air
was sweeter. Sex was amazing, revelatory. Everything
was better, and they didn't even notice. They trotted
along on their paths like the sheep they were.

Almost everyone he'd ever met was a fool, with the
possible exception of Orrin. He would miss him. Everyone else was a touchy-feely sack of tears and fears, a tool
for him to use. But in a way, he'd been a fool as well.

If he'd known how it would feel to take a life, he would have done it long before. The rush of adrenaline when the lamp had connected with the back of Orrin Dawkin's head had been incredible, nearly indescribable in its wild joyousness. The feeling had coursed through his system like wildfire, making his heart pound and his breath come fast. It had felt so good, he couldn't think of words for it. It was better than drugs and better than sex, although the ecstasy had had something sexual to it. His cock had hardened as he looked down at what he'd done, at the way Orrin's blood and brains splattered across the tidily vacuumed living room carpet. The feeling had made him reel, it was so powerful.

He'd known then not to rush with Stacey. When you discovered nirvana, you didn't want to just visit it. You wanted to live there. It had been sweet, so very sweet, to watch Stacey's eyes glaze over and to see her head loll back like an old pudgy ragdoll. Then he'd released the cord the smallest amount and allowed the oxygen to rush into her lungs again. He'd watched as Stacey remembered where she was and what was happening to her; watched as the horror and the terror and the knowledge of her own helplessness had washed over her. Then he'd tightened the cord and done it again, and again.

After Stacey was finally dead, it had taken only a few quick strokes to make him explode inside his pants with a burst of rapture he'd never experienced before. He wanted to feel that again. He wanted to feel the power and the control and the sweet release. He was breathing hard just thinking about it. He slid the cord between his fingers again and replayed it in his mind all over again.

There had to be a way to make it happen. It was dangerous, though—so dangerous. He'd have to be smart and bide his time.

It had been easy to get a warrant for Lois Bradley's last known address on Acacia Avenue over in north Sacramento near Del Paso Heights. With two strikes against Lois already, Judge Neely had been willing to believe that she might be predisposed to committing a third crime worthy of a strike.

Josh stood to one side of the cheap hollow-core door at the entrance to her apartment, and Elise stood on the other beneath the air-conditioning unit that jutted from the wall. Their hands hovered near the weapons on their belts.

The long, low building was painted pink with turquoise trim in an attempt at whimsy, but the paint didn't disguise the boarded-up window in the back, or the parking lot with only a scattering of gravel over its hard-packed dirt. The whole neighborhood had a defeated air, as if it had nothing left to lose.

Lois had something left to lose: her freedom. Paperhangers like Lois were not generally violent. They worked behind the scenes. They weren't into direct confrontation, but as Elise had pointed out, that wasn't always the case. If push had come to shove for Lois and she had killed the Dawkins, then she'd graduated from white-collar crime to something much grittier. Shooting a cop would be another big leap, but it was unwise to ever underestimate a third-striker. When faced with spending the rest of their lives in prison, people tended to get unpredictable.

Every once in a while, Josh wanted to grab one of the habitual offenders and shake them. Did they want to go to jail for life? Was that twelve-pack of Coors they had stolen from the Circle K really worth a life sentence? Most of them couldn't think past the lovely melting sensation of the alcohol or the weed or the meth hitting their brains, making the rest of their troubles slide away for a while. Forget that the troubles would come back tenfold once the high had worn off. That was too far away to think about. All they were thinking about was the next six-pack or the next hit off the pipe.

"Ms. Bradley," Elise said, pounding on the door. "Open up. It's the police. We need to talk to you."

Josh listened intently, but heard nothing. Lois Bradley could be gone or she could be good at keeping quiet.

Elise knocked again. "Police, Ms. Bradley. Open up now."

They waited again. Still nothing. Elise nodded at him and he reached for the doorknob. It turned in his hand—the door wasn't locked. He looked up at Elise, eyebrows raised. She tilted her head toward the door, giving her opinion that they should go in. He'd stay high, she'd go low since Josh was more than half a foot taller.

Josh silently mouthed "one-two-three" to Elise, then shoved the door open.

CHAPTER
7

Aimee finished writing up notes on the client she'd seen that afternoon. He'd been anxious about a date he'd set up with a woman he'd met at Match.com. Sometimes Aimee felt like she should pay all the matchmaking Web sites commissions; they drummed up plenty of business for her.

But today it had been hard to pay attention. Marian's little bombshell about Taylor's personality change after her family moved to Sacramento had Aimee itching to get back to her files. Maybe that was the key piece she needed to form the other puzzle pieces into a coherent picture.

It was much earlier than she usually left the office, but she was exhausted. She folded up her files and shoved them into her briefcase. She'd look at them at home, if she could keep her eyes open long enough.

In the waiting room, Julie O'Neal, one of the other therapists that Aimee shared spaced with, was struggling to put the water jug on top of the dispenser. Aimee dropped her briefcase and helped her right the bottle.

Julie brushed her hair from her eyes. "Thanks. I thought I was going to lose that one."

"You should have asked for help," Aimee said. "Those things weigh a ton."

Julie grimaced. "Louis and Carol have gone home and I didn't want to bother you today."

"I'm fine. Tired, but fine."

"Are you sure?" Julie put her hand on Aimee's arm. "This can't be easy for you."

"It's easier for me than it is for Taylor." Aimee shut her eyes for a second, trying to clear the image of Taylor's white, grim face as she left Mercy General for an indefinite stay at Whispering Pines.

Aimee opened her eyes to find Julie staring at her, her face serious. "Did she do it, Aimee? Did she kill her parents?"

"No. Absolutely not. Taylor's not violent." Aimee willed herself to believe that. *Could* Taylor have been part of this? Detective Wolf had said she was a suspect, but how could she be?

Julie sat on the back of one of the waiting room's overstuffed armchairs. "Are you really sure?"

Unspoken was the fact that Aimee had been fooled by a client before. She was still paying the price for that mistake. When Kyle had changed suddenly from a victim to an assailant, she had spent a week in the hospital with a broken jaw—and the two years since then second-guessing herself. But not this time. Taylor needed someone who believed in her. "I'm sure."

Julie nodded. "Okay, then. What do the police think?"

That was an excellent question. It was nearly impossible for Aimee to figure out what was going on behind Detective Wolf's controlled façade, or to figure out the feelings that fluttered through her when his watchful gaze landed on her. "I wish I knew. I don't think they're ruling anything out yet."

Julie stood up and gave Aimee a quick hug. "Good night, then. If you need to talk . . ."

"You'll be the first person I look for," Aimee assured her, and headed toward the door.

"Aimee." Julie stopped her.

"Yes?"

"Be careful."

With the exception of the crappy fourth-hand furniture, Lois Bradley's apartment was empty.

Bradley had packed and left in a big hurry. She left food in the refrigerator, trash on the floor, and no forwarding address. According to the property management company, she'd paid through the end of the month, two weeks from now. In Josh's experience, people who lived on housecleaner's salaries and rented month-to-month didn't waste two weeks' worth of rent, even if it was a cruddy efficiency in a questionable neighborhood.

Bradley's apartment was one of a series of tiny rooms for rent in a long, low cinderblock building. It looked more like a motel, with numbered doors opening onto a covered sidewalk with jasmine trailing up the wrought iron posts. It would seem pretty to anyone who didn't realize that the plant was like a weed out here. If someone didn't cut it back, it would take the damn posts down.

Josh leaned against the wall by the third door down. "Your dedication is impressive," he told Elise while she knocked. "Misguided, but impressive."

Elise shot him a look. "It's basic police procedure, Wolf. You're supposed to canvass the neighborhood."

"I know. I also know exactly what basic police procedure gets us most of the time." Nobody ever saw anything or heard anything—not in neighborhoods like this. It wasn't easy to scrape up rent, and they had bills to pay and troubles aplenty. If they had seen or heard anything, half the time they were afraid to say so. The other half of the time they had a bone to pick with the police, and would keep whatever information they had to themselves just for spite.

Josh looked at his watch. "You want to knock on doors, get yelled at by people, and receive noise complaints for parties that happened last month, be my guest. I'm thinking one of us ought to go back to headquarters and start checking Ms. Bradley's known associates, or at least call her boss."

"And one of us would be you, huh?" Elise asked, knocking again on the door.

"You're the one obsessed with basic police procedure," Josh answered with a shrug.

The door opened. The man who opened it was an inch or so shorter than Elise, which would make him five foot six. His scant hair was white and cropped close to the scalp, but his mustache was a luxurious affair that extended down the sides of his mouth in a classic Fu Manchu. He wore khakis belted low under a protruding pot belly and a plain white T-shirt, and he smelled of cigarettes and Aqua Velva. It almost made Josh homesick. The guy could have been his uncle Dean's double.

Elise flashed her badge.

"Police," Uncle Dean's doppelganger said. "And here I haven't baked."

"That's okay," Elise said. "We're watching our weight."

The man chuckled. Elise had a way with the cranky ones, that was for sure. "What can I do for you, officer?"

Elise flashed the picture of Lois Bradley. "Are you acquainted with this woman?"

He took the photo, stared at it for a moment, and then handed it back. "Sure. She lives a few doors down. Or she did."

"What does that mean?" Josh leaned in, finally interested.

The man eyed Josh with suspicion. Josh did not have a way with the cranky ones. There might even be those who would argue that Josh *was* one of the cranky ones. "What'd old Wall-Eye next door tell you?"

Josh shrugged. "She said she had better things to do than keep track of her neighbors."

The man grunted. "Only thing she keeps track of is the level in the vodka bottle."

Elise lifted the photo again. "And what about this neighbor?"

"She hightailed it out of here a few hours ago. Ran back and forth to her car with a lot of boxes. Round here, that generally means somebody has to move in a hurry, and that generally don't mean anything good." He ran his hand over his head. "What'd she do?"

"What time did you see her loading her car?" Elise asked, ignoring his question.

"Probably around ten-thirty. I was done watching *ER* on that TNT channel, but it wasn't lunchtime yet."

Josh winced. Would his life ever get that small? Bounded by reruns and mealtimes?

Who was he kidding? It was damn close to that now. Substitute work for reruns and ballgames for mealtimes, and that pretty well summed up his existence.

"You know her?" Elise asked.

The man shrugged. "A little. She kept to herself. Went to work in the morning. Watched TV at night. Went someplace two nights a week. I figured it might be a class or something. She wasn't too chatty. Seemed a little shy."

Elise glanced over at Josh, and he knew what she was thinking. That didn't exactly sound like the life a dangerous felon. Then again, everyone always talked about what quiet young men serial killers were.

"Where'd she work?" Josh asked. They knew she was supposedly working for a housecleaning business, but it didn't hurt to ask the neighbors what Lois had appeared to be doing.

"Worked for one of them housecleaning places. Snappy Clean? Quick Mop? Something like that. She'd zip out of here around nine or so each day with a bunch of buckets and a vacuum cleaner in the back of her car."

Elise nodded and handed the man her card. "Thank you very much. Would you mind calling me if you see Ms. Bradley return?"

"Not at all," he said, and shut the door.

She turned to Josh. "Now, was that so difficult?"

"Was it so productive?" he countered. He'd known the second he'd walked inside her apartment that Lois Bradley was in the wind. Maybe it helped to know she'd left today and not in the middle of last night, but he didn't see how.

Elise sighed and headed back to the car. "Wanna talk to the Kwikee Clean guy?"

"Boy, would I!" Josh said with false enthusiasm.

"Fine, then. Shut up and drive." She threw the keys at him and got into the car.

Aimee felt her cell phone vibrate in her purse as she walked to her car, keys already in hand. She considered not answering—two more steps to the car, to safety. Ah, to hell with it. She fished for her phone, feeling vulnerable with her hand in her bag in the deserted parking structure. The prickle of unease she'd been living with for so long bumped up a notch as she caught a whiff of someone's stale cigarette smoke. She brushed her fingers against her container of pepper spray, then grabbed her phone.

The caller ID read "Unknown Name and Number." Probably another therapist; they all blocked their numbers. Discretion and all that. "Dr. Gannon," she said, balancing the cell phone on her shoulder and opening the car door.

"Oh, hi, Dr. Gannon. This is, uh, Dr. Brenner from Whispering Pines," a young man's voice said.

Aimee slid into the driver's seat. "How can I help you, Dr. Brenner?"

"I was hoping you could send over your files on Taylor Dawkin. Her aunt told me that you had been seeing her. I'd appreciate you sharing your notes with me."

Aimee pulled the car door shut, locked it, and stifled the impulse to ask Dr. Brenner how old he was. He sounded like a kid. *Focus on the positive.* He was calling her. "I'd be happy to share everything I know with you. I could bring the file by tomorrow, say around eleven. Would it be possible for me to see Taylor then, too?"

There was a long pause. "I think you may have misunderstood me, Dr. Gannon. I'd very much like to see your notes, but I don't think we really need to meet. As for seeing Taylor . . . well, I don't think that would really be appropriate at this time."

Aimee threw her head back against the headrest. Damn it all to hell! "I'm not sure my notes can completely capture the complexity of the case, Dr. Brenner. Given Taylor's present circumstances, I think some kind of continuity of care could be helpful to her."

"I'm certain you're selling your notes short, Dr. Gannon. I'm sure they'll be sufficient. Now, when can I expect them at my office?" Brenner's voice sounded cold.

Aimee held back a sigh. "I'll messenger them to you tomorrow."

"Thank you. I appreciate your cooperation."

"You're quite welcome." Aimee hung up the cell phone and rested her forehead against the steering wheel. She'd lost that battle.

Kyle watched from the shadows of the parking garage. It had been ridiculously easy to find Aimee's car. A

Subaru—like her, dependable but not boring. Classy, but not flashy. He smiled.

His heart had quickened as she walked into view. She was so exquisite. Even more beautiful than he remembered, thinking about her night after night in that miserable place, willing her image to stay sharp in his mind, hoping he'd dream of her.

She'd have to pay for those bad nights. She'd have to pay for sending him to that stinking Vacaville facility. How could she not have seen that they were meant to be together? He'd known she wanted it; he was sure of that. Then she'd clung to that stupid fiancé after he'd interrupted them, and cried. What was that about? Just a show for everyone else?

She'd definitely have to make amends for all of that— but first Kyle wanted to watch her for a while. He loved the way she walked, head held high, long legs striding out. She was amazing, like some graceful animal striding through the forest. It's what made it so sweet when he remembered her the other way. The way he'd made her be. They way he'd made her cower on the ground before him. He could see it in his mind right now. The way she'd looked up at him, like he was a god. He swallowed hard and took a long hard drag on the cigarette in his shaking hand.

Then something made Aimee stumble.

Kyle frowned. He watched as she fumbled in her purse, distracted. She was pulling out her cell phone. She glanced at the caller ID and flipped the phone open.

Kyle held his breath. He hadn't expected to get to

hear her voice again so soon. He hadn't dared to hope to feel how the soothing tones would cascade over his body like warm water. He bit his lip and leaned forward.

Damn. She'd gotten into the car after only saying a few words. Tears pricked at the back of his eyes. The tease. She'd gotten his hopes up and then dashed them without a second thought. She'd have to pay for that eventually, too.

He watched her inside the car. Had she locked the door? Some things didn't change. She was still so vulnerable. He couldn't believe she didn't know that yet.

But he knew—and he'd be watching.

CHAPTER
8

Josh watched Dave Bradley squirm behind his cheap-ass desk. Good—he deserved to squirm, if he'd created a situation that left two people murdered and their daughter institutionalized.

Mr. Bradley was the one who had hired Lois Bradley as one of his housecleaners and had given her the keys to the Dawkins' home. The same-last-name thing? Not a coincidence. Lois and Dave Bradley were cousins.

Dave Bradley had found out that the news-breaking brutal murders were connected with Kwikee Clean when he'd gotten a call from the woman scheduled to clean the Dawkin house at ten that morning with her usual partner, Lois Bradley.

The woman had arrived and found the place cordoned off with crime scene tape and police officers crawling all over it. As far as she knew, Lois had never shown up at all. Dave had still been puzzling about what he should do about that when Elise and Josh arrived. Puzzling apparently took the form of sweating enough to leave big wet horseshoes under his armpits and clutching and unclutching his fat white sausage fingers a lot.

When Josh told Bradley that his cousin had packed up her apartment and disappeared, Bradley had turned white and sank into the chair behind his desk.

"So you were aware of your cousin's record when you hired her?" Josh sat in the cheap office chair in front of the desk.

Bradley wiped his sweaty forehead with a tissue. "Yeah, I knew."

Elise opened the trifold brochure about Kwikee Clean she'd picked up in the reception area. "Says right here that all your employees are bonded."

Bradley nodded. His Adam's apple bobbed up and down visibly in his throat.

"Exactly how did you manage to get your twice-convicted identity-thieving cousin bonded, Mr. Bradley?" Elise asked sweetly. She tapped the brochure on the edge of the desk.

Bradley gulped again. "I, uh, didn't actually. There was no way. You can't get someone like Lois bonded."

"So you lied to all your customers?" Elise asked and then turned to Josh. "Does that sound like fraud to you? It sounds like fraud to me. Do you think the fraud division would be interested in hearing about this? I think they might."

"Maybe," Josh said. "But I think the ones who would really like this are those dudes on channel three who do those consumer protection spots. You know, the ones where they follow people around with their cameras and keep the businesses' names up on their Web sites for months and months and months."

"What do you think about that, Mr. Bradley?" Elise asked. "Do you think your customers would like to find out that you've been lying to them via a fraud investigation? Or do you think they'd prefer hearing about it on TV? Personally, I think people prefer TV. It seems more glamorous."

Josh could have stepped in, but he could tell Elise was enjoying this and she needed to let off a little steam. It was far better if she let the steam off at Bradley than at him. Come to think of it, her husband probably owed Bradley a big ole thank you, too. He'd be sure to mention it the next time they got together for dinner. They could all toast Dave Bradley.

"I didn't lie to all of them," Bradley protested. "Only to the ones that Lois cleaned for. And it's not like she was going to do anything wrong; she couldn't risk another conviction. It'd be her third strike, you know."

"We're aware of that," Elise said. "We're surprised that *you* were aware that your cousin was a career criminal when you started handing over the keys to people's houses. Did you give her a little map to where she could find their checkbooks and bank statements? Or did she have to find those on her own?"

Bradley shook his head, making his heavy jowls tremble a little. "You don't understand. Lois isn't a bad person. She got herself into some bad situations and tried to get out of them a little too easy. I've known her since she was a little kid. She was always trying to take the easy way out, but she learned her lesson. She didn't like prison. Said it was like living in hell."

"So she learned she didn't want to get caught," Josh said. "No more jail time for her."

"Exactly," Bradley said. "She hated prison. Said nothing was worth going back in there."

"Maybe she was so determined not to go back that

she was willing to kill," Elise said, her voice smooth and dangerous.

Bradley was such easy prey for Elise, it was almost cruel. It was like watching a cat play with a three-legged mouse.

"No, no, no!" Bradley protested. "I'm telling you, you got it all wrong. Lois wouldn't do nothing like that. She wouldn't hurt a fly. She was the one would always catch the spiders and put 'em outside instead of squishing them. Made the rest of the crews crazy sometimes."

"Spiders can't accuse you of identity theft and send you back to prison," Elise said. "It's easy to be nice to them."

Josh almost snorted. He happened to know that Elise felt about spiders the way Indiana Jones felt about snakes. She's sooner pop one with her 9 mm than let it share breathing space with her.

"No," Bradley said with great conviction. "Lois wouldn't do nothing like that. I know it. You've got to believe me."

No one wanted to believe that someone they knew could turn into a cold-blooded killer. No mother ever thought her baby could become a rapist or a thief or a murderer. But someone's baby had done this and had found it enjoyable. That was one bad baby.

Elise slid a pad of paper across to Bradley. "We need to have Lois tell us that herself. Think you could jot down the names of some of her friends or relatives that she might have run to?"

Bradley grabbed the pad and pen as if it were a life preserver.

Aimee started the tedious task of photocopying Taylor's file for Dr. Brenner. She watched the first pages chug through the machine, then leafed through the notes from her second meeting with Taylor. It had been a blustery day, windy and cold and gray. Taylor had worn an old army jacket that had seen better days and a pair of jeans that made her legs pipestem thin.

"How's it going?" Aimee had asked.

"Fine," Taylor had said sullenly.

"Taylor," Aimee had said.

Taylor had stared at her hands and said nothing.

"Look at me, please."

Taylor had heaved a sigh that could have swept away half the Midwest, but she had looked up. Barely. "What?"

"Do we have to go through this every time you come in? Do we have to start from scratch?" Aimee asked over arms she'd crossed on her desk.

A smile had quirked at Taylor's mouth. "I guess not."

Aimee had smiled back. "Well, that's a relief. So tell me about your week."

To Aimee's total amazement, Taylor had launched into a long and Byzantine description of high school hierarchies and shifting loyalties that left Aimee stunned. She'd scribbled notes as fast as she could, hoping she was getting names and affiliations correct. "And how does that affect you?" she'd asked once Taylor had finished.

"I don't know." Taylor shook her head. "I don't get it. I don't get why any of them did any of it."

Aimee had laughed. "I think most of us feel that way about our high school years. I still can't make sense of mine."

"That's what my mom says, too." Taylor was looking down again and plucking at her clothes. "She says none of this will matter to me in five years. I won't even be able to remember why I thought it was important."

"Do you think she's right?" Aimee had asked.

Taylor had shrugged. "Probably. I don't see how she could be right now, but she says that that comes with time."

"Do you often go to your mom to talk about your problems? Or to try and figure out things when you're confused?" A solid supportive connection with her mother could make a huge difference for any girl. For Taylor, it could be a lifeline.

A shutter had come down over Taylor's face. "Sometimes. At least, I used to."

"What made you stop?"

Taylor lifted her hands up in a helpless gesture. "It was fine when I was a little kid. She always seemed to know what to do, what to say. Now she's totally lame. She doesn't have a clue about what my life is like."

That echoed what Stacey Dawkin had told Aimee. She used to be close to her daughter; now there was a chasm that she couldn't bridge no matter how hard she tried. She didn't know what caused it. She just knew it seemed to have opened up a few months before, when Taylor's behavior changed so drastically.

"Have you tried to explain it to her? Have you tried to tell her what your life is like for you?"

Taylor rolled her eyes. "What's the point? Her solutions to things were great when I was in preschool and my biggest problem was that Connor Sigal was always taking my crayons. Things are different now. It's not as easy as asking somebody to take turns."

"So what's your biggest problem now?" Aimee asked softly.

Taylor had frozen and started examining her fingernails again.

"Taylor?" Aimee had prompted.

"I don't even know," Taylor had half whispered down into her lap. "I don't know why I feel this way inside. I only know that some times I feel like I'm going to burn up from the inside out."

"Taylor, tell me about cutting yourself," Aimee said, her voice soft, but firm.

Taylor had stayed very still. She shut her eyes. "I don't know. It makes me feel . . ." Her voice trailed off.

"Do you feel numb otherwise?" Girls got overwhelmed and shut themselves down. They cut themselves to make sure they could feel something, anything. Seeing their own blood flow wasn't part of a death wish or a suicide attempt; it was actually an attempt to make sure they *weren't* dead, that they were still living, breathing beings with beating hearts still in their chests.

But Taylor was shaking her head again. "No. It's not like that. It's like I'm feeling and thinking too much.

My head feels like all my thoughts are whirling around in it so fast that it's going to spin right off. When I cut myself, it slows everything down. It focuses me and I can think. It's like a relief."

They were getting somewhere important. "How long have you felt this way?"

A wind gust shook the panes of glass in the window and a tree branch scraped the outside of the building. "I don't know." Taylor wrapped the army coat tighter around herself, losing her thin frame in its ratty bulk.

"Have you always felt like this?" Aimee pressed.

"No. Not always. There were times when everything was okay. I could think just fine." Taylor leaned forward as if she was as interested in hearing her own answers as Aimee was. "Then sometimes I'd feel like this, like I couldn't possibly make sense of stuff."

"When were the times when things were okay? When did they stop?" Maybe Taylor's behavior change coincided with when the "okay" times stopped.

"I don't know. They just did. It's not all the time, anyway. It's just something that I need to do, you know, to get focused," Taylor said with her eyes cast down.

Aimee's heart clenched. She could see how hard it was for Taylor to talk about her self-mutilation. The shame that came layered on top of the pain of the behavior itself was another hurdle they were going to have to jump together. "It's okay, Taylor. No one's judging you for this."

Taylor's head shot up and her eyes blazed. "Are you fucking kidding me? Everybody judges me for this. Everybody."

"Who judges you, Taylor?" Aimee sat back in her chair, glad to see the fire in Taylor's eyes. Turning the anger outward instead of inward was a huge step.

"My mother. My father. Other kids at school." She ticked the list off on her fingers with their chewed cuticles and black fingernail polish. "I'm a freaking cliché. The emo girl who cuts herself. I hate it. I hate me. I hate everything."

Then she had begun to sob, and she hadn't spoken again for the rest of the session.

Now Aimee thought about the blank look on Taylor's face as she had rocked herself. What was going on inside? What horrors was she protecting herself against? What things that she didn't want to feel were lurking inside there with her?

She placed a new set of papers into the photocopier. In the back of the file were some drawings Taylor had done during the three months they'd been seeing each other. Aimee unfolded the top one, a self-portrait. Taylor had drawn herself as a small figure in the lower corner of the paper. The figure's face was stark white limned in black. The body of the figure was black with a red circle in the center of it. But that wasn't what Aimee found herself staring at. It was the repeating pattern of trisected rectangles and circles across the top of the page.

She picked up her cell phone and dialed.

"Wolf here," Josh said.

"Detective Wolf, this is Aimee Gannon."

Damn, he liked the way her voice sounded even over the static of a cell phone. "What's up, doc?"

"I've found something in my files on Taylor Dawkin that I think you should see."

"That's great. What is it?" He gave Elise a thumbs-up sign.

"You know the pattern that was on the walls at the Dawkins'? It's in a drawing she did for me months ago, too."

That was interesting, but hardly conclusive of anything. "Is there anything else in the drawing?"

"It's a self-portrait. There's just that pattern and Taylor very small underneath it. Detective Wolf, I need to see her. This is important; I'm sure of it. But the psychologist at the facility doesn't want me to see her."

"Do you think it might get her talking?" Anything that might break through to her would help.

She hesitated. "I don't know, but I think it would be a first step in that direction."

For crying out loud, could a shrink ever give a definitive answer? Still, a step was a step. And it wouldn't exactly bother him to spend more time with Dr. Gannon. "Tell me again the name of the place they stashed Taylor, and I'll meet you there tomorrow morning."

CHAPTER
9

Aimee swung her car into the Whispering Pines Center parking lot, tense with excitement. She was on to something, she was sure of it. She was going to be able to help Taylor. Her shock over the murders was gone, replaced by anger. Anger was good, much better than fear. Anger burned clean.

She cruised down the parking lane, finding a spot. A vintage green sports car angled across two spaces; she could construct an entire personality profile based on that parking job. It was probably a he. He'd be controlling and manipulative, extremely precise and ordered in his ways. Perhaps a victim of some kind of abuse as a child, he tried to create order in his outer life to keep the chaos inside himself under control. No wonder the guy was visiting someone when in a mental institution—he probably drove everyone around him crazy.

When Aimee entered the lobby through the automatic sliding doors, Detective Wolf unwound himself from one of the scratched chairs.

Aimee's pulse picked up and she frowned. Fine, he was gorgeous. But she didn't need to get involved with a cop—that would be just too clichéd.

"Thank you for meeting me." Aimee walked toward him, eager to get this process started.

"Thanks for calling." He smiled down at her.

She stared up into his dark eyes and felt a buzz in her bloodstream, a connection she hadn't felt with anyone for a very long time. "I had ulterior motives," she said.

Those were to see her patient, right? Not to stare up into those dark depths or admire that strong jaw. She was betting that Brenner would step aside to let Josh Wolf talk to Taylor.

"I gathered. Ready?" He smiled and gestured to the booth.

Aimee nodded. He took her elbow and a shiver ran up her arm. She sidestepped away. He was a distraction; she needed to be focused if she was going to help Taylor.

"I'm Detective Wolf. I'm here to see Dr. Brenner," Josh said through the round metal grate.

The woman shoved a clipboard with a sign-in sheet through the Plexiglas slot and clicked on her microphone. "I'll let him know you're here." She clicked her microphone back off and picked up her phone.

Josh and Aimee both signed in and waited until one of the attendants, a short, round-faced woman with dusky skin and sleek black hair pulled into a tight bun, ushered them in and led them to Dr. Brenner's office on the second floor.

The attendant knocked on an oak door recessed into the deep blue wall, and a voice told them to enter. The attendant opened the door.

"Come in. Come in," a voice from inside the office said.

The attendant glided away and Aimee and Josh went into the office.

Dr. Brenner was tall, thin, and pale, his coloring a rarity in California where just walking to your car could put color in your skin. He looked beyond beleaguered. The circles beneath his eyes were dark and purple. His eyes were tinged with red, and his hair stuck out like he'd been running his hand through it.

Wolf settled himself in one of the chairs across from Brenner's desk, crossed one of those long legs over the other, and leaned back. Purposefully nonconfrontational, or just playing his cards close to his chest, Aimee wondered? If it came to a pissing match, she had no doubt who would win. By the way Brenner's Adam's apple bobbed, he apparently didn't have any doubts, either.

"Thank you for seeing us, Dr. Brenner. I'll cut to the chase here. We need to see Taylor Dawkin," Josh said.

Brenner sat down somewhat uncertainly. Aimee could understand why. It was Brenner's office, but Wolf had made it clear within seconds who was running the meeting. "We?" Brenner asked.

Aimee leaned forward and offered her hand. "I'm Dr. Gannon. We spoke on the phone."

Brenner's lips drew tight. "And I'm certain I made clear that while I would very much value seeing your notes, I don't think it's in Taylor's best interests to see more than one therapist at a time. She's already confused and frightened. She needs stability."

Wolf remained leaning back in his chair. "This isn't necessarily about Taylor's best interests, doctor. This is about a homicide investigation. Dr. Gannon is acting as a consultant for the Sacramento Police Department. She has valuable insights into the Dawkins' family dynamics and into Taylor especially. We need her in there, and we need her in there today."

Brenner cleared his throat. "Well, if that's the case, I . . ."

"I assure you, it's the case." Wolf never raised his voice, but something in his tone made Brenner shrink back.

"Very well, then."

Aimee and Josh both rose from their seats. "Thank you so much, doctor," Josh said.

Aimee set a packet down on his desk. "Here are photocopies of my file on Taylor. I'd be happy to discuss any of it with you. My card's in the file." She doubted Brenner would call her, but it was worth the chance.

Brenner nodded and summoned another aide to take them to see Taylor. He apologized that he wasn't going with them, because he was behind in his paperwork.

Aimee and Josh fell into step as they walked down the hall behind the aide. Aimee leaned in and whispered to Josh, "Consultant?"

A smile quirked the edge of his lips. He leaned down and whispered, "The pay's not great and the hours stink. Sure you're interested?"

His low voice against her ear sent a tingling vibration down her neck. "Definitely." She swallowed hard, not entirely sure what she'd just agreed to.

He straightened and looked down at her. "Good. This isn't exactly the part that I excel at."

She gave him a smile. "We're even, then. I'm not so hot at the part you just took care of."

That earned her a rumbling chuckle. "Guys like Brenner don't give me any trouble."

He probably ate the Brenners of the world for breakfast.

The aide opened the locked doors of the ward. Someone screamed from one of the back rooms; a blank-faced woman shuffled down the hall, clinging to the walls like they were life support. Aimee walked through in front of Josh, his large, hard hand on the small of her back. This time, she didn't pull away.

"They're in the day room," the aide said.

"They?" Aimee asked.

"Oh, you're not Taylor's only visitor today," the attendant said. "She's quite the popular girl. They often are, at first."

After a while, family and friends stopped coming. It wasn't nice, but it was true. People didn't get that good-deed feeling after visiting a friend or relative in a mental hospital. Too often, the patients couldn't or wouldn't mirror the care and concern being offered them and people eventually drifted away. Psychological wounds took as long to heal or longer than physical ones, and people lost patience after a while. Unless they'd been through it themselves, they often didn't understand why someone couldn't "just get over it."

Danny certainly hadn't understood why Aimee couldn't.

They turned the corner into a large open room filled

with long tables. The far wall had high windows through which you could glimpse the trees outside, partially obstructed by reinforcing wires. Taylor and her visitors sat at a table near the windows.

On the surface, Taylor looked better. The cuts no longer oozed. She still sat with her arms tightly around her and rocked forward and back, but she was in a chair now and the rocking was less frantic.

Aimee's heart clenched. She hated that this was progress. It wounded her to have such a bright girl with so much potential brought down to this level. It made her sick that someone this young had had to endure this much physical and emotional violence. It was the way the world worked too often.

Marian Phillips sat next to Taylor, knitting something. Next to her was a man Aimee recognized from somewhere. He was tall and broad-shouldered, with a full head of neatly barbered dark blond hair and one of those suits that made a person realize why expensive suits cost so much. It took a second for recognition to hit her. He was the man in the photos with Orrin. He had to be Carl Walter, Orrin's business partner and daredevil playmate.

He stood as they approached, and extended his hand when they introduced themselves. "Carl Walter." His handshake with her lingered a little longer than Aimee was comfortable with.

"Carl is . . ." Marian's voice trembled. "Carl was Orrin's business partner."

"And a family friend," Carl said, crossing his hands in front of himself.

Marian smiled up at Carl, her look adoring. "A dear family friend."

And a possible source of information, as someone who'd known Taylor for a long time. "It's nice of you to visit Taylor," Aimee said.

Walter's mouth drew down. "It's the least I could do. Orrin was like a brother to me. I've known Taylor since they moved to Sacramento. I can't believe this is happening."

"Mr. Walter, my partner and I would like to stop by and talk with you sometime soon about Orrin." Josh moved off to the side with Carl to make an appointment.

"Hi, Taylor." Aimee placed her hand on Taylor's back. Taylor didn't shy away, but she didn't look up, either. Aimee straightened. "Any change?" she asked Marian.

Marian shook her head. "Not really. I did get her to eat, but only a bit. They say she's barely slept, too."

"They should be able to do something about that with medication," Aimee offered.

Marian looked distressed. "I know, but somehow I don't want her so snowed under that she can't talk. What must she have seen, to make her like this?"

"She saw too much, that's for sure," Aimee said grimly.

Taylor began to rock a little faster.

"Maybe we should talk outside," Aimee suggested. She looked over at Josh, who nodded.

Carl and Marian followed them out into the hallway. Aimee turned and nearly bumped into Carl, who was so close on her heels she almost tripped over him.

He was solid, muscled like a rock under his tailored clothing, and he wore enough cologne to make her want to sneeze. She stepped back and thought she caught a ghost of a smile on his lips.

"I'm glad you're both here. We have to make Taylor feel safe if she's going to come through this. Knowing that there are people to protect her will help so much," Aimee said.

Carl took a step toward Aimee, his hand on her arm, warm and strong. "Of course," he said with a slight catch in his voice. "Anything for Taylor. I feel like she's practically my own daughter."

He was handsome, but he knew it, too. He was too confident, too assured. His stance was too studiously casual. There was something else about him, too. Something in his eyes.

"Dr. Gannon," Wolf said, clearing his throat and reminding Aimee that they were here for more than a social call.

"I was hoping we could have a few moments alone with Taylor," Aimee said, looking from Marian to Carl. There was no telling how things would go with what Aimee planned to do. She'd just as soon not have an audience or any distractions.

"Do you have a lead?" Carl asked. "Something solid?"

Aimee shook her head. "No, but there are some things I want to follow up on with her. At least as much as I can right now."

Marian frowned. "Why can't we be there?"

Aimee took Marian's hand in hers. "I think Taylor is trying to communicate with us, but something's stopping her. I'd like to remove as many variables from the process as possible until she feels like she can talk again."

"But—" Marian began to protest.

"This is a police investigation, Ms. Phillips," Wolf cut in. "If we need to talk to Taylor alone, we'll do it."

Aimee glared at him over her shoulder. It was fine with her if he intimidated the heck out of Brenner, but not so fine if he pulled that macho act with Marian.

"I think it would be easier on all of us, especially Taylor," she said.

Walter stepped into the fray. "Come on, Marian. I'll buy you a coffee."

Aimee threw him a grateful smile as he shepherded Taylor's aunt down the hall.

Josh glared at Carl Walter's retreating back. That guy was all shiny shoes and carefully styled hair and clothes way more expensive than Josh's police salary could ever provide. Josh had seen him when he came into the hospital while Josh waited for Aimee in the lobby. He hadn't thought much of him then, and his opinion wasn't improving. He didn't like how close Walter stood to Aimee or how often he found an excuse to touch her. And that smile that Aimee gave him? Josh was definitely not crazy about that.

He liked it much better when she was smiling up at him, which she was *not* doing right now. Instead she was walking back into the room where Taylor Dawkin was sitting. Fine, then. Straight down to business was fine with Josh.

Aimee sat down next to Taylor. Josh took the chair on the opposite side of the table.

"Hi, Taylor," Aimee said in that sweet contralto. "How are you doing?"

The kid said nothing. Did Gannon really expect her to start chatting? He leaned back in the chair and crossed his arms over his chest.

"I know you're frightened, sweetheart. I know this is hard, but it's very important." Gannon reached into her briefcase and pulled out a file folder. "I found some drawings in your file that you did for me back when you first started coming to my office. I was hoping we could talk about them."

Taylor didn't look at Aimee, but she did make a little snorting noise and Josh thought the rocking might have slowed.

Aimee took a piece of drawing paper out of the folder and spread it open on the table. "Do you remember this drawing, Taylor? You said it was a self-portrait. Do you remember drawing it?"

Taylor snorted again and the rocking picked up speed.

"You told me that the drawing was of how you felt sometimes. How sometimes you felt so tiny and insignificant and things were pressing down on you, threatening to squash you. Do you remember saying that?" Aimee put her arm on Taylor's shoulder. The girl flinched away.

"Taylor, can you look at the drawing?" she asked.

Taylor rocked faster and didn't look at the drawing.

Aimee took a deep breath and let it out slowly. She traced the design at the top of the drawing with her fingertips. "Can you tell me what this design means, Taylor? I know it must be important, because you drew it again at your house. Is there something you're trying to tell us, Taylor? Can you help me understand what it is?"

Taylor's rocking was now full-on frantic. Damn— this was just a colossal waste of time.

"Please, Taylor, help me understand what this means so I can help you." Aimee held the drawing up in Taylor's view.

Taylor stopped rocking and looked. Josh held his breath. Then she let out an enraged cry and ripped the drawing from Aimee's hands. In seconds, it was just a pile of shreds on the floor and Taylor was clawing at her own face. Josh was around the table and had the girl restrained before her nails could do much harm, but the girl continued to twist and kick and shriek until two orderlies and a nurse with a hypodermic arrived.

CHAPTER
10

Josh took Aimee's arm and steered her out toward the lobby. Her muscles were tense. She kept her focus on the door, waiting for the attendant to unlock it and let them out.

The door buzzed and Josh pushed it open.

"Thank you," she murmured.

As she passed by, he caught a whiff of her scent, something light with a hint of citrus. *Down, boy.*

They walked silently out of the lobby and into the parking lot. A light breeze lifted Aimee's hair and Josh glanced up at the sky. It was starting to cloud over.

Aimee stopped at the curb. "Are you okay?"

It wasn't *his* patient who'd gone apeshit. The full force of her concerned gaze hit him in the gut, but he needed to stay focused on what he'd come to find out. He cleared his throat. "Fine. How about you?"

She gave a short, tight smile. "I was looking for a reaction. I certainly got one."

"True that. What the hell did it mean?" He was more convinced now that the girl had the capacity to be violent.

"It means that Taylor's frightened. I think it also means that whatever happened to Stacey and Orrin is linked to whatever made them bring Taylor to me in the first place." She shook her head. "I wish I knew what it was, or how it was linked."

If they really were and this wasn't some elaborate ruse on the part of a crazy teenager. "What are the chances that Taylor's faking?"

Aimee's eyes widened. "*Faking?* Faking a near catatonic state? You've got to be kidding me."

"I don't think the question is very humorous," he said, stepping off the curb so they were on eye level. Lord, if those blue eyes could twist him up when she was looking up at him, he'd had no idea what being face-to-face with her would be like. His chest was as hot and tight as if he'd just run a superfast 5K.

"You're right," she said, glaring at him. "It's not funny. I can't believe you'd even consider it."

The spark was back in her eyes. Damn, he really liked that fire in her. "It's my job to consider it. I'd be irresponsible not to pursue it as a possibility. I'm not accusing her of anything; I'm only asking your professional opinion, especially as someone who knows Taylor well."

That gave her pause. He watched as she bit her full lower lip, and wondered what she'd do if he offered to take over the task. He was sure he could do a great job.

"No," she said. "I don't believe she could fake this. This is real. That child is scared literally out of her mind. I told you before. Taylor's not violent."

Josh's jaw dropped. "She just tried to claw her own face off! How can you say that?"

"She was expressing her fear and rage in the only

way she could. Besides, her violence has always been directed at herself, not anyone else."

"Can you say that with one hundred percent certainty, doctor? Could you really say that anybody absolutely is not violent? You and I have seen too much of human behavior to think that a person wouldn't have a breaking point. You yourself said that Taylor was in a fragile state. Maybe something pushed her over the edge, just like you pushed her over the edge today." The kid could have done it; Josh was sure of it. There was a lot of anger in that little package.

A shadow flashed over her face; his question clearly bothered her. "Something definitely pushed her over the edge, but not to violence against another person." Her words were firm, but her tone didn't have the confidence it had had a moment ago.

"She was pretty violent with herself," Josh pointed out. It wasn't just today's episode. It had taken a certain amount of violent effort to get enough blood to decorate the walls. Could those cuts mask scrapes on her arm from her mother's attempts to defend herself?

"That's typical of female victims." Gannon sounded confident again. "Men are much more likely to strike out when they've been a victim. Women—girls—are more likely to turn that anger inward into self-destructive behavior."

That was an interesting point, and possibly another lead to follow. "What exactly do you think Taylor was a victim of?"

Gannon shook her head. "I still don't know. I've

been going over my session notes and if there's something there, I'll find it."

"What about the symbols?" Josh pressed.

Gannon rubbed at her forehead with her thumb. "I'll keep looking. You'll be the first to know if I figure out how it relates to what happened to Taylor's parents."

Josh's eyebrows rose. That last statement was carefully put: she'd committed only to sharing information if it pertained to the case. Shrinks—couldn't trust them farther than you could throw them.

He gestured toward the parking lot and they walked to her car, his hand at the small of her back. "Do you know anything about Taylor having a boyfriend? Someone her parents weren't thrilled about?" he asked.

Aimee sighed and leaned against her car. "I know a bit."

"I wish you'd mentioned that." Just friggin' perfect. What else did she know that she wasn't volunteering? "Is there a reason you withheld that information from us?"

"Withheld that a rebellious teenage girl had a boyfriend her parents didn't like? It doesn't exactly sound like a news flash to me. Does it to you, Detective?" Aimee's voice was just as sharp as Josh's as she looked up at him.

Damn, he wished she wouldn't do that. He was pissed at her; he didn't want to go all weak-kneed and dreamy. He put his sunglasses on as if they would shield him. This woman had him twisted up in knots, and he wasn't even sure whether to trust her or not. "I suppose not, but it would have been handy information to have. Do you have the boy's name?"

Aimee gritted her teeth. "No. Taylor always referred to him by a nickname. I can look it up if you'd like. I'm sure I have it in my notes."

"We have the nickname. It's Flick, in case that jogs anything in your memory."

Aimee shook her head. "That was how Taylor always referred to him. I didn't press for his real name; I didn't want to make him more of an issue than he already was. Flick was more of a symptom of Taylor's core problem than the actual problem itself."

"If you come across anything that would help us find him, I'd appreciate your calling me." Josh watched while she unlocked the car and got in.

"Is he a suspect?"

Josh wasn't falling into that one. "We have some information that indicates this Flick was with Taylor that night. We need to check it out."

"But you think he might have seen something?" she pressed. "Or be involved somehow?"

"It wouldn't be the first time that a couple of teenagers decided to take out one set of their parents." Especially hopped on hormones and X.

Aimee shook her head. "No. Absolutely not. Taylor may have been trying to make her mother's life hell, but they were way too connected. She wouldn't have allowed her security blanket to be torn away like that."

"Then the best way to prove that is to talk to the kid. You sure you don't have anything?" Josh leaned down to look into her eyes, searching for answers in those blue depths.

"I can't help you." She stared back at him, unblinking.

"We don't have to be on opposite sides here, Dr. Gannon." He leaned closer to her. He couldn't help it.

"I hope you're right about that," she said, lifting her chin.

Their lips were so close, it took almost nothing to brush his mouth against hers, to caress the softness of that full lower lip with his own. It was only a brush and only for a second, but fire raced through Josh's veins. He pulled back and searched her face. Her cheeks were flushed, her eyes wide. Her breath came in short pants, smelling of cinnamon. That one brief taste of her had been intoxicating, but he needed more. He leaned back in.

She stopped him with her hand on his chest.

"Aimee," he said, trying to read what was going on inside her head, inside her heart.

She fisted her hand in his shirt and pulled him to her.

This kiss was no delicate brush of lips. This time her lips parted under his and her head tilted back, allowing him to explore and tease, to taste her sweetness.

"Definitely the same side," he murmured against her lips.

"I'm not so sure," she said, pushing him away. Still staring at him, she closed the door and started the engine.

Kyle nearly bit through his lip to keep himself from screaming. What the hell was Aimee doing? Who was that guy? Why was he standing so close to her? Why didn't she move away? It was disgusting how she let him practically rub against her. Pervert.

How could she have allowed him to touch her like that? She wasn't there for anyone's taking, she belonged to *him*. He'd gone to jail for her. How much more would he have to do before she understood that they were meant to be together?

He had watched the whole interaction from behind the low shrubs on the hillside that sloped up from the parking lot. The guy looked like a cop. He had that walk and that way of looking around him all the time. Kyle had had to shrink down underneath his shrub to avoid being seen. That pissed him off. Hiding like that made him feel small, like he was a little kid again, hiding in his closet or under the bed. Hoping like crazy that his brothers wouldn't find him. That he would be left alone at least for a little while.

He didn't feel like that when he was watching Aimee, though. He felt more like a hunter, like he was waiting patiently for the deer to walk into the clearing. It had been so easy to follow her here. What a joke this place was—cushy digs for the crazy kids of the rich. This was probably where that patient of Aimee's was put after someone offed her parents. Oooh, poor little rich girl has to be locked up in some hoity-toity spa.

He'd seen the girl when she'd come to therapy. He hadn't known she was Aimee's patient, but there was something about her that Kyle had found appealing. Maybe it was that she looked a little like Aimee with the black hair and the blue eyes—except Aimee's hair was real, not dyed like the girl's. This chick was nothing but a pathetic poser. She probably needed to be locked up.

Of course, they had said Kyle needed to be locked up and they had been wrong. That was a terrible place. He hadn't belonged there at all. This place wasn't anything like the hellhole they'd housed him in for all those months. Little Silver Snatch wouldn't have lasted ten minutes in Vacaville.

Kyle returned his attention to the scene below. The guy was walking Aimee to her car now. He was *touching* her. He had his hand right on her back and she was doing nothing to get away. This would not do. No. It would not do at all.

The other one—Danny—had gone. Kyle was sure of that. There was no sign of his car anywhere near Aimee's condo, and Kyle hadn't seen him coming or going. He hadn't met Aimee at any of the places Kyle had followed her to. So who was this new guy, and what the hell did he think he was doing, putting his filthy paws all over her like that?

Now the pig was kissing her! And Aimee was kissing him back! What the hell was going on?

Kyle was *not* about to have someone else move in on his territory. Was she willing to give herself to anyone who offered? Was she just another slut?

He would have to teach her. He would have to show her that he was the only one for her. He had almost done it before—he'd come so close. Then that stupid Danny had ruined all of Kyle's plans. He nearly screamed again, just thinking about it. He'd had her.

Had her right where he wanted her, and it had all been snatched away.

He shut his eyes and started to count to ten, trying to get the red to recede from his brain so he could think. He would get her back again.

He knew just how to do it, too.

Jesus, Mary, and Joseph, what the hell had he done?

He'd kissed a civilian involved in a homicide investigation in a public parking lot. What was he thinking?

He *hadn't* been thinking, obviously. At least, not with his big head. The little one was clearly thinking overtime.

Josh rubbed his face as he drove, flicking on the windshield wipers as the spring storm swept in and traffic on I-50 slowed. He resisted the urge to hit the horn. It was just a little water, people. Not a reason to slow to a crawl on a fifty-five-mile-per-hour road.

So Aimee Gannon was attractive. So she was just his type. So there was something about that measured control of hers that had him wanting to make her shudder with pleasure. He was an adult and a peace officer, for crying out loud, not a horny teenager.

At least she wasn't a witness or a suspect. If she were, he and his happy dick would be in *big* trouble now.

He drove back to headquarters, strode past the news crew parked in front with a "no comment," and vowed to focus solely on work.

Aimee gripped the steering wheel with both hands as she drove out of the parking lot. She wanted to press the accelerator down and streak away, wheels spinning and back end fishtailing. She fought the instinct down. *Breathe. Keep breathing.*

Had she really just let the detective who might be trying to make a case against her client put her in a lip lock in the middle of a parking lot?

Let him? Hell, she'd practically dragged him into her car!

The car shimmied a little as the wind picked up. A storm was coming in. She opened the car window and let the cool air stream against her hot cheeks. She gulped in the rain-tinged breeze.

She'd go back to the office. She'd focus. She'd spend more time with Taylor's file. Maybe something more would shake loose. The picture still wouldn't come clear. How could it, when she was boiling over with lust? She had to get her hormones under control.

But sexual attraction wasn't why her insides were roiling, or why she was gripping the steering wheel so hard. She was on overload. Taylor's reaction had brought it all to a head, and it was all catching up with her now. The scene at Taylor's house. All that blood. The symbols scrawled on the wall.

Aimee merged onto the interstate, heading back into Midtown. When raindrops splattered on the windshield, she rolled up the windows and switched the wipers on.

Detective Wolf wasn't doing much to leave her feeling settled and calm, either. Aimee doubted he had any control over the heat that rolled off him like a palpable force, or the smooth grace with which he moved. He definitely couldn't control the way her stomach tightened when he put his hand on the small of her back, or the way her heart had started to pound when he'd leaned into her car to talk to her, his lips close to hers. Or the way she'd practically devoured him when he'd kissed her.

She'd been glad to have him walk her to her car; he was so reassuring. Maybe it was his size. His height. The broad shoulders. The wide strong hands. The absolute maleness of him.

Aimee took another deep breath. That disturbing sense of being watched had been more intense than ever today. She had felt as if she was under observation from the moment she had left the condo. Ever since she'd been notified that Kyle had been released from the state mental hospital, she'd been on edge, convinced that danger lurked around every corner. She glanced at her purse where her pepper spray was stashed, and hoped like hell she was better prepared this time. She had a restraining order. She was on guard all the time. She was no longer as naïve and trusting as she had been. Kyle had taken that from her as surely as she had helped the authorities take his freedom from him a few months later.

On the other hand, it could all be in her head. She rubbed the back of her neck at the place where the hairs prickled when she walked alone, but the sensation wouldn't leave.

Even while Kyle had been locked up, that feeling of being watched, tracked, and hunted had stayed with her. She jumped at shadows and lashed out at everything around her. It had stayed with her longer than Danny had. Danny with his eyes full of sympathy and soul-shattering pity. Aimee clenched her teeth. She didn't need anyone's sympathy. She didn't want anyone to feel bad for her. She was fine. She just needed some more time. But Danny hadn't understood that, and eventually he'd gotten tired of trying and left.

She shook herself. Naturally, having been attacked by another violent patient would stir up her anxieties; it was called retraumatization. It was why the nice young accountant Aimee saw on Friday afternoons was claustrophobic. Every time she had to go into a small, dark place, she reexperienced her mother locking her in a closet as punishment. She hyperventilated every time she had to retrieve a suitcase from the storage space in the basement of her apartment building. It didn't matter how safe she knew the space was. On some level, she again became the seven-year-old girl who was trapped and didn't know if anyone would ever come to let her out.

Which was exactly what Aimee suspected was happening to Taylor.

At least Aimee and the accountant had the advantage of knowing what had caused their original trauma. They knew why they behaved the way they did, which was a huge step in learning to deal with it. But Taylor had been as bewildered by her own behavior as her parents had been.

Aimee pulled into the parking garage for her office, gathered her briefcase and her purse before she unlocked her car, and stepped out. This feeling of being watched was only the accumulation of stress and tension coupled with a nasty case of déjà vu. Though being able to understand it intellectually didn't make it go away, it lessened the impact.

She hit the remote to lock the car and headed for the stairs, repeating to herself that she was safe as she fingered the pepper spray in her purse.

When Aimee reached her office, a girl, maybe sixteen or seventeen years old, although it was hard to tell under the white pancake makeup and thick mascara, shot up from where she sat in the hallway. "Where's Taylor?" she demanded. "What have they done to her? Where the hell is she?"

CHAPTER
11

After talking to Lois Bradley's sister, Josh stood up and spoke to Elise over the wall of his cubicle. "The sister's lying." No one would admit to having seen Lois since she'd hightailed it out of her neighborhood. "She says she hasn't seen Lois or heard from her in over a week, but it sounded rehearsed. I don't buy it."

"Want to go check it out?" Elise offered.

"What else we got?" The crime scene techs had been working their asses off and evidence was starting to pour in. Until Josh and Elise figured out what mattered, though, it was just stuff.

"Doc Halpern called. Our perp has to be at least six feet, based on the damage to Orrin Dawkin's skull." She tapped her pen on her desk.

"That lets the girl off the hook." Taylor Dawkin was only about five foot four.

"Depends on how tall the boyfriend is," Elise said, flipping through a folder. "Clyde pieced together the wine bottle Taylor used on herself."

Josh raised one eyebrow. "Was it a good vintage?"

"It was a custom bottle from an e-commerce company and the Dawkins had close to a case of the stuff. Might be worth paying a call on the company. It had

Taylor's fingerprints on it, but it had four or five other sets as well that they haven't identified yet."

Josh pinched the bridge of his nose. Finding Lois Bradley seemed like the hotter lead. "Let's wait to see if they get hits on the other prints. Did you get hold of Sam Parker?" Parker was with the sheriff's office. He'd had the misfortune of catching a weird-ass culty ritual murder the year before. Elise had thought it would be a good idea to let him take a look at what Taylor had drawn on the wall to see if he could make anything of it. Maybe the symbols were some sort of cult thing.

"Yep. I sent him photos of the crime scene. He said he'd take a look and get back to us ASAP."

Josh had looked some stuff up on the Internet. He hadn't seen anything connected with Satan worship that looked like what Taylor had drawn on the walls and, frankly, the Web sites had given him the heebie-jeebies. What the hell was wrong with these people? Didn't they have any idea how much evil lurked right outside their front doors? You didn't need to manufacture this stuff; it was out there waiting for you. They should be building barricades against it, not inviting it in.

Elise shrugged. "So let's go talk to the sister. The wine bottle and the bloody walls will still be here when we get back."

Josh rose. "And Lois Bradley might be halfway to Mexico already." He grabbed his suit jacket from the back of his chair. It was a hell of a lot easier to get answers in person than it was over the phone. It was too easy for people to lie when they didn't have to look you in the eye. It was too easy to miss the telling detail that could help unravel whatever web of deceit the person had woven when you weren't there watching them, too.

They were halfway through the maze of cubicles when Ed from financials caught them. Ed was a tall, lanky guy with a beaky nose, a bald head, and watery brown eyes half-hidden under droopy lids. He always reminded Josh a little of a vulture, but he was Josh's kind of vulture. There was no one better to pick over the remains of someone's financial life and pull out the tidbits that could really bring an investigation together. "Hey, guys, you might want to see this," he said.

"You got something already?" Josh's pulse quickened. He loved it when things started to come together.

"I got something. Maybe not what you're looking for, but I thought you should know about it." Ed rubbed his hand over his shiny pate. "Orrin and Stacey Dawkin were broke."

Elise shifted her weight onto one leg and rested a fist on her hip. "In that crib? Those people were broke? How the hell did that happen?"

Josh wondered, too. That house was worth a ton. It wasn't some crappy McMansion in Elk Grove.

"They had a second and a third mortgage, plus car loans and a boat loan. Credit card debt, too. Four cards totally maxed out and two more that were creeping up. They had debt up to their ears. I'm not sure your identity thief would have found much to steal."

"She wouldn't have known that, though," Elise said,

glancing over at Josh. "She would have thought the same as we did, that they had pockets worth picking."

"Where was the money going?" Josh asked. Gambling? Drugs? Those would be two very popular choices for people getting in over their heads financially. They would also be two very popular choices that might lead to homicide. Neither of those worlds was exactly overflowing with law-abiding citizens.

"I'm not sure yet," Ed said. "I've got some more digging to do. I thought you'd want a heads-up on their financial situation."

They thanked him and he headed back to his basement cubicle.

"You still want to shake down the sister?" Elise asked as they headed out the door.

"Seems worthwhile," Josh said.

"Anything worthwhile at the loony bin where they locked the kid up? Did Gannon's hot lead pan out?"

Josh shrugged, acting nonchalant. "Can't say, really. Taylor went apeshit when she saw the drawing, but I still don't know what it means."

"Did Gannon have any ideas?"

Other than to let him put his tongue down her throat? "Nothing specific. She thinks the murders are tied to something that happened when Taylor was a kid. Other than the drawings, I don't see how they're connected and that seems pretty loose."

Elise shrugged into her jacket. "It didn't hurt to make contact with the new shrink. Make sure we hear anything Taylor says or does that might help us."

"Yep." Josh pushed the door open and held it for Elise.

"She didn't do this, Josh." Elise slipped her sunglasses on.

"If she didn't do it, she saw something. I'd put money on it." He slipped his sunglasses on, too, even though the sun didn't bother him one bit.

Aimee glanced behind her. She was alone. Her heart pounded in her chest and her mouth went dry. The girl took a step toward her. Aimee took a deep breath and resisted the urge to take a step back. She would not be pushed. Her hand dropped inside her purse and touched the pepper spray.

"Taylor isn't here," Aimee said, her voice calmer than she felt.

"Where is she, then? What are they doing to her?" the girl screamed, her fists clenched at her sides. "They're brainwashing her, aren't they? I won't let them fucking do it. You've got to let me see Taylor! I'll report you!"

"No one is trying to brainwash Taylor. They're trying to keep her safe." Aimee kept her arms at her sides, remaining as physically nonconfrontational as possible. Being aggressive in response would only fuel the girl's fire. She swallowed her fear and stood her shaky ground.

The girl rolled her raccoon-ringed eyes. "Safe from what? Safe from thinking for herself? Safe from her friends? Who's keeping her safe from *you*?"

"We're trying to keep Taylor safe from herself," Aimee said, not raising her voice.

"What do you mean, she has to be kept safe from herself? What'd she do? Did they lock her up? Where?" the girl demanded.

"Let's sit down and I'll explain to you what's going on." Aimee walked past the girl, unlocked the door to the office, and gestured to the couch and chairs. "What's your name?"

The girl sat down, her eyes wary. "I'm Caitlin. You're her shrink, right?"

"I'm Dr. Gannon," Aimee said.

"She talked about you." Caitlin relaxed a little bit into the couch.

So apparently whatever Taylor had told Caitlin about her was good. That would make this easier. "I guess you've heard about Taylor's parents."

"Who hasn't? Everybody at school is talking about it, and nobody knows where Taylor is. No one will tell me anything. I called her house, her cell, the police station."

"You must care about Taylor a lot to go through all that trouble." Aimee kept her eyes on Caitlin and her voice low.

Caitlin's eyes filled up with tears. "I do. I need to know she's okay. I need to know what they're doing to her. I wanted to help her. I mean, my parents are fucking idiots, but that doesn't mean I want someone to kill them. They're saying at school that she found them. She's gotta be totally freaked."

"I'm glad you understand how upsetting that was for Taylor. She *is* having a really hard time. So hard that she can't have many visitors yet. Things are getting a little bit better. If you give me your phone number, I'll call you when she can have visitors and you can go see her then."

Caitlin looked hard at Aimee. "You promise they're not doing a *Girl, Interrupted* thing to her?"

"I promise," Aimee said, fighting a smile.

Caitlin chewed on her lower lip. "Taylor said you were okay. She said she kind of trusted you."

"I'm glad." Aimee pulled two business cards out of her wallet and handed them to Caitlin. "Jot your number down on one of them and I'll keep it, and you keep the other one. You can call me and I'll let you know how Taylor's doing, okay?"

"Okay," Caitlin said. She wrote down the number and handed it to Aimee, tucking the other card into her backpack.

Aimee stood and headed toward the door. "Caitlin, there is one thing you might be able to do to help Taylor."

"Name it." Caitlin got up from the couch.

"I need to know where I can find Taylor's boyfriend, the boy she called Flick."

Lois Bradley's sister, Tammi Paston, was a hard-faced woman with teeth that looked like the "before" in a cosmetic dentistry ad. She lived in a rat-trap duplex on Northrop Avenue. "I'm telling you," she said for the fourth time, "I haven't talked to Lois since last Thursday night. She was supposed to come over, but she called and said she was too tired from cleaning all day. I haven't heard from her since."

"Is that typical?" Elise asked. "Do you often go for days without speaking to your sister?"

The woman looked over at Josh and rolled her eyes. He so was not used to being the good cop, but he smiled and shrugged. The woman turned back toward Elise, her eyes narrowing. "She's my sister, not my kid. I don't keep tabs on her."

"So you're not close," Elise said.

"I wouldn't say that, either." The woman was getting impatient. Behind her, the theme music to *Sponge Bob Square Pants* played loudly. "Look. I haven't talked to her. I haven't seen her. Not in a few days. We usually talk once a week or so. It depends on what's going on. What do you want with her, anyway?"

"She's a person of interest in a homicide investigation," Josh said, leaning against the doorframe and smiling down at her. "We need to ask her some questions."

The eyes narrowed further. "You're looking for the wrong person. Lois tried to cash a few checks that weren't hers. Other than that, she's harmless."

There it was again. Nobody thought their relative was all that bad. It was just a few checks that didn't happen to actually belong to her that had gotten her into trouble. No big deal.

"Maybe. Maybe not," Elise said. "We need to talk to her and find that out."

Tammi chewed her lip. The volume of the TV behind her went up a few decibels. "You kids turn that crap down," she yelled over her shoulder, then turned back toward Josh and Elise. "Person of interest, huh? In a homicide? Sounds important."

Josh leaned forward a little more. "It is, Tammi. Very important."

She smiled. "So is finding her worth some cash?"

Aimee sat in her office and tapped Josh's card against her desk. Her heart picked up speed at the thought of talking to him again. She still couldn't believe that she'd kissed him like that. She ran a finger across her lips, marveling at how his lips had sent her reeling.

She took a deep breath and dialed Josh's cell phone number.

"Detective Wolf."

The familiar growl of his deep voice started a vibration that ran down her nerve endings. "I've got some information for you on Taylor's boyfriend."

"On Flick? Great, what do you have?" Enthusiasm lit his words.

"I'm afraid it's not much, but I did find out where he works." It was all Caitlin would give her, but it was something.

"It's a start. Where does he work?"

"Hot Topic. At Arden Fair Mall."

"Great. Thank you." He was clearly going to hang up.

"Wait. Could I talk to this boy when you pick him up?" Flick might know something about the symbols, or something that might help her get inside Taylor's shell.

"You want to question my suspect?" He didn't sound pleased.

"No, of course not. I'd like to ask him some questions about Taylor to see if I can find out anything that I might use to help her. Because we're on the same side, right? Because helping my client doesn't have to be mutually exclusive from helping with your investigation?"

"I did say that, didn't I?" He chuckled. "Fine. I'll let you know when we track him down. I can't promise anything, but I'll try to get you a few minutes with him."

"Thank you. Also, I'd really like to get back in to see Taylor again." As long as she was on a roll, she might as well go for all the prizes in the basket.

There was a hesitation on the other end of the line. "Because she was so helpful the last time?"

Aimee closed her eyes, trying to block the image of Taylor clawing at herself. "No. Because I need to make sure she's okay, and I doubt they'll let me in again without someone forcing the issue."

"So what will you do when you get there? Bring more drawings?"

"No! I really just want to make sure she's all right. Maybe sit for a while near her." She'd pushed hard enough for now.

"What the hell will that accomplish?"

"I need her to feel safe with me again, and that might take some time."

"Aimee—"

She interrupted. "Please, Josh."

There was that hesitation again. She felt like she could feel him breathe, sense his chest rising and falling. "Aimee, this is a homicide investigation. There's not really time to sit around and do nothing."

"Not for you, but for me. I just need you to get me in the door," she pleaded.

It took him a long while to answer. "All right."

They arranged a time to meet and hung up.

Aimee glanced up at the clock. She had a few minutes before her next client showed up, so she opened Taylor's file again. She was convinced that here lay the key that would help her unlock Taylor from her prison.

CHAPTER
12

Lois Bradley had come with them docile as a lamb, murmuring a quiet protest as they'd cuffed her and put her in the back of the car.

Josh looked at her through the peephole in the interrogation room. They'd put her in one of the cushy rooms, one with a chair and carpeting and a table, but it was still an interrogation room, and Lois Bradley clearly knew what that meant. She sat at the table, her hands clasped in front of her, her head bowed down, the picture of defeat. Josh felt a stab of pity for the woman. What chance did you really have in life when your own sister would rat you out for sixty bucks?

Elise opened the door and strode in. "Hello, Ms. Bradley."

Lois Bradley looked up, her eyes full of tears. "I didn't do anything. I swear I didn't do anything. I don't even know what happened to those people."

"Those people?" Elise said, sitting down across from Lois. "Which people would that be?"

A look of confusion passed over Bradley's face. Josh read it all too easily. She was asking herself if she'd made a mistake already. She was thinking maybe she was protesting that she didn't have anything to do with the wrong crime.

She wasn't wrong, but it was good to let her sweat a little bit. Josh sat down next to Elise, who didn't take her eyes off Bradley.

"Which people are you talking about, Lois?" Elise asked again.

"The D-d-dawkins," Bradley stammered out. "This is about them, isn't it? I swear I didn't have anything to do with it. I don't even know what happened. I just know I got to their place to clean, and there was yellow tape and cops everywhere. I turned around and left. I didn't have anything to do with whatever happened there."

Josh leaned forward. "Those people are dead, Lois. That's what happened there. Somebody killed those people. You know anything about that?"

"Oh, no. No, no, no," Lois moaned. She wrapped her arms around herself and rocked. "Those poor people."

"Poor?" Elise leaned in now, too. "Why do you say that? They look like they had it made. Big house. Big cars. A boat. A cabin in Tahoe. Poor, my ass."

"Things aren't always what they seem from the outside." Lois Bradley leaned forward. "When you clean people's houses, you learn more about them than most people see."

"Like where they keep their spare checkbooks?" Josh asked. "Or what their credit card numbers are?"

"No! I swear, I am out of that kind of business forever. I never want to go back inside. Never."

That was the opening Josh had been looking for. "You want to stay out of prison bad enough to kill somebody who caught you stealing, Lois? Is that what happened?"

The woman's eyes went wide. "No, that's not it. I'm working hard. I'm checking in with my P.O. I'm staying away from bars. I'm one hundred percent clean."

Josh leaned back. Interrogation was a dance. You had to know when to lead and when to follow. "So how come you said the Dawkins were poor? What was so poor about them?"

Lois looked down at her hands. "They weren't so happy. You'd think a house like that, a life like that, they'd be happy, but they weren't. Mrs. Dawkin, well, she drank. I'm pretty sure of that. White wine isn't a man's drink, and there were an awful lot of empty Chardonnay bottles in their recycling."

"A lot of people drink wine, Lois. That doesn't mean they're unhappy."

Lois shook her head. "It wasn't just that, either. She seemed . . . lonely. I don't know."

"You can tell whether someone is lonely by their garbage? What are you, the trash whisperer?" Josh shook his head.

"Not just their trash. Their sheets. Their magazines. Their shoes. Where their stuff is. You can just tell." Lois looked from Elise to Josh and back to Elise again.

Josh knew what Lois meant. He'd learned a hell of a lot more about people from where their stuff was and what was in their garbage than from interviewing them. People lied. Garbage didn't. "Okay. So Stacey Dawkin was lonely. Who isn't, now and then? That still doesn't tell me why you said they were poor people."

"Well, there's that daughter of theirs. That one's trouble." Lois nodded her head.

This could be interesting. "What made her trouble?"

"She was into all kinds of stuff. I found empty booze bottles under her bed. Roaches on the windowsill. Pecker marks on her window from her skanky boyfriends hanging around outside. That girl's bad news. I'm telling you, if you're looking for an inside job, you should be looking at that girl."

Aimee had suspected sexual abuse from the start, given Taylor's constellation of symptoms. Taylor had seemed completely baffled when Aimee brought up the subject, but many survivors of sexual abuse went years without any memory of what had happened, especially if the abuse occurred when they were children. The trauma and the confusion were so great that they blocked the event entirely. Then suddenly one day, something would trigger a memory. It might be a certain smell or going to a certain place or having a child of their own to protect, but the memories could come flooding back and be completely overwhelming.

Aimee believed that Taylor had been on the verge of having that flood come back, and she'd hoped to keep the memories from drowning Taylor when they rushed over the emotional dams she had built. Maybe the trauma of her parents' murder had made them all come back at once, and without anyone there to help, Taylor had gone under the pounding waves. Could it have to do with those patterns of circles and squares?

Aimee couldn't figure that out without knowing what the symbols meant.

She did find one interesting item in her notes. During one session, she'd asked Taylor how she'd felt about moving to Sacramento. Taylor claimed not to really remember much from that time period. When Aimee had pressed, Taylor had said that Sacramento sucked then as much as it sucked now, a typical sentiment. Lots of things in Taylor's life sucked.

Aimee tapped her pen against her teeth. Some kind of trauma had happened to Taylor around the time that her family had moved to California; she was sure of that. Marian Phillips's comment about Taylor's personality change, coupled with Taylor's lack of memories, was like a giant red arrow screaming "look here." And something had happened six months ago to bring it all back and send her into a tailspin.

Nothing in her interviews with the Dawkins seemed to help. When she had started probing their memories in that meeting, Orrin Dawkin had immediately gotten angry.

"What exactly are you getting at, Doctor?" Orrin Dawkin had countered, frowning. "If I knew something had happened to my daughter years ago, don't you think I would have done something about it then?"

"Sometimes parents don't know something has happened or can't prove something has happened, and are reluctant to take action on just a bad feeling or a suspicion. Can you recall any moments like that? Moments that you were uneasy? Or when Taylor seemed frightened out of proportion about something or someone?"

"How about you stop beating around the bush, Dr. Gannon? What exactly are you implying here? Are you implying that someone has hurt my little girl?" Mr. Dawkin had leaned forward in his chair, his eyes narrowed into a squint. Mrs. Dawkin had reached out for her husband's forearm.

To restrain him? Aimee had wondered. Or to calm him? Either way, it was an interesting response to her husband's sudden aggression.

"Yes," she had said, not backing down. "I'm concerned that someone could have abused Taylor sexually."

"And you think it was me?" Dawkin was almost out of his chair, despite his wife's restraining hand. "With my little girl?"

The fact that Dawkin had brought up sexual abuse himself made Aimee doubt that he was responsible, although fathers were generally the first people to come under suspicion for that kind of crime. It sickened Aimee how many men tried to justify raping their daughters, stepdaughters, granddaughters, and nieces, leaving a trail of destruction. But Mr. Dawkin didn't look interested in justifying anything. He looked like he might be physically sick.

"Not necessarily you, Mr. Dawkin," Aimee had said. "Is there anything that could have triggered Taylor's recent behavior change that could be a reminder of something in the past?"

Mrs. Dawkin had shaken her head. "I've racked my

brain. We lead a pretty boring life. We have a routine that works for us and it doesn't vary much. I can't think of anything that changed that could have sent Taylor reeling like this."

They had left promising to keep thinking about what Aimee asked, in case something jogged their memories. That had been the last time she'd seen Orrin and Stacey Dawkin.

She shuddered. Could they have remembered something that started this whole terrible mess?

Elise and Josh left Lois Bradley cooling her heels in a holding cell. They'd check out her alibi—a woman named Joanne Crowley who'd been with Lois at the community college from six-thirty to nearly ten o'clock—as soon as they were done with Carl Walter.

Dawkin-Walter Web Consultant's offices looked like pretty much every other set of offices for every other company whose purpose Josh couldn't figure out. He decided it was the fault of the Management Consultants Gone Wild mentality of the nineties, with even itty-bitty businesses having mission statements about leveraging worth and maximizing potential that made it damn near impossible to figure out what anybody did for a living anymore. The police force was no exception. They were supposedly "striving to be proactive" and "anticipating trends," among other things. At least "cop" was still a recognizable profession. For now.

He held the door to the glass and steel block open for Elise, glancing around the parking lot. Someone was doing okay. There was a red Mercedes CLK class convertible and a silver Lexus RX in the lot. Inside, the carpeting was beige. The walls were a slightly different shade of beige. A young woman with long, blond-streaked brown hair and tired eyes looked up from her computer. "Can I help you?"

Josh flipped open his badge. "We have an appointment with Carl Walter."

Her face crumpled and her eyes filled with tears. "Is this about . . . Orrin?" Her chin quivered.

"I'm afraid so," Josh answered. The receptionist was certainly going to miss old Orrin. In fact, it looked like she was going to miss him a lot. He wondered what that meant. He glanced over at Elise, who raised her eyebrows infinitesimally. Yeah, she'd caught it, too.

"We're all crushed," the receptionist said. "Crushed."

"I take it you and Mr. Walter were close," Elise said.

Josh let her take over; it seemed the right time for that woman-to-woman touch. It always impressed him how easily Elise could move from that girly compassionate stuff to being one of the guys. The woman was a chameleon.

"We were. He was awesome to me. Awesome." The receptionist pulled a tissue from the box on her desk and blew her nose. "He was helping me figure out what I wanted to do, so I could go back to school. My dad's so pissed at me for dropping out that he won't even talk to me about it, but Orrin was amazing. Totally amazing."

"How was he helping you. . . ." Elise let her voice trail off. "I'm sorry. I didn't catch your name."

"Oh," the girl said. "My name is Caroline. Caroline Trevalayne."

"I'm Elise Jacobs. It's nice to meet you."

Caroline smiled and ducked her head. "Nice to meet you, too."

"So how was Mr. Dawkin helping you?" Elise shifted her weight onto one foot.

"Oh, he'd take me out for coffee a couple of times a week and we'd talk. I really felt like things were becoming clear. He had so much vision." Caroline's hands rose in the air like little doves attempting to wing away as she spoke.

Josh again got the infinitesimal eyebrow raise from Elise. CEOs of even small companies did not generally spend time taking their receptionists—their young, leggy receptionists—out for coffee to hear about their hopes and dreams unless they were looking for their phones to be answered in private.

"It's like he could see people so clearly. Completely clearly." Caroline's face crumpled again. "I'll really miss him."

Elise put her hand on Caroline's forearm and said, "We are so sorry for your loss, Caroline."

Caroline sniffed and straightened herself. "Thank you," she said as if she were Dawkin's grieving widow. Josh thought about what Lois Bradley had said about Stacey Dawkin being lonely and sad. Would she have been as broken up over Orrin's death?

"Do you think you could let Mr. Walter know we're here?" Elise asked.

Caroline's hand went to her mouth. "I'm so sorry! I totally forgot."

Elise smiled. "That's okay. It's important that we know as much as we can about the victim in these cases. You were a big help."

The big eyes went liquid again. "I was?"

"Absolutely," Elise assured her.

Caroline hit some buttons on her phone and said, "The police are here to see Carl. It's about Orrin." She paused for a moment and said, "I'll tell them."

She hung up and looked up at Elise. "Carl will be right out to talk to you," she said, as if a great honor were being bestowed.

"Thank you."

Josh and Elise moved off to the side of the reception area to wait. "Think we should talk to some of the other female employees?" he asked in a quiet voice.

"Couldn't hurt. I wonder how many young women Orrin was totally, totally awesome to," Elise said with a smirk.

A few moments later, Carl covered the reception area in a few long strides. "Detective Wolf," he said and extended his hand to Josh.

"Mr. Walter, I'd like you to meet my partner, Elise Jacobs," Josh said after shaking Walter's hand.

"It's a pleasure, Detective," Walter said. "Or would be if it were under different circumstances."

Elise nodded, noncommittal but polite.

"Thank you for taking the time to meet with us," Josh said.

"Anything to help you get to the bottom of this tragedy."

The man was a little too good looking for Josh's comfort. He'd thought his original reaction to him had been because of the way Carl had stood so close to Aimee at the hospital; he hadn't liked the proprietary air with which Carl had placed his hand on Aimee's arm. But his reaction here was just as negative as it had been the first time. He smothered it. It wouldn't help get him what he wanted at the moment. "We appreciate it. Could we speak in private?"

"Of course." Walter led the way down the corridor to his office.

Naturally, the guy had a corner office. Josh thought about his industrial-grade carpet-covered cube and stifled a sigh. Perhaps his mother was right and he should have gone into a different line of business.

"What can I tell you?" Carl said after they'd all sat down.

"To start with, can you think of anyone who might have wished Mr. Dawkin harm?" Elise asked.

Carl turned slightly to look at her. "What exactly do you mean?"

"Is there anyone who might have held a grudge against Mr. Dawkin? Anyone who was angry with him?"

Walter sighed. "The business climate is pretty cutthroat these days. There are any number of people who are jealous of our position in the industry, and a few more who might have been looking to take advantage of what they might have seen as deep pockets. But people angry enough to kill Orrin? And Stacey along with him? I can't imagine."

"We need names, Mr. Walter," Elise said, her fingers laced in her lap, her voice respectful but very definite.

"Names?" Walter repeated as if unfamiliar with the term.

"Yes. Names of business associates who resented Mr. Dawkin's success or had some sort of bone to pick with him. Names of competitors who are a little more cutthroat than the others. Names of disgruntled employees."

Walter's eyebrows went up a bit on the last. "Did Mr. Dawkin have some problem with a disgruntled employee, Mr. Walter?" Josh asked.

Walter leaned back in his big black leather chair and frowned. "Name me a firm that doesn't have a disgruntled employee or two."

"I'm sure everyone has them. *Not* everyone gets their head bashed in in their own living room. We need to check out everyone, Mr. Walter." Elise's voice never rose, but the steel in her tone was unmistakable.

"Including me?" Walter said, leaning forward.

"Do you have a reason for wanting Mr. Dawkin dead, Mr. Walter?" Josh kept his voice even, although his pulse began to pick up. There were two reasons for most murders: sex and money. Who better than a business partner to have a money motive for murder?

Walter shoved back from his desk. His face flushed scarlet. "Of course not! I was being facetious. Orrin was like a brother to me. I'm going to be lost without him."

"Then you won't mind telling us where you were on Tuesday evening," Elise said pleasantly as she pulled out her notebook.

"I . . . I . . . wait a second. Let me think here." Walter's eyes darted back and forth between the detectives.

Elise smiled blandly, her pen poised over the notebook.

"I, uh, I worked here until six-thirty or so and then went to the gym. I stopped for a cup of coffee at a Starbucks near there. I go there all the time; they'll probably recognize me and you can check with the gym. You have to swipe your membership card to go in."

Elise scribbled it all down, along with the name and address of Carl's gym and which Starbucks he went to.

"Now," said Josh. "What about the names of those disgruntled employees and business associates?"

Walter began to list people and spell their names. There was nothing like being asked for your alibi to make giving up someone else's name more palatable, Josh thought wryly.

"We don't have particularly high turnover here, considering what this industry is like," Carl said. "We've had a few people leave to go on to other opportunities who we would have been happy to keep. We've had a couple more move away after realizing what it costs to live out here. I don't suppose you're interested in any of those people."

"Not really," Josh said, keeping his eyes on Walter's face. Most people had some kind of "tell" when they lied. It's what professional poker players relied on and cops, too. Walter looked unhappy and uneasy, but he didn't look like he was lying. There was no downward glance to the left. No nervous picking at his fingers or compulsive shuffling of papers on his desk.

"You want the dirt, then," Walter said and shifted in his chair as if the plush leather had suddenly become too warm.

"If you feel like cutting to the chase, then yes, we want the dirt," Elise confirmed.

"The only person we've let go where there's really been bad blood was a young woman who worked on our administrative side. Her name was Doreen Hughes." Walter looked out the window.

"Bad blood in what way?" This was finally getting interesting.

"Orrin had to fire her. It was quite unpleasant. He went through the trouble of firing her with cause. It's not much fun, but financially for the company, it was the better decision."

"And what was the cause?"

Walter steepled his fingers and looked at Josh over the top of them. "Doreen had a drinking problem. Serious enough that if she wasn't drunk at work, she certainly reeked of booze. More than one of her coworkers noticed it. She was a bright young thing, one of those smart kids who hadn't quite found her way. Orrin was encouraging her to go back to school. We have quite a generous tuition reimbursement program here."

A bright young thing being taken under Dawkin's

wing? That had a familiar ring to it. "That was kind of him."

"We consider it an investment in our future. Good people are hard to find, and we try to hold on to them." Carl looked Josh directly in the eye.

The guy was just a little too sincere. There was something about true believers that always made Josh a little wary. "So what went wrong?"

"Well, like I said, the girl apparently had a drinking problem. It wasn't too long before her work suffered. She'd come in late, take long lunches, that kind of thing. Then she'd go to Orrin and try to cover it up. In the end, we had to let her go. On her way out she made some . . . ugly accusations." Walter's gaze went back to the windows.

"What kind of accusations?" Josh asked, although he was guessing he already knew the answer to that question.

"Doreen claimed that Orrin had made improper advances to her and that when she'd refused him, he sabotaged her. She said she was going to bring a sexual harassment suit against the company." Walter rubbed the furrow between his eyebrows with his thumb. "It was exactly the kind of publicity we did not need."

"And?" Josh asked. They'd run Orrin and Stacey Dawkin's names through the system. If any kind of case had been filed he'd have known about it already. Nothing had been filed except a complaint against a contractor three years earlier regarding the remodeling of the Dawkins' bathroom.

"And we paid her some money to go away," Walter said, his words tumbling out fast.

"A lot of money?" Elise asked, her head tilted to one side.

"I guess it depends on your version of a lot," Walter answered with a rueful smile. "When it's coming out of my pocket, it tends to look like a lot to me."

"Could we have a ballpark figure?" Josh asked.

"Six figures," Walter said. "Is that specific enough?"

That was serious money in Josh's book. Very serious.

"We get the idea." Elise glanced over at Josh and started to rise. That was his cue to ask any last questions he might have. He stood, too.

"Thank you for taking the time to talk with us," Elise said.

As they were turning to leave, a young man came into the room. "Oh," he said. "Dad, I'm sorry. I didn't know you had someone in here."

"That's all right, Sean." Walter motioned the young man in. "This is Detective Wolf and Detective Jacobs. They're here to talk about Orrin and Stacey."

The young man gulped. "Here? They don't think anyone at Dawkin-Walter Consulting is involved, do they?" He glanced at Josh and then Elise and then back to Carl.

"No, of course not. They're gathering information. Detectives, this is my son, Sean. He moved back to California and joined the firm about six months ago. He's been working quite closely with Orrin on the administrative and financial side of the business." Walter stepped over to his son and put his arm around his shoulders. The resemblance was striking. Sean had his father's hair, his height, and his broad shoulders. He had the same slightly Slavic high cheekbones and chiseled chin. He was a looker, all right.

He definitely lacked his father's self-assurance, though. Sean nodded at his father's statement, but offered nothing of his own.

"Can you think of someone who might want to hurt Orrin or Stacey?" Elise asked Sean.

Sean stepped backward as if he'd been shoved. He glanced at his father, whose expression was one of polite interest, and didn't say anything.

Carl said, "It's okay, Sean. If you have something to tell them, by all means, do it now."

Sean looked slowly away from his father's face, first to Elise and then to Josh. "Nothing that I can think of."

"If you think of something, we'd appreciate it if you'd give us a call." Josh gave business cards to Sean and to Carl. "Anything at all. Even if it seems minor to you."

When they were at the door, Josh remembered one more thing he wanted to ask about. Feeling way too Columbo-ish, he turned in the doorway. "One more thing: did either of you see Orrin or Stacey on that day?"

Carl gave his head a shake. "Orrin had been working from home quite a bit. We spoke on the phone a few times and e-mailed, but I didn't actually see him."

"How about you, Sean?" Josh asked.

"I, uh, I brought some papers over to him that day."

"Really? Around what time?" That was interesting.

Sean licked his lips. "I'm not really sure. After lunch, I think."

"And how did he seem?"

"Seem?" Sean looked so confused, Josh was starting to wonder if he spoke fluent English.

"You know, did he seem nervous? Like there was something on his mind?" he pressed.

"No. Not that I noticed. I mean, Orrin was a very intense person." Sean glanced down to his left. "He always had something on his mind. He was always thinking about something. It's part of what made Dawkin-Walter Consulting so successful. Orrin was always looking for an edge. But no, there didn't seem to be anything worrying him in particular."

Elise reiterated their request to call them if anything came up or they thought of anything, and they left.

Josh tossed Elise the keys and got into the passenger seat. It was her turn to drive. She got in, turned on the car, and cranked up the air conditioning to blow the warm air out of the car before she shut the door. "So I wonder what young Sean is lying about."

CHAPTER
13

"We've got a footprint." Clyde was nearly dancing by Josh's cubicle. "A bloody one."

"And it's not ours? You're sure of it?" The Dawkin place had been covered with footprints by the time the crime scene unit got there. It was nobody's fault: the first officers on the scene had had no idea what they'd been walking into until they were already in the middle of it.

Clyde nodded. "Positive. I checked."

"What about the guy who found them? Norchester? You sure it's not his?" The man had hightailed it out of the Dawkin home as fast as he could, intent on making it out the door to puke. He wasn't thinking about not disturbing a crime scene, and it would have been easy for him to track blood out.

"Not unless he was wearing shoes way too big for him," Clyde said, clearly very happy with himself. "Dude's a size nine, and even with just a partial—we've got a heel and part of the sole—this guy's at least an eleven. I'd put my money on eleven and a half."

"Great!" Elise said. She'd stood up in her cubicle the second Clyde had started talking and had come around behind him. "Anything specific about the shoe that'll help us?"

"You're the detectives," Clyde said. "I'll send you up a copy. See what you can do with it."

"Thanks so much," Elise said, her eyes narrowed.

Elise stayed in the entryway into Josh's cubicle after Clyde walked away, drumming her fingers against the metal edging. "Told you it was a man. Not many chicks out there wearing men's size eleven and a half shoes. I'm barely a men's seven and a half." She looked down at her long, elegant feet.

Josh leaned back in his chair. "One shoe print does not a perpetrator make."

"But it means somebody besides Taylor was there to walk through the blood. If it wasn't the perp, he still knows something he should be telling us. Who walks out of a house like that and doesn't call the cops?" Elise's fingers had picked up pace in their drumming.

Josh shot a rubber band at her hand, hitting her knuckle. "No doubt. I'm just sayin' that I'm not getting all excited over a partial footprint. It *would* eliminate the kid, though."

"That would be nice," Elise said. "You eliminate our paperhanger yet?"

Josh sighed. He had indeed. Lois Bradley's alibi with Joanne Crawley had checked out. So much for sewing this case up fast and easy. "She was in a math class at the community college from six-thirty to eight-thirty and then meeting with her study group until ten. Damn her."

"It is truly astonishing, the nerve some people have. Imagine trying to better herself that way, and just when we're trying to pin a double homicide on her, too." Elise shook her head. "I've pieced together what I can of the Dawkins' final night. As far as I can tell, Orrin never left the house that day. Stacey bought . . ." Elise paused and looked at her notebook. "Chicken breasts, couscous, some frozen vegetables, and two bottles of Chardonnay at approximately three-fifteen from the SaveMart on Elk Grove Boulevard."

"Two bottles?" Josh asked, thinking about what Lois Bradley had said about Stacey Dawkin hitting the sauce.

Elise shrugged. "Maybe she was stocking up. Maybe she was going to sit in her living room and get quietly plowed in ladylike fashion. Maybe she was going to pour it in the tub and bathe in it."

She was right; two bottles of Chardonnay meant nothing. "I don't see anything there," he said. Nothing in Stacey or Orrin's last day sounded like it could have predicted the hideous way their night would end.

"Me neither," Elise said. "One more thing, about Dr. Gannon . . ."

"Yes?" It wasn't like his partner to be coy.

"I figured out why she's so familiar."

"Yeah? Why?" Josh sat up straighter.

"Remember the shrink who was attacked by one of her patients two years ago?"

"You're kidding. That's her?" Josh sat back in his chair.

"Mmm hmm. The guy stalked her. Found out when she'd be alone and tried to rape her." Elise kept her voice flat and even.

"Who stopped him?"

"According to the file, it was her fiancé, a Danny Stannard."

Josh wasn't sure which he found more irritating: the fact that Aimee Gannon had a fiancé, or the fact that knowing she had a fiancé made his teeth clench. Why the hell had she kissed him like that if she had a fiancé?

"Apparently he kept calling her and she didn't answer. He got worried and went to her office. He kept the guy from raping her, but the guy had beat her up pretty bad."

Josh sighed. "What happened to the perp?"

"State mental hospital."

"For how long?" Josh asked.

"He got out six weeks ago," Elise said.

Elise's cell phone rang. She flipped it open. "Jacobs here." After a moment, she stood up a little straighter and looked over at Josh with her eyebrows raised. "We'll be right there," she said and snapped the phone shut.

"Where exactly will we be, and why?" Josh asked, already standing up.

"We'll be downstairs talking to Ed, because he knows why the Dawkins were broke."

Carl Walter whistled to himself as he walked out into the parking lot. Last night's thunderstorm had blown through and left the air rain-washed and clean. God, it was good to live in California. If someone else had been with him, he might have remarked about what a lucky man he was. He'd act humble and grateful, as he knew he should act. Underneath though, Carl knew that people made their own luck. He certainly had.

His car was a case in point. He's always wanted a vintage sports car. He'd had this one for more than ten years and he kept it spotless. That wasn't luck. That was good planning and taking care of what needed to be taken care of. He whipped the handkerchief out of his pocket and rubbed a spot off the finish of his green Mercury Cougar. He never used the handkerchief except on the car. Really, blow your nose in something and then stick it back in your pocket to carry around all day? The amount of bacteria that would contain was disgusting. But his mother had always insisted that a gentleman carried a handkerchief, and Carl was damned if he was going to be anything but a gentleman. He carried it in his personal kit that he always kept in the breast pocket of his suit. The kit that helped him take care of his daily business without exposing himself too much to other people's germs.

Carl got in the sports car and pulled out of the lot. Taking care of business in general was going to be a lot more difficult without Orrin. He'd never find anyone as simpatico to his way of thinking as Orrin had been. There were so few people of that caliber, so few people who thought the way he did and had the brains to put it into practice. Meeting Orrin had been like finding a long-lost brother and far more providential.

He did have Sean. That was some relief, but Sean was . . . weak, flawed. Carl blamed the boy's mother. It certainly didn't come from his gene pool; he came from a long line of strong men. Sean could probably fill the gap until Carl found someone he could trust in the CFO position, but not much more.

Carl cursed the circumstances that had brought this all about. Fate certainly dealt some harsh hands, but he'd handle it. If nothing else, he could always count on himself.

He turned the corner into his neighborhood. Sarah and Thomas would be waiting to have lunch with him. He knew that Sarah would already have lunch on the table by the time he walked in the door. She liked to please him and she knew that would make him happy. Finding her had also been providential luck. No, that wasn't true. He'd searched a long time for a woman who was right for him. He never wanted to make the same mistakes he'd made in marrying Sean's mother. That had been a disaster. He probably was lucky that she'd done no more than leave him and taken Sean with her. Having Sarah in his life was the result of Carl's own hard work.

And little Thomas. He was on his mind nearly all the time. Such a sweet boy. Carl had high hopes for him. It was like getting a second chance to do things differently than he had with Sean. He'd learned from his mistakes. He was still winning the little boy's trust right now, but he was making good progress, and so much more sweetness would come of it. Carl was sure of that. It was well worth putting in the work.

Carl sighed. Orrin had had no second chances. That girl of his was even weaker and more flawed than Sean. Carl couldn't believe what he'd seen at that mental hospital the day before. It had taken everything not to physically recoil from Taylor as she rocked back and forth, practically drooling with all the drugs they'd pumped into her system. Carl doubted that she'd ever snap out of it. If she did, would she be able to piece together a cohesive narrative of what had happened that night? The kid had had a screw loose for years. Orrin hadn't wanted to admit it and Stacey had tried to cover it up, but Carl knew. He had a special sense about those things. He could sniff out the weak ones.

He'd stop by Whispering Pines again this afternoon and see how she was doing. He'd keep a close watch on her progress, maybe send Sean to monitor it, too. That way, Carl would know what was coming and be able to direct it.

Yes, sending Sean was the way to handle it. Now that he knew what his plan would be, he felt much better. It was good to be in control. He hadn't thought that he'd minded sharing the power with Orrin. He'd been happy with the way they'd divided the company, with Orrin taking care of the finances and Carl directing the technical end of things. Now, though, he was starting to realize that it might be even better with Orrin gone. He'd never say that out loud to anyone, of course. There were so few who would understand. But he knew the truth of it himself, and that was all that counted.

Carl pulled into his driveway and got out of the car, looking around the yard with a critical eye. The lawn service was supposed to have been there that morning. Had they slacked off on the mowing because of the rain? He'd measure later. You had to watch people every damn minute.

When Carl pulled open the front door, Thomas was in the family room watching that show about the boy aardvark. Sean had liked those books when he was a kid, too. "Hey, kiddo. What's Arthur up to?" he asked.

"Losing a tooth," Thomas said, looking up at Carl. "Is it time for lunch?"

"Just about." Carl picked the little boy up, tossed him in the air, and blew a big raspberry on his tummy.

The child giggled in response. "Stop," he squealed. "Stop! That tickles!"

"It does?" Carl roared. "Does this tickle?" He blew another raspberry.

"Yes! Yes! It does! Stop it! Stop it!" The little boy kicked his feet ineffectually, and Carl set the boy down.

"Hey, Dad," a much deeper voice said from the hallway.

Carl hadn't realized Sean would be here. It seemed like every time Carl was trying to spend time with Thomas, he'd turn around and see Sean watching. How long had he been standing there watching them now?

"Hi, Sean," Carl said. "I'm glad you're here. I was hoping you could stop by and check on Taylor today. I'm not going to have time and I want to make sure she knows we're around."

Sean nodded his assent, but there was something in his eyes that chilled Carl. He had seen it before when he was playing with Thomas and his older son was around. The briefest of shadows crossed Sean's face when Carl paid attention to the little boy. It would only be for a second, then it would disappear. But for that brief second, Carl was afraid of his own son.

———

"Whatcha got, Ed?" Elise strolled into Ed's crowded cubicle and, as usual, propped her hip on the desk.

"I got the reason your vic was leveraged up to his eyeballs, is what I've got." Ed rocked his office chair onto its back legs and patted his chest with pride. His heavy-lidded eyes had a sparkle to them.

"Do tell," Josh said, leaning up against the cube entry.

"Dude was a day trader," Ed said, as if that explained everything.

"A what?" Elise asked.

"A day trader. He traded stocks. He'd keep 'em for a few hours, ride their momentum up—or, in Orrin's case, down for the most part—and then sell." Ed brought his chair down onto the floor.

"Is that legal?" Elise asked.

"Yeah. I mean, there are rules, which it looks like your guy was a little dicey on, but nothing that would have interested the SEC. His problem was he got stuck with some margin calls." Ed shook his head like a teenager's parents shake their heads over a speeding ticket.

Elise drummed her fingers. "What the hell is a margin call?"

"Say you bought some securities with borrowed money," Ed began.

"Borrowed from where?" Elise cut in.

Ed looked up at Elise. "That's an interesting question and I'll get to that in a minute, but I can only explain one thing at a time."

Elise sighed. "Fine. Go ahead," she said, still drumming her fingers.

"Okay. Let's pretend that you bought some securities

with borrowed money. Then those securities tanked and their value dropped below a certain point. The broker might make a margin call and force you to deposit money into the account to bring it up to a certain level." Ed looked over at Josh, who nodded that he was following the explanation.

"But if you borrowed the money to buy the securities in the first place, where would you get even more money to deposit into the account?" Elise wasn't drumming her fingers anymore.

"Therein lies the rub, sweetheart." Ed smiled sadly. "You'd have to borrow more to cover the margin. Then because you were already in over your head, maybe you'd borrow even more to make more investments, to try to come back from your losses."

"This is starting to sound like those guys who end up losing their houses at blackjack tables," Josh said.

"The similarities are striking," Ed said. "Some of the government Web sites post a quiz to see if you have a gambling problem on their day trading pages."

Elise looked over at Josh. "Remember those photos in the hallway of the house? All those photos of Orrin skydiving and rock-climbing and scuba diving?"

What Josh remembered was watching Aimee Gannon stand in front of the photos in a pair of slacks that cupped her ass in a way that made him jealous of the fabric, but she had a fiancé. She should have worn a ring. A woman should make it clear that she was taken. It was just plain cruel to let a man dream. "I remember."

"Those are the playtime of somebody who likes to take risks. What's riskier than being a gambler? And what's even riskier than gambling with your family's security?"

Josh straightened up and said to Ed, "So you're telling us that Orrin Dawkin had gutted the value of his house and lost everything he had doing this day trading?"

"I haven't nailed down all the specifics, but it sure as hell looks like it."

"You think he might have borrowed more? Maybe from somebody he shouldn't have been doing business with?" Josh's mind raced. Loan sharks didn't generally kill people who owed them money; it made them difficult to collect from. But maybe if you got in deep enough, they might decide to cut their losses or make an example of you for other upstanding citizens.

"Could be," Ed said. "I'll keep digging and see if I can track from where and when money came in, and to where and when it was going."

"What do you think?" Josh asked Elise. "Russian mob, maybe? They play pretty rough."

"Some of those Asian dudes aren't all sweetness and light, either," Elise observed.

Something still didn't feel right, though. "I can see bashing a man's head in over money, but the torture aspect of Stacey's death doesn't feel like the product of a business deal. It felt personal."

"I know. Maybe whoever they sent was a little more suited to the job than anyone knew, and got off on it."

Josh nodded. "Let's let Ed figure out if this is turning into a RICO case that the feds'll rip out of our hands."

CHAPTER
14

Aimee had had an early appointment with a professor at Sac State who was, in Aimee's opinion, trying to figure out how to leave her husband. Breaking up a relationship wasn't easy. Although with Danny, it had taken less than a year to go from wedding planning to divvying up CDs, dishes, and furniture.

She had a two-hour break before she had another client, enough time to meet Detective Wolf and check in on Taylor—assuming they'd let her in after the way things ended yesterday. She tried to still the butterflies in her stomach at the thought of seeing Josh again.

After parking at Whispering Pines, she sat for a moment in her car. How long would Taylor be in this place? It was going to get terribly hard for Marian Phillips to stay down here. Eventually she'd need to go home to Redding, to her own life. There was no way she would be able to begin to process her grief over her sister's murder while she was here in crisis mode. Plus Marian had her own life to get back to, her own home and her own children who would need her. Would Taylor be ready to go with her? Would Taylor *ever* be ready to leave this place? Aimee had to believe that she would.

She walked across the parking lot, enjoying the

feel of the sunshine on her shoulders. The sensation of being watched wasn't nearly as strong today. How much of it had had to do with yesterday's dark clouds and stormy weather? What a weenie! She'd come a long way since Danny's departure gave her a wake-up call that her life was off the rails, but she still had further to go. She glanced up at the surrounding hills and saw nothing but bushes and scrub oak.

Inside, she sat in the reception area to wait for Detective Wolf. He strode through the doors less than five minutes later, his long legs eating up the distance between them. "Dr. Gannon," he said.

"Josh." She stood to face him. "Thanks for coming. I appreciate it."

"Don't thank me. We're not through those doors yet." He started past her to the reception booth.

"Wait." She reached out and grabbed his arm. "I think we need to talk."

He looked down at her hand on his arm and then back up to her face, his eyes hard. "What about?"

She gaped at him. "Yesterday? In the parking lot?" *When you kissed me and took my breath away?*

He clenched his jaw. "I apologize. If you'd like to lodge a formal complaint, I'll make sure you have the appropriate names and contact information."

Aimee drew back and dropped her hand. "I don't want to lodge a complaint, I—"

"Excellent. You can be assured that it won't happen again. Now, we both have work to do." Josh gestured for her to walk in front of him to the reception area.

Aimee, stung and confused, did as he suggested.

He'd been right to be doubtful. The receptionist took one look at them, squinted her eyes, and started dialing her telephone. Brenner was down in the waiting room in a matter of seconds.

"I simply cannot let you compromise my patient's condition any further for any reason. I have no idea how far you set her treatment back yesterday, but I will not allow it to happen again." He crossed his arms over his skinny chest and glared at Aimee.

She deserved the reprimand. She'd had her reasons, though. "I assure you that I don't have any intention of upsetting Taylor further today, Dr. Brenner. It was important that I find out if seeing that drawing would get her to start communicating. Surely you see that. There's so much at stake here."

"And now she may not communicate for months." Brenner pressed his lips into a tight line.

"I disagree," Josh said from behind Aimee. He didn't move, but he made his presence felt. "Taylor communicated more yesterday when she ripped that drawing apart than she has since we found her."

Brenner took a step toward Josh. "In any kind of trauma work, revelations surface when they're ready to surface. Rushing them can only set the process back."

Josh straightened to his full height and looked down at the other man. "That may be, but this isn't just about trauma work, Dr. Brenner. It's about finding out who killed that girl's parents. You can let my police consultant in to talk to her now, or I can come back later with a court order. But trust me, when I come back, I'll be cranky."

Brenner backed away a step. "It seems I don't have a choice, then."

Josh shepherded Aimee past the other man and through the door. "No, you really don't."

"He's right, you know," Aimee said quietly to Josh as they climbed the stairs to the locked ward.

"About what?"

"About trauma work, and letting people's memories and feelings surface when they're meant to. I can't force her." People had tried many ways to do that and it simply didn't work.

He shrugged. "If you say so."

"What's happening with the investigation?" she asked.

Wolf glanced down at her and cocked his head to the side. "You don't really expect me to answer that, do you?"

"Have you found Flick?"

He looked at her again and didn't answer.

"Do you think he's involved?" she pressed.

"Dr. Gannon—" Josh started.

"Aimee," she interrupted.

"Dr. Gannon," he repeated, his voice firm. "I cannot discuss details of an ongoing homicide investigation with you."

What bee had gotten in his bonnet? She'd hoped he'd at least let her know whether Taylor was still a suspect. She'd hoped to have him put his hand on the small of her back so she could feel the warmth spread through her. She'd hoped to see the way his sudden quick smile transformed his face, and to feel the shiver down her spine that came after he spoke low and close to her ear.

Aimee straightened her shoulders. It was just as well. She was here for Taylor, not to flirt with the cop who might be trying to lay the crime at Taylor's feet.

They found Taylor in the common room again. She sat hunched over in her chair, rocking slightly, with the stuffed dog that Marian and Aimee had found, clutched in her lap. This time she was with a young man whom Aimee hadn't met before. He leaned in toward Taylor and spoke very softly with a very intent look on his face. Aimee strained to hear him.

"I am so sorry, Taylor. I can't tell you how sorry I am," he said. "If there was any way I could make this up to you, I would. I hope you know that. I hope you can hear me." He sat up, a distressed look on his face, and noticed Aimee and Josh.

He stood up fast, as if he'd been caught with his hand in the cookie jar. "Detective Wolf," he said, his voice wary.

Aimee walked toward him. "Hi, I'm Dr. Gannon, Taylor's therapist."

"Ohhh," he said, his brow uncreasing. "I'm Sean Walter. I worked for Taylor's father."

"Nice to meet you," Aimee said, shaking his hand. He didn't have that same magnetic pull that his father had, which was fine with Aimee. Carl Walter made her a little uncomfortable.

"I just wanted to see Taylor and let her know I was thinking about her. I'll get out of your way," he said.

"That's okay," Aimee said, placing her hand on Taylor's shoulder. She was relieved that the girl didn't shy away from her touch. "I don't want to interrupt. I can go get a cup of coffee and come back if you'd like."

Taylor's hand reached up and closed over Aimee's.

Kyle couldn't believe Aimee was visiting Little Miss Fancy Pants again. She'd never come to visit him. Not once, and he'd been in Vacaville for months. What was so special about this stupid girl? So her parents were dead. Boo hoo hoo. Kyle's mother had died when he was little, but that hadn't gotten him any traction with Aimee.

He lit a cigarette and took a deep drag, his fingers trembling. There'd been a moment as Aimee walked through the parking lot that she'd glanced up at the bushes that hid him. She couldn't see him, but could she sense him? Did she know he was watching? He licked his lips and his heart beat harder at the thought. They were connected. He knew it. That glance proved it.

Then, of course, the pig had shown up. Aimee still allowed that asshole to be around her. He would have to do something about that. He wasn't sure what yet, but he'd come up with something.

First he had to find a way to communicate with Aimee, to let her know he was here. He knew all about the stupid restraining order, so he'd have to be careful. He needed a plan.

Kyle started to map out his strategy.

Aimee almost jumped when she got a reaction from Taylor. Taylor still kept her eyes cast downward and her free hand still clutched the stuffed dog. The hand she'd put on Aimee's was like ice. Aimee closed her other hand over it to warm it.

"No, no," Sean said quickly. "There isn't anything to interrupt. We were all done."

Josh cleared his throat and Aimee looked up at him. "Dr. Gannon, if you have what you need from me, I need to be going." He walked out of the common room without saying good-bye.

Aimee sighed and watched his retreating back. What the hell had happened? How did he go from kissing her until she could barely see straight to giving her the cold shoulder? Why?

Sean headed toward the door as well, but before he got there, his cell phone rang. He gave Aimee and Josh an apologetic smile. "Excuse me," he said, pulling the phone from his pocket and flipping it open.

"Hello," he said into the phone and listened for a moment.

"Bingo? You mean Thomas's puppy?" he asked, then listened again. His brow creased. "No. Not since last night. I think I saw him in the laundry room when I got home from work. Have you checked all the closets?" He listened again. "Of course I'll come help look. He's probably just asleep somewhere."

He snapped the phone shut and shook his head. "My little brother has apparently misplaced his puppy. I've been summoned home to participate in the great puppy hunt." He smiled.

Aimee sat down next to Taylor and rubbed her back. "How old is your brother?"

"Five," Sean said. "He's actually my stepbrother. Or, I guess, my stepbrother-to-be. My father's remarrying. Thomas is his fiancée's son from a previous marriage. He's a great kid."

"With a lost puppy," Aimee said.

"Yes, so I need to be going, I guess. It was nice to meet you." Sean walked out the door and Aimee turned her attention fully to Taylor.

"Hi, Taylor," she said softly. "How's it going?"

Taylor kept rocking, but she didn't let go of Aimee's hand.

"Are you feeling any better?" Aimee felt a little stupid continuing to ask questions when she was getting no answer, and she sighed and patted Taylor's back. For now, all she could do was to let Taylor know she was there ready to help her when Taylor was ready to receive help. They sat for a while in silence.

Marian Phillips bustled through the door and stopped short when she saw Aimee. "What are you doing here?"

Aimee stood. "Marian, I'm so sorry about yesterday," she said.

"You're sorry?" Marian marched across the room. "I'm supposed to be protecting this child. I trusted you. When I came back from lunch, they had her in restraints and so drugged up she couldn't even open her eyes."

This was her fault; there was no getting around it. "I rushed the process, Marian. I shouldn't have. But I think it was important to try."

"I'm not willing to lose my niece by trying to find her parents' killers." She glared at Aimee.

"This is as much for Taylor as it is for anyone else." Aimee explained to Marian about finding the pattern drawn on the self-portrait from months before.

Marian sank down in a chair next to Taylor. "The same pattern as the one on the walls? What does it mean?"

Aimee sat down next to her. "I'm not sure, except that it means something to Taylor."

Marian nodded and looked around. "Did Sean leave?" she asked.

Aimee nodded. "Something about a missing puppy. He had to go help find it."

"He was that kind of boy, always helping out. I was glad to see that he'd turned into such a nice young man. I haven't seen him in years. When Carl and Nancy split up, Nancy went back to the Midwest. She was raised there and her parents were still there. She took Sean with her. I suppose he came back for visits now and again, but I never saw him. Stacey said he decided to come back and work for his dad and Orrin after he graduated. Orrin was very complimentary about his work. He's apparently a very bright boy with a head for finance. And I think Taylor liked seeing Sean. She rocked a little bit faster when he came in." Marian pulled her knitting out of her bag.

"Were they friends before Sean left?" Aimee asked. Taylor had never mentioned Sean in their sessions, but if he'd been gone for a long time, there was no reason that she should.

Marian smiled. "I think Taylor had a bit of a crush

on him. She used to follow him around all the time. You saw how handsome he is, just like his father. He was a beautiful boy." Marian blushed a bit.

Aimee nodded. "They're both very good looking men."

"Amen to that, sister," Marian said feelingly. "Sean must have been in his early teens when he left. He never had any of those awkward phases preteen boys usually go through."

"It's nice that he gets along so well with his father's new family. Not every adult child is so happy about a parent remarrying, especially when it brings new children into the picture."

"I know!" Marian exclaimed. "It's as if he's been waiting his whole life to have a little brother. He spends a lot of time with little Thomas, really dotes on him."

"That explains his rush to get back to help with the puppy hunt," Aimee observed.

Marian pulled out her knitting. "That and he may have felt a little awkward around you. He's very shy. Stacey mentioned that he seemed more withdrawn than he had as a kid. It's odd. I remember him being more charismatic, a real leader. But I guess people change in all kinds of ways."

Aimee crouched down to eye level with Taylor and put her hand on Taylor's arm. "Hey, Taylor, I brought you something." Aimee laid out the art supplies on the table in front of Taylor.

Taylor remained still.

"I thought you might want to do some drawings,"

Aimee said as if it were the most normal thing in the world. "Dr. Brenner said I could leave these supplies here for you to use any time you want."

Taylor clutched Sammy the dog tightly in her left hand, but moved her right hand to rest on the box of chalk.

Aimee could see that Marian had noticed, too. She put her hand on Marian's arm and gave a small shake of her head. When Marian's brows drew down in confusion, Aimee touched her finger to her lips. Marian nodded. She started to chat about real estate prices while both women pretended not to watch Taylor.

Taylor flipped open the box of pastels and ran her fingers over the chalks. She still didn't appear to be looking at Aimee or Marian, but Aimee was certain she was aware of their movements, and kept hers slow and still. Taylor barely seemed to be looking at the box of pastels, either. She kept her head down and continued to rock steadily and to keep the stuffed dog clutched in her lap.

Then Taylor took a piece of chalk from the box and tentatively started to draw. From the corner of her eye, Aimee could see the marks she made were barely visible. She could also tell that it was getting harder and harder for Marian to pretend not to be looking. Over the next few minutes, Taylor began to make more definite marks. Her arm moved with more energy and she would stop rocking for a few seconds now and then.

Aimee and Marian were no longer pretending to talk, but they kept their distance. This was a huge breakthrough for Taylor, establishing a connection with the outside world. She had to be allowed to express herself without pressure, without judgment, without questions.

She filled one page, ripped it off the tablet, and started on the next one. She drew faster, and her gestures were larger. Aimee held her breath. She desperately wanted to grab the sheet that Taylor had turned upside down on the table and flip it over to see what secrets it might reveal, but she couldn't. Not without risking that Taylor would stop drawing completely.

Taylor filled a second sheet and ripped that one off the tablet, casting it on the floor. It landed face up.

Taylor had drawn the same set of symbols she'd drawn on the walls of the living room.

CHAPTER
15

Once Josh had rejoined Elise, their next stop was to see the president of the company that had created the custom wine bottle Taylor had used to gouge herself. They'd called ahead to let Garrett Cohen, president and CEO of Sac City Data, know that they were coming, but they hadn't told him why. It was often as informative to find out why people thought the police were asking them questions as to get the answers to the questions themselves. Josh often got some pieces of information by letting people talk on their own.

Sac City Data was housed in a square two-story glass and steel box in Roseville. They took up the eastern half of the first floor. The offices were nice, but not too nice. The guy at the front desk had black spiky hair and a Bluetooth earpiece and wore jeans and an untucked dress shirt that screamed "trendy." It wasn't easy being a hipster in Roseville, and Josh almost felt sorry for the kid. "Can I help you?" the young man asked as they walked in.

Josh flashed his badge. "We're here to see Garrett Cohen. He's expecting us."

Spiky Hair's eyes opened a fraction wider. "I'll buzz him right now."

A few minutes later, a heavyset man with pale red

hair and freckles across his doughy face trundled out of the back rooms. "Detective Wolf? Detective Jacobs?" he said tentatively and stuck out his hand.

Cohen was younger than Josh expected, but it seemed like everybody was, these days. How somebody who looked barely old enough to get into a bar could own and operate a company that employed thirty people was a mystery to him.

Cohen led them through the maze of cubicles to his corner office. The inside of Sac City Data didn't look all that different from the inside of the police department. The cubicles were a little bigger. The carpet was a little cushier and significantly less stained. The cube walls came up a little bit higher and looked a little sturdier. Basically, though, there wasn't much difference.

Cohen settled his bulk behind his desk. The blinds were pulled against the glare of the sunlight and possibly against the view of the parking lot. He took a swig from the Rockstar energy drink on his desk.

"Thanks for taking the time to see us," Josh said, sitting down across from Cohen.

"It's no problem at all. Can I get you guys some coffee? Maybe a soda?" There was some sort of inherent reflex in people that made them want to treat a visit from the police like a social call. Cohen licked his lips as if he was thirsty, or perhaps nervous. It wasn't an uncommon reaction to having the police show up on your doorstep, either. Even people without so much as a parking ticket got tense when a detective asked for a few minutes of their time.

"We're fine, thanks." Elise sat next to Josh and got

right down to business. "Did your company have a wine custom bottled and labeled recently, Mr. Cohen?"

Cohen looked startled. "Yes, we did. We had a Merlot put in custom bottles to celebrate our launch about a month ago. We opened the virtual doors on this puppy and we wanted to do something special for everybody who worked on it, and for our first customers, too."

Elise plunked one of the bottles they'd found in the Dawkins' wine rack down on Cohen's desk. "Is this the wine you had bottled?"

Cohen picked up the bottle. "Yes, this is it. Was there something wrong with the wine?" He snapped his fingers. "Oh, my God! Was this one of those counterfeit wines I've been reading about?"

Josh ignored the other man's question. "Is there a reason that a man named Orrin Dawkin would have had a bottle of the wine?"

Cohen paled behind his freckles. "This is about Orrin Dawkin? I should have realized that when you called. I couldn't believe it when I saw it on TV. I couldn't imagine who would do something like that to him and to his wife, too. Do you guys think the daughter did it?" Cohen leaned forward.

Elise barely blinked, but Josh saw her jaw clench. "The wine bottle, Mr. Cohen? Why would Orrin Dawkin and his family have had a bottle of the wine you had specially bottled for your company?"

Cohen focused on the bottle in front of him. "Oh, yeah. Orrin's company did most of the programming behind our launch. Without Carl's programming, we would never have gotten off the ground. I sent a bunch of bottles to Carl and Orrin and to their office."

"Sent? As in through the mail?" Elise asked.

Cohen shook his head. "No. I gave them to Carl Walter and his son, Sean. They came to the launch party. Orrin couldn't make it, so I sent bottles for him and for their office with them." He blushed a little. "I'd had a little to drink by that time. I think I sent them out of here with a case or two. I was feeling pretty magnanimous."

"So you did business with Walter-Dawkin Consulting?" Elise asked.

"Quite a bit," Cohen said. "Like I said, they were responsible for pretty much all the programming behind the scenes of our Web launch. Well, them and some of their subcontractors. Although that seemed to be a sore point."

"Sore point with whom?" Josh leaned forward, and Cohen leaned back. The dude might be president and CEO, but he was no alpha dog. Carl Walter probably had him cowering in a corner and peeing on himself.

Cohen's forehead creased. "Nothing, I guess. It was just something weird at the launch party. I'd gotten the bill from Orrin for the last bit of programming, and he had two subcontractors on it. It's cool. Everybody subcontracts. I mean, I was subcontracting my software engineering needs out to them, right? It was just that Carl had blown a bunch of smoke up my ass about how he oversaw all the work the company did, and was responsible for the quality assurance on it. I felt a little ripped off when I found out they were using subcontractors. I mean, how's he supposed to do quality control when the stuff is all done in India or something?"

"Good point. So what seemed to tick Walter off about the subcontractor thing?" Josh asked.

"It was weird," Cohen said. "I ribbed Carl about it at the party a bit and he didn't seem to think it was funny. I got the impression that the fact that they were using subcontractors was news to him. He wanted to know their names and which invoice they were on, and a bunch of stuff that I would have thought he could look up easier in his own files. I made some smart-ass remark about it. Like I said, I'd had a little to drink and was probably a little looser than I should have been. Anyway, Carl got pretty huffy, and so did his kid. Although it's hard to read that one. He gives me the heebie-jeebies." Cohen gave a little shiver.

"You mean Sean Walter?" Elise asked, her head cocked to one side. She often homed in on things a witness would say that another investigator would blow past, and those offhand remarks often seemed to be the very point the case turned on.

"Yeah. Sean's kind of . . . twitchy. It's weird. Carl is so smooth and so assured and so . . . charismatic. People are drawn to him. You should see it when he walks through here. Half the women drop whatever they're doing and stare, and I'm not just talking about the young ones. The kid is practically a carbon copy of him, lookswise. Same build, all tall and broad-shouldered. Same dark blond hair cut the same way. Same clothing style, even. Personality, though? It's a totally different deal. At the party, he sat in a corner looking miserable while his father held court by the shrimp cocktail."

"Did he seem to know anything about the subcontractors?" Josh asked.

Cohen shook his head. "No. He seemed as surprised about it as his father, but he told his dad he'd look into it for him."

"Do you think you could get us the names of those subcontractors you mentioned?" Josh asked.

Cohen said he could have them in a couple of minutes, and excused himself to go talk to his accounts payable department. He was back in less than five with the names jotted down. Josh and Elise thanked Cohen again for his time and headed out.

Damn it. Damn it. Damn it. What had the shrink heard him say? Sean pounded his fist on the steering wheel. He couldn't even remember what he had been saying when she'd walked in. He'd been so startled, he'd lost track of everything but the need to act normal in front of her.

Crap. How the hell did you act normal in front of a shrink? They didn't think anyone was normal. They saw neuroses behind every tree and psychoses under every rock.

Maybe she'd only seen him talking quietly to Taylor. That would be good. And really, it was all he had done. He'd just wanted to talk to her. He'd been trying to talk to her alone since he came back to California six months ago, but she dodged him all the time.

Then, with her dyed hair and pierced eyebrows and

weird clothes, she seemed unapproachable. She clearly didn't want to talk to him. Maybe it was best to leave it all alone.

He doubted the shrink would agree with him. His own shrink back in Minnesota sure hadn't. He'd wanted to examine every detail, every memory. And what had it gotten Sean? He'd thought it would get him a chance at a regular, normal life, something he hadn't been sure he would ever be able to have. Instead, Sean felt worse since he'd come back to California than he had in years.

He wondered what went on behind that calm façade Taylor's shrink projected. He was sure psychologists all went into the mental health profession to heal their own wounded psyches and to pretend to be superior. This one was all smooth dark hair and sweet low voice on the surface, but he bet she did something psycho when she was alone. He could sense those things. He knew who was vulnerable and who wasn't. He bet she ate entire gallons of ice cream and then made herself barf. Or maybe she had sex with strangers she picked up in bars. She had no right to look at him the way she had. She was every bit as damaged as he was; he'd bet money on it.

What had that look she'd given him meant? What had she heard? Damn it. He didn't know why he was torturing himself about it. It didn't matter. He hadn't really said anything. Taylor would understand what he was trying to tell her. Nobody else would, because nobody else knew what had happened the summer that the Dawkins moved to California. Then his mother had whisked him away to Minnesota that fall, saying she wanted half the country between her and Sean's dad.

That was another worry—his dad. Sean had thought being back here would be easier. He thought he was ready to handle it, but it was way more difficult than he'd expected. Seeing his dad with a new wife and a new son was torture. Sean felt like needles were being stuck in his skin every time he watched Carl play with Thomas. It didn't help that Thomas was the quintessential all-American kid, all cowlicks and freckles and puppy dog tails. They might as well call him Opie and send him off to go fish in the crick.

Maybe he should call his therapist back in Minnesota. Seeing his dad with Thomas made the bad feelings start up again with a vengeance. He'd thought he'd had it under control, and wouldn't have come back if he hadn't thought he could manage it. God, he wanted a drink. He wanted to dull the pain and the rage and, most of all, the shame. He wanted to crawl under a rock.

As he drove back toward Dawkin-Walter Consulting, he wondered what the shrink was doing now. Was she asking Taylor questions? Would Taylor ever respond?

And if she did, what would she say?

The inside of the store throbbed with music. Josh felt like his chest was vibrating with the pulse of the bass.

Elise shook her head at him. "I can't believe you knew where this place was."

He shrugged. "I bought a present for my niece here last Christmas." Josh went to the front counter, leaned over, and shouted to the girl at the cash register, "I need to speak to the manager."

She turned. Her hair was razor cut, short in back and longer in front, with tendrils falling over her eyes. Several strands had been dyed bright pink, with a few acid green ones thrown in for contrast. She had on a black fishnet hoodie with her thumbs stuck through the cuffs, layered over a black camisole and a pair of jeans so tight, Josh wondered if the girl had any circulation in her legs. Her face was pasty white. Her eyes were ringed with kohl black liner, and a smudge of pink the same shade as her highlights colored her eyelids. "I am the manager," she shouted.

He flashed his badge. "Turn down the music so we can talk. Please."

"It's store policy," she shouted back, glowering out from beneath her bangs. "They tell us what to play and how loud to play it. I could get in trouble for turning it down."

"You could also get into trouble for not turning it down. Turn it down now." Josh leaned over the counter and glared.

The girl heaved a sigh and went into the back. A second later the music went off, although Josh felt like his breast bone continued to vibrate.

The girl came out and went back behind the counter. "What do you want?"

"You got a kid working here named Flick?" Josh asked.

"Yeah. Why? What'd he do?" She slouched onto the stool by the cash register.

"We're looking for him," Elise said, not bothering to answer the girl's question.

The girl inspected her fingernails. "Yeah, well, he's not working right now."

"I can see that," Elise said, her voice still pleasant, although Josh wondered how long that would last. "We'd like to know his real name and his address and phone number."

"I'm not supposed to give information like that out. It's, like, personal, you know," she said, still looking down.

"It's okay," Josh said. "We're, like, the good guys. You can trust us."

She rolled her eyes. "So you say."

"So my badge says," he replied, relaxing his posture. "Why'd you think Flick did something? Has he been in trouble before?"

She shrugged. "Nothing I know about for sure."

"Then why did you ask what he'd done?" Elise leaned in now, too. "Has he given you any trouble?"

The girl hesitated for a few seconds. "It just seems like things go missing sometimes after he's been on shift. Nothing big. Some metal studs, some earrings. Stuff like that."

"You think he took them?" Josh asked.

"Or maybe looked the other way when someone else did," the girl said. "I don't know."

"And who takes the fall for that kind of thing? Who gets in trouble if there's too much shoplifting?" Elise asked.

"Manager," the girl mumbled.

"And that would be you." Elise sighed and looked over at Josh. "It's always the same, isn't it? The responsible ones taking the fall for the irresponsible ones. I hate to see that happen."

"I'm not taking the fall for that creep," the girl said hotly.

"You will be if you won't give us his name and address," Elise said. "You really think your boss is going to thank you when I have to go get a search warrant and get their lawyers involved?"

The girl looked stricken.

"I'm not asking for state secrets here. I just want the name, address, and phone number of one kid who's already a pain in your backside," Josh said.

"I'm not supposed to," she answered, but she looked less sure of herself. "It's against store policy. I could get into a lot of trouble."

Josh smiled. "I promise you will not get into trouble for this. No one will ever even know you gave us the information. And if they did find out, they'd probably give you a raise."

She chewed on the fishnet hoodie where her thumb came through. "Really?"

Josh straightened up. "Cooperating with the police on an investigation? Absolutely. It's promotion material." He turned to Elise. "Don't you think?"

Elise nodded. "Absolutely."

"Wait here," she said. "I'll be right back."

The girl went into the back again and returned in two minutes with a sheet of note paper. On it were scribbled a name, an address, and a phone number. "He's

wrong, because without knowing that, I can't be much help."

Louis was such a man. Carol hadn't wanted someone to fix the problem. She wanted to bitch a bit, to complain, and to be consoled. Fixing it, if there was anything to fix, could wait.

She waved Louis's comment away. "I'm sorry. I'm feeling touchy about it. I'll go over my notes and see if I can come up with something concrete to discuss next week." She turned to Aimee. "You're the one who probably really needs to talk. How's Taylor? How are you?"

"Taylor's still not speaking. And me? I'm exhausted."

Julie reached over to pat Aimee's leg. "I bet. Have you been out to see her at Whispering Pines?"

"Pretty much every day. Her aunt's been there nonstop, too, and her dad's business partner and his son have visited."

"That's great that she's got so much support," Carol said. "That should help her to start feeling safe again."

"I hope so. There've been a few little signs. She touched my hand today, but she still won't meet my eyes or speak."

"Do you know what's going on with the investigation? Do the police suspect her of being involved?" Julie asked.

"I don't know anything concrete. I honestly don't know what the police suspect or don't suspect." Aimee thought uneasily about Josh Wolf's sudden chilliness today.

"What about you, Aimee?" Louis asked. "What do you suspect?"

Aimee looked up, a little surprised. "I have no idea who might have done this. I can't imagine that Taylor could have been involved."

"Are you sure?" He scanned Aimee's face as if looking for clues.

"I'm sure, Louis." Damn him. He had years more experience than she did, and had always been their unacknowledged leader and mentor. He was also almost always the one most willing to play devil's advocate. While it was a technique worth using, it was the last thing she needed right now. She was second-guessing herself enough without him jumping on the doubting bandwagon. "Taylor's anger has always been self-directed. That hasn't changed. She cut herself pretty severely before she was found."

"Do you think it was a suicide attempt?" Julie asked

Aimee shook her head, unsure of what she should and shouldn't say. The agreement was that everything said within this room stayed within this room, but the stakes were much higher than they'd ever been before. "No. If anything, I think it was an attempt to communicate, like her cutting has always been."

"By the way, I meant to tell you that you're an idiot," Elise said. It amazed her that such an intelligent man could be so stupid.

"Excuse me?" Josh turned to look at her in total shock.

"What part of that sentence don't you understand?"

"I don't understand any of it." He tossed the map

and the piece of paper with Brent Mullen's—aka Flick's—address on it to her. "Figure out where we're going, would you? You might as well do something useful while you're calling me names."

Elise snatched the map from him. He truly *was* an idiot. Aimee Gannon had had a fiancé two years ago, but maybe the whole thing had fallen apart. Elise hadn't noticed any rings. "Take one-sixty," she said and folded the map back up.

"So why am I an idiot?" Josh flicked on his turn signal and changed lanes.

"I don't know, Josh. Maybe it's genetic. Or maybe your mama dropped you on your head as a baby."

"Very funny. Tell me one thing I did wrong."

Elise shifted in her seat to face him. "You got your panties in a twist because you found out she had a boyfriend two years ago, didn't you?"

Josh glared at her. "My panties are not in a twist, and it was a fiancé, not a boyfriend."

"Fiancé shmiancé," Elise said.

"There's a difference. Maybe not to you women, but to us guys there is. We're the ones who shell out the big bucks for the fancy ring. We're the ones who have to get down on one knee. We're the ones who open ourselves up to rejection. A fiancé is something substantial." His jaw was clenched.

Elise threw her hands up in the air. "Oh, for Christ's sake, what is this? *Sex and the City for Men*? So Holly dumped you and gave back your ring. It was three years ago. Pawn the damn thing and move on with your life, would you?"

"I already pawned it."

"Seriously? What'd you get for it?"

That earned her another sidelong glance.

"And the moving on thing?" she asked, knowing the answer to that all too well. Her partner had only taken the occasional woman to dinner and a movie since Holly had moved to South Carolina to take an assistant professorship.

"I'm working on it."

"Well, maybe you need to work on it a little harder," she suggested.

"Maybe I need to solve this damn case," he said.

"Maybe you need to turn right on Vallejo."

Josh pulled the car over in front of a two-story single-family home whose garage was bigger than his apartment. "Nice digs."

Elise took in the old trees, big lawns, and expensive cars. "It doesn't suck."

They walked up to the front door. He rang the bell and they waited. Elise was about to give the bell a second jab when the door opened.

The woman behind the door was plump, with mousy brown hair and glasses. "Yes?" she said expectantly.

Josh flipped open his badge. "Mrs. Mullen?"

Her eyes narrowed. "Yes," she said, but her tone was a lot less friendly.

"Would you be Brent Mullen's mother?"

She crossed her arms over her chest. "Why?"

"We need to speak to Brent. May we come in?" He moved forward.

She stayed in the doorway, arms still crossed. "You got a warrant?"

"Excuse me?" Josh stopped short.

"A warrant," the woman repeated slowly as if Josh were dim.

Elise knew she should be helping him out, but right now she was enjoying this.

"No. We're not here to search your home or to arrest Brent. We just want to talk to him."

"About what?"

Josh was clearly at a loss about how to proceed. So Elise stepped in. "Is Brent friendly with Taylor Dawkin? We understand they're acquainted."

"If you already understand that they're acquainted, why are you here asking me if they're friendly? You're not going to believe anything I say, no matter what. That's how you people operate, isn't it? Make up your mind about a kid or a situation, and don't let the facts muddy up your hypotheses."

"Us people?" Josh repeated, looking over at Elise.

"Yes, you people. You police try to barge in here, civil rights be damned, wanting to question my son about this or that. You never have evidence, you never have a reason. I'm tempted to charge you all with harassment. What do you think about *that*?" Mrs. Mullen was right up in Josh's face now, or as close as she could be considering the height difference.

"What else has little Brent been questioned about?" Josh wasn't giving up any ground.

"You think that's funny? You think you're some kind

of comedian? Your sarcasm isn't going to make me want to cooperate with you. In fact, I doubt there's anything that *would* make me want to cooperate with you. Now get the hell off my property and stay off it, unless you have a warrant." Mrs. Mullen slammed the door in their faces.

When Josh turned and looked at Elise, his face a mask of bewilderment, she could barely keep from doubling over with laughter.

In almost perfect mimicry of Mrs. Mullen, Josh said, "You think that's funny?"

She thought it was so damn funny, she damn near peed her pants.

Then Josh's cell phone vibrated in his pocket. He fished it out and flipped it open. "Wolf," he said.

"Hey, Josh, it's Ed."

"Why, Ed, it's delightful to hear from you." Josh glanced over at Elise. She nodded to let him know she was listening as they walked back to the car.

"Remember those subcontractors you asked me to look into? The ones you said had done some work for Dawkin-Walter Consulting?"

"Yeah. What about 'em?" Josh motioned for Elise to drive.

"Well," Ed said with a note of triumph in his voice, "they don't exist."

"What the hell does that mean?"

"It's complicated. When are you going to get back to the office?"

"After we talk to Doreen Hughes," Josh said as Elise pulled away from the curb.

"See you then."

It only took them fifteen minutes to get Doreen Hughes's house.

A ponytailed blonde with a narrow face and a wide mouth opened the door. Josh guessed her to be in her late twenties or early thirties. The hair looked expensive, glossy, with multiple shades of blond streaked in. The clothes were casual—capris in some kind of nubby-textured fabric and a silky tank top—but not cheap. "Doreen Hughes?" he asked.

Her eyes narrowed with suspicion. "Who's asking?"

Elise flipped her badge open. "Police."

The skinny eyebrows raised on Doreen Hughes's forehead. "Is this about Orrin Dawkin?"

Josh and Elise exchanged a glance. "Yeah, it is," Josh said.

Doreen stood aside to let them into the condo. "I wondered when you'd get around to me."

Killing the puppy had been a mistake. He knew that now. He couldn't even really say how it had come about. A cluster of things had come at him too fast from too many different directions; otherwise he would never have lost control like that. He had a plan. He knew to stick to the plan.

He fingered the lamp cord again, sliding it through his fingers, wrapping it around his hand. He knew he should throw it out, but every time he looked at it, he felt a little bit of the rush he'd felt when he'd used it to choke the life out of Stacey Dawkin.

Here, in private, when he could really look at it and

touch it, it practically sang to him of all the power he had now. He'd been playing with the cord when the puppy had scampered toward him and then squatted and peed on the carpet.

A submission pee-er, that's what Sarah said the puppy was. When he sensed someone higher in the pack nearby, he peed. Well, little Bingo had gotten that right. *He* was the alpha dog, and he'd shown that little pee-er, too. It had struggled and writhed, twisting under his hands as he slowly, slowly, slowly choked the life out of it.

It had been so satisfying to watch the life drain out of it, and to know that only he had the power to grant the little shit life or death. It had been completely up to him. He needed a better hiding place for the body, though. The spot under the bushes would work for only so long. The body had to be better disposed of before someone stumbled across it.

But killing the dog had been an amazing relief of the tension that had been building. The police had been around asking questions. That psychologist was prying into things. His schedule had been disrupted. The noise in his head had been building, building, building, until he could barely hear himself over the roar.

Everything had stilled as the dull glaze had spread over the puppy's eyes. It wasn't gone, but he doubted anything could ever make it go away entirely. Killing Orrin and Stacey had brought him closer to peace than anything he'd experienced in years. He could think clearly.

Still, killing the puppy had been a mistake. It had added to the chaos in the house. Thomas was upset, which made Sarah distraught, which made the volume of the noise rise. He knew he should wish he hadn't done it. It was like so many other things he'd done and pretended to say he was sorry about, but didn't really regret.

The only important thing? Not getting caught.

"I can't tell you much. They made me sign a confidentiality agreement." Doreen Hughes sat on her leather couch.

"But there's no love lost between you and Orrin Dawkin, right? You had some hard feelings?" Josh sat on a chair opposite Doreen Hughes.

Doreen laughed. "Why would I have hard feelings toward Orrin Dawkin? I get to live like this and go to school with no loans, all on his dime."

"Must have been a nice settlement, then," Elise observed as she sat back in her chair. Her arms were at her sides, open, nonthreatening.

"No more than I deserved." A hard edge crept into Doreen's eyes.

"He must have done something pretty heinous." Josh took his cue from Elise and leaned back, too.

Doreen's lips tightened for a moment and then she shook her head. "I can't say anything. I signed the papers. I took the money. I'll stick to it."

Josh held his hands up in front of himself. "We understand. I was just saying it must have been a nice settlement. So, where were you on Tuesday night at around nine-thirty?" Josh asked, leaning forward again and watching Doreen's face carefully.

She smiled, her generous mouth pulling wide. "At my uncle Howard's birthday party with about twenty-five members of my family."

"Got any names and phone numbers so we might check that out?" Josh asked pleasantly, wondering what the big joke was.

"Why don't you ask Uncle Howie yourself? You work with him. You probably know him as Captain Howard Gibson."

Elise and Josh had left Doreen Hughes and headed directly to headquarters and Ed's office in the basement.

"Okay, Ed, give it to us with both barrels smoking." Elise plopped herself down on the edge of Ed's desk. Josh took up his usual post against the cubicle entrance.

"Those subcontractors you asked me to check into are front companies. They exist on paper only," Ed said. "Dawkin set it up very cleverly; I don't know how long it would have taken me to find them if you hadn't pointed the way."

"So what did they front for?" Josh asked.

"They were front companies for Orrin Dawkin. He was using them to embezzle money from Dawkin-Walter Consulting. He was siphoning off the company profits to cover his day trading debts."

CHAPTER
17

"Enough!" Simone panted. She bent over, hands pressed to her knees, and took in great gulps of air. "Are you trying to kill me?"

Aimee laughed and pushed up the sleeves of her shirt. It had been chilly when they started; now she was dripping with sweat. "Sorry. I was trying to run some of the cobwebs off my brain." She crouched down and unlaced her shoe partway to release the apartment key she'd tucked into the laces.

Simone straightened up, her face serious now. "This case is really getting to you, isn't it?"

"I wish it wasn't." Aimee unlocked the door. "You wanna come up for coffee?"

Simone glanced at her watch and shook her head. "If I go straight home, I'll have time to shower before Connor's soccer game. Whatcha doing tonight?"

"Not much. I thought I'd catch up on my billing."

"Girlfriend! Say it ain't so! It's Saturday night—date night. How am I supposed to live vicariously through you if you're going to live like a freaking nun?" Simone winced and rubbed at her side. "Come over tonight. Brian rented a movie and we'll throw something on the grill. You can beat us all at Boggle."

"Oooh," Aimee cooed. "Sounds pretty wild."

"Better than catching up on billing. See you around six? If we don't feed the kids by seven all hell will break loose."

"Sounds great. I'll bring ice cream."

Josh sprawled on the uncomfortable plastic bench two stores down and across the hallway from Hot Topic. He held a newspaper, but he wasn't really reading it. Instead he scanned the throng of people walking by and inwardly cursed Brent Mullen's mother. It would have been much easier to pick Brent up someplace less crowded. Someplace where no one would be likely to snap Josh's picture with a cell phone camera during the takedown. He'd probably be on freaking YouTube before the day was out.

Elise sat next to him and filed her nails.

"Incoming," she said. "Six o'clock."

Josh glanced over the top of the paper. Brent Mullen was walking straight toward them, heading to Hot Topic as if he didn't have a care in the world. Josh waited until Brent had walked past them and then he rose. Elise stood up, too, and they walked up behind Brent together.

"Brent Mullen," Josh said.

Brent looked over his shoulder and without a second's hesitation took off down the mall.

Josh smiled over at Elise. "I love it when they run."

"Go get 'em, tiger," she said, smiling back.

Josh took off at a run. It wasn't hard to keep Brent in sight. The purple-tipped mohawk that stood up a good six inches from his head made him easy to spot, and there weren't many places to go in the mall that weren't dead ends. Josh dodged a young woman with a stroller and zigzagged around two white-haired ladies in Rockports. He closed the gap between Brent and himself to a matter of yards. He didn't get up every morning at five-thirty to run six miles for nothing. Hearing Brent's wheeze, Josh mentally patted himself on the back for never smoking.

In four large strides, he grabbed Brent by the collar of his leather jacket. He yanked backward and Brent's feet went out from under him. Josh twisted to make sure Brent's head didn't bounce on the hard tile floor, deftly rolled the boy onto his stomach, and planted his knee in the boy's back.

Elise caught up with them as Josh snapped the cuffs on Brent. He said, "Hi, Brent. My name is Detective Wolf. I'd like to talk to you."

"I got nothing to say to you," Brent said, his face pressed against the floor.

"Then you probably shouldn't have run," Elise said philosophically. "That makes us think that you've got lots to say to us." They hoisted Brent to his feet.

"You're making me late for work, man," he grumbled.

As they marched him toward the exit to the mall with everyone staring, Elise said, "You should really reconsider the running thing. I hate it, but my partner here absolutely thrives on it. Hence his ability to knock you to the floor in about forty-five seconds. Plus, we're going to have to call your mother to come get you from the station once we're done chatting. We can't wait for another opportunity to talk with her. She's a charmer."

Just seeing the door to the facility made Aimee feel uneasy. Was this how Danny had felt, coming to visit her in the hospital day after day after what had happened with Kyle? She'd been in for close to a week, and he'd been by her bedside every day. If this was how he'd felt, she wished she'd been a lot more sympathetic.

She got through the reception area without any hassle this time, but when she got to the locked ward, she wasn't buzzed through. Instead, a nurse came out to talk to her.

"I'm sorry," she said. "This isn't a good time to visit Taylor."

Aimee immediately went on alert. "What's happened?"

"I'm sorry, but are you a family member?"

"No, I'm her therapist."

The nurse's brows drew down and she was clearly flustered. Still, she said, "You'll need to talk to Dr. Brenner. I'm sorry. I simply can't say any more without his permission. Do you need someone to show you to his office?"

"No. Thank you," Aimee said. "I can find my way."

Aimee hurried to Brenner's office, worry quickening her footsteps. She knocked on the closed door and heard a muffled "enter" from inside.

"Dr. Gannon," he said, rising from behind his desk and extending his hand.

She took his hand, but didn't sit down. "The nurse wouldn't let me in to see Taylor. What's happened?"

"We had a situation with Taylor last night after her aunt left." Brenner sat, eyeing her with caution.

"What kind of situation?" What had happened to the girl? And how?

"She, uh, managed to unscrew the screen around the lightbulb in her bathroom and used the broken bulb to cut herself pretty severely." Brenner seemed unwilling to look Aimee in the eye and instead examined some of the folders on his desk while he spoke.

Aimee was astounded. She couldn't believe that the girl who had done nothing but sit and rock and clutch a stuffed dog had managed to work up the energy and nerve to do something like that. She remembered the way Taylor had taken her hand, though, and drawn those symbols on endless pieces of paper. She had been starting to come out of her state. It was a precarious moment, poised between the pain of reentering the real world and the safety of her cocoon. "Stitches?"

He shook his head. "No, no. But there was a lot of blood and it was upsetting for everyone."

Which everyone was that? The staff at these places seemed inured to things like blood and screaming. "What's being done?"

"Well, we stepped up the Ativan for the time being." Brenner still didn't meet Aimee's eyes.

She'd expected that, but it didn't please her. "So you're chemically restraining her."

"I prefer to think that we're calming her down so

we can deal with the situation." Dr. Brenner's lips tightened.

Aimee needed to be careful how hard she pushed him. She could lose access completely if she didn't step lightly. "Can I see her?" Aimee asked.

"I don't think that's wise right now. We need to get the situation back under control before she has more visitors. She's had quite a parade through here the past few days. Perhaps that's what's upsetting her." Brenner sat back down, a smug look on his face.

As much as she wanted to go over his desk and pop him, that wouldn't get her what she wanted. She wished she'd brought Josh with her again.

"I understand," she said. "Will you call when she can have visitors again?"

"Of course," Brenner said.

Aimee got up and he rose as well. "I'll see myself out," she said.

What had upset Taylor so much? Aimee was so deep in thought that she nearly ran right into Sean Walter as she walked outside. "Excuse me," she said, losing her balance for a moment. "I'm sorry."

He caught her by the elbow to steady her. "That's okay. Are you all right?"

"Fine." She smiled up at him. "Just lost in thought. Are you here to see Taylor?"

"Yeah, I wanted to give her this." He held out an Aerosmith CD. "I know it's lame, but I used to listen to this a lot during a kind of dark time in my life. I thought maybe she'd want to listen to it. I want to do something to help, but I don't know what kind of things would be of any use."

Aimee looked at the CD. She recognized some of the songs: "Love in an Elevator," "Janie's Got a Gun," "Monkey on My Back." "I don't think it's lame, Sean. Unfortunately, Taylor can't have visitors right now. She had a setback yesterday. They won't even let me in to see her until they're sure she's calmed down. Even then, I'm not sure when they're going to let her have things like CDs." *Especially this dark and angry CD.* Aimee took a closer look at him. He seemed so blandly pleasant.

Sean looked crestfallen. "When do you think I could give it to her? Maybe next week?"

Aimee started toward her car. "It's hard to say. It could be weeks before she feels safe enough to talk and interact, or it could be days. There's no way to know for sure."

Sean grimaced. "It's hard to keep coming out, not knowing if I'll be able to see her or not."

"Would you like me to hold on to the CD and give it to her when she's ready?" Aimee offered.

Sean smiled. "That would be fantastic. Are you sure you don't mind?"

"Of course not." Aimee slid the CD into her brief-case and opened her car door. "I'll call and keep you posted on her progress, too, if you'd like."

"That would be great. Thanks so much. I'd really like to keep close tabs on her progress. So would my dad. Taylor's like family."

Aimee looked into Sean's handsome face. He was

the person closest to Taylor's age who had known her when she'd first moved to Sacramento. "Sean, do you remember anything significant happening the summer that Taylor and her family moved here? Something that might have upset her? Or even something weird happening that you didn't quite understand?"

Sean took a step back. "Like what?"

Aimee sighed. "I don't even know myself. I'm grasping at straws. I think something may have happened to Taylor that summer that's somehow linked to what's going on now."

He shook his head. "Nothing comes to mind, and my mom and I moved soon after that. Taylor and I only overlapped here for a few months."

Sean shut her car door and headed to his car.

There she was! God, he loved the way she walked, the way her hair lifted in the breeze and flew back behind her, the long strides of her legs. At night, he'd lie in his bed and dream about what she'd look like walking toward him. She'd have that half smile on her face, the one where the very outer parts of her lips turned down just the tiniest bit, like she was trying not to smile. Kyle's mouth felt dry, and he was breathing fast. It happened almost every time he saw her. But why was she back outside already? She'd just gone in. He'd been hoping to have a chance to look in her car.

Kyle bit his knuckles in frustration underneath the bush. Why the hell did she drive all the way out here and then turn around and walk back out?

And the pretty boy was back. The stupid shit looked

like a male model. Kyle hated him on sight. Some people got handed too much on their silver platters. He was too young to have earned that Saab. It wasn't fair that Kyle had to drive a piece-of-shit old Ford. It wasn't fair. If Kyle ever got him alone, he'd take that pretty boy down a peg or two. The thought of what he might do to the sissy boy made him pant a little more. He'd learned a lot in the state mental hospital, though not as much as his older stepbrothers had taught him about making someone suffer. Oh, he could have a lot of fun with Mr. Fancy Pants.

He was giving something to Aimee. Kyle peered down through his binoculars. A CD? How junior high. You didn't give a woman like Aimee a CD. She was amazing. Unique. A gift to her would have to be as amazing and unique as she was. The only thing possibly more embarrassing would be a mix tape. Who did this asshole think he was?

Kyle dropped the binoculars and gnawed on the side of his thumb. He'd done it so much, the skin there was getting pulpy. It helped him think, though, so he gnawed it some more. He should try and figure out who this dillhole was. Then he could make sure Aimee knew this wasn't a guy she should be around. He could make sure that Aimee saw through him. Kyle could use him to send Aimee a message.

Kyle wriggled out from under the bush and took off down the hill for his car. He'd follow the guy. He'd find out who he was, and then he'd make sure Aimee knew what a poser he was.

That would be Kyle's gift to her. It would be special

and unique. It might frighten her, but in the end, she would realize that he'd done it in her best interests.

"I didn't have anything to do with Taylor's parents getting whacked," Brent insisted.

"So what exactly *did* you two kids get up to that night?" Josh asked, leaning his chair back on two legs.

"Nothing." Brent kept his gaze down on his hands in front of him.

"Oh, come on, Brent. We know she crawled out of her friend's window to see you that night. What exactly did you do?" Josh kept his tone light.

"I told you. We didn't do anything." Brent still did not look up.

"I find that hard to believe." Elise leaned back in her chair and laced her fingers behind her head. "According to some of the e-mails we've read between you two, you've done plenty on other nights. Why would this night be any different? And, by the way, Brent, do you understand what statutory rape is?"

That question made Brent look up. "How the hell can it be rape if the chick practically tore my pants off?"

"Whether she said yes or not doesn't matter, Brent. Taylor's only seventeen; she's a minor. According to your driver's license, you turned twenty last month. According to state law, that three-year age gap makes it a crystal-clear case of statutory rape." Elise gave Brent a big sweet smile.

"I didn't do anything with her." Brent looked back down.

Elise shrugged. "Maybe not that night, but I'm

guessing by what we saw on her computer that you did sometime. I'm also guessing that with a little DNA cross-matching, we'll be able to make something stick."

Brent threw himself back in his chair, his mohawk barely shifting, and shrugged his shoulders. He was a nice-looking kid, Josh had to admit. Tall, broad shouldered, and long legged. The parts of his hair that weren't purple were a sandy blond. His features were sculpted.

"Shit," Brent said. "Shit. Shit. Shit. I knew that chick would be trouble. She had trouble written all over her."

"But?" Josh asked.

"But she was like totally into it. She was all over me. It's not so easy to say no, you know?" Brent looked at Josh pleadingly.

This wasn't a group therapy session, it was an interrogation. Still, you often got more information if the subject thought you were on their side. Josh gave him a smile. "She was pretty hot?"

"You have no idea," he moaned. "Plus she had this thing about doing it in garages."

"Garages?" Elise repeated.

"Yeah. You know, where we might get caught. And it was like having the cars around totally turned her on. Freaky, but *so* worth it."

"So did you go to a garage on Tuesday night?" Josh asked.

Brent made a disgusted noise. "No. That's what I thought we were going to do. She'd even jacked a bottle of wine from her old man's wine fridge, but she was all freaky that night."

Elise leaned forward. "Freaky? How was she freaky?"

"I don't know how to describe it. Freaky, okay? Like one second she'd be all over me, practically sticking her tongue down my throat and grabbing my dick through my pants. The next second, she was all shaky and crying. That's why I took her back when I did. I didn't need the hassle, man. There are plenty of other chicks who want a piece of me without getting all weird." Brent pushed away from the table. "I took her back to her tight-assed girlfriend's place and went down to the Avalon to meet up with my peeps."

"What time did you get to the Avalon?" Elise asked.

Brent shrugged. "Probably around nine-thirty."

"And you were there until when?"

"Close to midnight."

Josh shoved a pad of paper across to Brent. "Write down some names and numbers. We're going to need your peeps to verify where you were."

Brent took the pad and pen and started writing.

Elise gave a little head jerk to Josh. She wanted to talk.

Josh nodded and stood up. "We'll be back in a minute, Brent."

They both stood up and walked out.

"Hey!" he called after them. "Hey! Where are you going?"

Josh shut the door without answering. It wouldn't hurt the little creep to sweat it out for a few minutes. "What's up?" he asked.

"Does this kid remind you of anybody?" she asked. "Somebody involved in the case?"

"I can't think of anybody else with a purple-tipped mohawk. What are you trying to tell me?"

"Look past the dyed hair and the piercings, Josh. This kid is the spitting image of Sean Walter."

Carl stepped into the garage. Most people didn't like a detached garage these days. They wanted the convenience of never stepping outside, of going from one climate-controlled environment into another. Carl had always liked having the separate structure. He liked the garage being its own place, separate from the rest of the house.

Sarah teased him. She said it wasn't a garage—it was a shrine to his car. She was right, in a way. He did love the Cougar. He liked that it had its own sacrosanct place. It wasn't a shrine, though. It was a place he could go to think, with the excuse of changing the oil or checking the washer fluid. Sarah was content to leave all that up to him and he was happy to take of it for her. He was happy to take care of her and Thomas. Period.

He let himself in through the side door and nearly jumped back out when he saw Sean. The garage wasn't a place Sean spent much time without duress. Sure, Sean liked the Saab Carl had bought him as a graduation present, but he'd never been a car guy the way Carl was. Carl had never figured out what Sean *was* into, after he and his mother had left. He wasn't sure he wanted to know.

"Hey, son, what are you doing out here?" Carl asked.

Sean seemed equally startled to see his father. He put the shovel he was carrying into its place on the wall with gloved hands. "Putting away my tools when I'm done with them, like you taught me," he said with a tight smile.

"What were you doing with the shovel?" Carl came a little closer. Sean had cleaned off the shovel, but not completely. Some dirt and grass clung to the bottom of the blade.

"Remember Sarah said she'd like a crape myrtle over on the west side of the house?" Sean said, stripping off the latex gloves.

Carl smiled. "Sarah knew what a crape myrtle was?" Gardening was not exactly his fiancée's forte. That was okay. She had other things to recommend her.

Sean smiled back. "She said she wanted one of those pretty trees with the purple flowers, and I knew what she meant. I heard something on the radio about now being the time to plant them, so I stopped by the nursery and picked one up and planted it over on the west side of the house. Sort of an early Mother's Day present."

Carl pulled a pair of latex gloves from his personal kit, slipped them on, grabbed one of the thick blue work towels off the roll, and wiped the dirt and grass off the bottom of the shovel. "You went out and did that in the dark?"

"Doesn't take much light to dig a hole. Besides, I had a flashlight." Sean shrugged and started for the door.

"Sean," Carl called to him before he left.

Sean turned slowly around. "Yeah, Dad."

"It means a lot to me that you're accepting Sarah and Thomas. Not every child would be so welcoming to a new family coming in. I've seen how much time you spend with Thomas and all the things you've done to gain his trust." Carl's voice caught a little in his throat. That was a good touch. He wanted Sean to hear the emotion in his voice. "I wanted you to know how much that means to me, how happy that makes me."

Sean cocked his head to one side. "It's my pleasure, Dad. Thomas is a great kid and Sarah is really sweet. They've been awfully good to me, too. Not every new wife-to-be would want her grown stepson coming home for an indefinite period of time."

"She is sweet, isn't she?" Carl liked to hear that other people thought highly of Sarah. He was proud of his fiancée. She was exactly what he'd been looking for for years and years. "And Thomas. What a kid, eh?"

"Yeah," said Sean. "He's a real peach. I love him to pieces."

Carl smiled, remembering when he used to say the same thing about Sean. He turned to leave the garage.

Sean stopped him. "Dad?"

Carl turned. "Yes, Sean."

"I love you, too, Dad. I wanted you to know that. I love you a lot."

S ean walked into the house from the garage. That was one mess taken care of. His hands were still shaking, but that was okay. As long as he could keep cleaning up the messes, maybe everything would be okay.

Right now, he needed a little space. He needed to be someplace safe. He looked down at his clothes, covered with dirt. He'd clean up, and then get the hell out of this house for a while.

He went into the bathroom, stripped off his shirt, and started running hot water into the sink.

"Whatcha doin'?"

Sean smiled. Thomas was peeking around the doorframe. He had on red and blue Spider-Man pajamas that had black webs under the arms. Sean remembered having pajamas a little like those. They had been Superman pajamas with a detachable cape, and he remembered feeling like he could fly when he had those pajamas on. He wondered if Thomas felt the same way. He wondered if Thomas felt like he *needed* to fly away, the way Sean had by the time he was only a little bit older than Thomas was now.

"I'm shaving," Sean said.

Thomas looked serious. "How do you do that?"

Sean scooped the little boy up and plopped him down on the counter next to him. "I'll show you. Hold out your hand."

Thomas held out his hand and Sean marveled at the chubby perfection of it. He squirted a little shaving cream into it.

"You put the shaving cream on your face like this." He lathered up his own face to demonstrate.

Thomas copied him and then looked in the mirror and giggled. "I look like Santa Claus."

"Maybe I should sit on your lap and ask you for a present," Sean teased.

Thomas rolled his eyes. "You can't sit on my lap. You're too big. You have to get your own presents."

"Truer words have never been spoken, my brother." Sean looked around the bathroom for something safe Thomas could use to scrape off the shaving cream. He grabbed a toothbrush from the drawer.

Thomas crossed his arms over his chest. "That's not a shaver. That's a toothbrush."

"It'll be your pretend shaver. Use the non-bristly end."

Thomas didn't uncross his arms and didn't take the toothbrush.

"It's that or a washcloth, my man," Sean said.

"Okay." Thomas took the toothbrush, but made a face.

"Now, here's the tricky part. You have to scrape all that off without cutting yourself or making a big mess." Sean started shaving and Thomas imitated his movements.

"You're a natural at this."

Thomas looked up, his eyes big and round. "I am?"

"Absolutely. You were clearly born to shave. I've never seen a five-year-old shave like you do."

Thomas's chest puffed up a little, and Sean hid a smile behind his razor. He remembered what praise from a grown-up had meant to him when he was a little guy. He remembered especially how it had felt when his dad had praised him. Carl had been his hero.

"Now you wipe the rest off." He got a washcloth wet and handed it to Thomas.

Thomas looked at the washcloth and then back up at Sean. "You said it was the toothbrush *or* the wash-cloth. I used the toothbrush. Why do I have to use the washcloth?"

The kid had a point. "I'm sorry, it's the toothbrush *and* the washcloth. I'm going to use my washcloth, too."

"That's okay. It was just a mistake. Everybody makes mistakes. Ms. Barnett says so." Thomas wiped the last of the shaving cream off his face. Ms. Barnett was his teacher and apparently the arbiter of all that was good and right in the world.

"Thanks. I appreciate you cutting me some slack." Sean ruffled his hair, picked Thomas up off the counter, and set him down on the floor before wiping the last of the shaving cream off his own face.

"Sean?" Thomas asked. "Is lying the same as keep-ing a secret?"

Sean froze for a moment. "No. Not exactly."

"But sometimes you have to lie to keep something

secret, right? Like our secrets. Sometime I might have to lie to keep those."

"Yeah, you do sometimes have to lie to keep something secret. But the best way to keep a secret is to not say anything at all." Sean kept his eyes on Thomas's to see if he understood.

Thomas nodded solemnly.

"Sounds like you've got a lot on your mind, buddy." Sean busied himself at the sink.

"I guess I do."

Sean glanced at his watch. "Listen, kiddo. I've got an errand I need to run, but I'll come back as early as I can, okay? And you and I can talk. Maybe we can play our special game tonight, too. It's Saturday, so you can stay up a little later than usual."

Thomas nodded and started to walk out of the bathroom. He turned in the doorway. "I don't know if I like our special game, Sean. It makes me feel funny."

Sean's heart pounded. "You'll get used to it. Then it won't make you feel so funny anymore. Okay?"

Thomas nodded again. "You promise you'll come back early?"

"I promise."

Sean went into his room and shut the door, trying not to let it click. He opened the closet door then and stared at the pair of shoes sitting in his closet. They would have to be disposed of and soon. It had taken him a while to notice the streaks and stains on them, and a little longer still to realize what they were. He'd watched enough TV shows to know that he could clean them all he wanted, but trace evidence would still remain on them. They couldn't be found in this house.

He had no idea how long it would take the police to figure out what had been going on behind the scenes at Dawkin-Walter Consulting, but he was pretty sure they would figure it out eventually. That Detective Wolf didn't strike him as stupid.

It would only be a matter of time before they went from looking into things at Dawkin-Walter to taking a good long look at the Walter household. He'd stick the shoes in his gym bag to carry them out of the house, and toss them into a Dumpster. Even if someone found them, they would never be able to trace them back to this household.

Just in case, though, Sean pulled on a pair of latex gloves—he always kept some handy—and picked up a spray bottle filled with ammonia and water and started wiping down the shoes.

That was one sick twisted son of a bitch. Kyle dropped the binoculars. The view into the bathroom had been obstructed, but he'd seen enough to make him want to puke. The pretty boy sicko really knew how to manipulate. He had that little kid eating out of the palm of his hand.

Kyle knew his type. One of his stepbrothers had been the "good cop" to the other two brothers' "bad cops." He had won Kyle's trust with presents and treats and the thing that Kyle had craved more than anything else: attention. He'd made Kyle believe that he'd cared. He'd convinced Kyle that he liked him. Then he had turned Kyle over to his brothers to be tortured and abused.

Aimee was the one who had helped Kyle see it. She was the one who had shown him that the kindness that Warren had shown him had all been an act. She'd led him through the steps that helped him realize that it wasn't because Kyle was weak or unlovable. His brothers had been cruel and abusive, and blaming himself was wrong. In a way, it wasn't fair to blame them either. Warren and Gary and Bill had learned their craft at the hands of a master. Or should he say mistress?

Pretty boy was leaving the bathroom now. Kyle figured he must be getting ready to go out. That was just fine with him. He'd seen everything he needed to see, and he knew exactly where he needed to go to get a very special present for Aimee. He hoped she'd understand the message he was going to leave her. But of course she would. She was smart. Really smart. Then she'd know that Kyle only had her best interests at heart. She'd know he was only doing this for her own good. She needed to understand that he was the one for her. She'd helped him understand so much; now it was his turn to help her.

He knew where this creep's secrets were buried now. Literally. He hugged himself and chuckled at his own joke. He'd show those secrets to Aimee. She might be a little scared at first, but then Kyle was sure she'd be grateful. Just like he'd been grateful to her for showing him so much, even though talking about it and thinking about it had been scary for him, too.

Kyle imagined Aimee thanking him. She'd walk up to him with that long stride of hers. She'd smile. She'd open her arms to hold him. He imagined himself pressed against the softness of her breasts, inhaling the light fresh scent of her hair. His hands would circle her waist and pull her closer to him. She'd murmur encouragement in his ear. She'd tell him how thankful she was he had come into her life. She'd tell him how strong he was, and how smart. She'd thank him for showing her the truth about the people around her and tell him that he was the only one she trusted, just as she was the only one he trusted. They would be together forever. A team. Facing the world and beating the bullies who tried to tear them down.

He touched himself through his jeans. His cock was hard and pulsing. He glanced around. He was well hidden; no one would see him. He could uncover the pretty boy's secrets a little later.

He rolled over on his back, unzipped his jeans, and closed his eyes. As he grabbed hold of himself, he imagined Aimee again walking toward him with her arms open.

"Well, who doesn't like a good ratatouille?" Simone asked, as the same-named movie ended. She sat curled up in the corner of her couch, sipping a glass of red wine.

"Me," her husband, Brian, answered as he scooped their youngest off the floor where he'd fallen asleep. "I hate eggplant; it's slimy. Even when it's not being made by rats."

"Do you think you can wake Dylan up enough to get him to pee before you put him in bed?" Simone asked.

"I'll give it a try." Brian walked out of the room with Dylan draped over him.

"You two need to go brush and pee, too," Simone said to the two older boys.

"Mom!" Connor, Simone's oldest at the ripe old age of eleven, blushed. He cast a sidelong look at Aimee, who was ensconced in her own corner of the couch with her own glass of red wine. "Could you be a little more discreet?"

Simone's eyes widened. "This from a child who just yesterday ran naked from my house to watch the garbage truck?"

"It wasn't yesterday, Mom," Connor protested, turning even redder. "It was like five years ago."

"Fine. Please go get ready for bed, Connor. You, too, Jackson." Simone made a shooing gesture with her hands.

As the two boys headed out of the room, Jackson said, "Yeah, Connor, go pee."

"Shut up!" Connor gave Jackson a little shove.

Jackson shoved back and the two were off down the hallway in a jostling match.

Simone rolled her eyes. "What did I do to deserve this much testosterone?"

"Married a guy with good Y chromosome swimmers?" Aimee smiled. Simone loved being the queen bee in a house of men. She also liked to complain.

"There should be some kind of test they have to take before you agree to procreate with them," Simone grumbled.

"You're lucky, and you know it." Aimee stood up and yawned. It had been a long week. She'd felt the tension melt away from her as she'd eaten the burgers that Brian grilled and drank the good wine he'd poured. Part of her didn't want to leave. Another part of her couldn't wait to get home and into her own bed.

"I should go. I think it's past my bedtime, too." She shivered a little. It was a lonely drive between Simone's house and her condo late at night.

Simone's watchful gaze stayed on Aimee's face. "Do you want Brian to drive you home? I could bring your car over to your place tomorrow morning, and you could drive me back after our run."

That sounded good. It also sounded way too chicken shit. "It's not far, and I didn't have that much to drink."

"I don't think you're too drunk to drive. You know that isn't why I offered." Simone's lips pursed in irritation.

"I know why you offered, and it's exactly why I'm saying no. I'm fine. I've moved on."

"And it's time you moved on in some other ways."

Aimee started putting her shoes back on. "Like what?"

"What were we doing here tonight?"

"Having dinner and a movie." She smiled. "It's the classic American date. What's wrong with that?"

"What's wrong is that you shouldn't be dating Brian and me. You should be dating a real guy, having a real date."

"Are you trying to tell me that you're just not that

into me? That you don't want to take our relationship to the next level?" Aimee teased.

Simone grabbed a pillow and threw it at her. "I just think that you deserve better."

Brian walked in. "I'm feeling left out here. Do I at least get to watch?"

Simone launched a second pillow at her husband.

Aimee hugged her friend good-bye and let Brian walk her to the curb.

"Hey, listen," he said awkwardly. "I kind of heard what you and Simone were talking about. She's right, you know. It's been a year since you and Danny broke up, hasn't it?"

Sometimes the pain of breaking off her engagement seemed like it had happened yesterday. Other times, it seemed like the woman who had fallen in love during weekend trips to Napa and ski getaways in Tahoe was a complete stranger. Brian was right, though. It would be a year next month since she'd given Danny back the ring that had belonged to his grandmother, and watched him walk out the door without a backward glance.

"About a year. Yes."

She beeped the car open.

"Danny was a fool," Brian said. "He should have stuck with you."

"He did his best, Brian. It's not that easy." Aimee gave Brian a hug and got into her car. He waved and headed back inside as she drove down the street. He was a good guy and he meant well; he simply had no clue.

Traumatic events left marks. When the shock and numbness had worn off after the attack, Aimee had become powerfully angry. At first she didn't realize it. She'd had trouble sleeping, trouble eating. She hadn't wanted to go out with friends. Danny had tried to tempt her with a trip to wine country to revisit some of the places where they'd first fallen in love, but she'd wept so hard while trying to pack, he'd canceled the trip.

Strange, how easy it was to recognize depression in someone else and how hard it was to see it in oneself. The anger hadn't been easy for her to see, either. She'd only recognized how angry she was when it was time for the trial.

Her thirst for vengeance had been nearly insatiable. While she couldn't lie when asked about Kyle's violent tendencies, she couldn't defend him, either. She hadn't explained to the jury why Kyle had fixated on her—that she was the first woman entrusted with his care who hadn't abandoned him or betrayed him.

Of course, that was no longer true. She *had* abandoned him. And when she hadn't explained that to the jury, she'd betrayed Kyle every bit as much as his stepmother had when she'd allowed her own sons to use him as their personal punching bag and worse.

Worse yet, she'd betrayed herself.

Everyone expected her to press charges against Kyle, but she didn't have to do it with as much gusto as she had. How could she claim to be a person who spoke out for those who couldn't speak for themselves when she'd gone back on those convictions the second it became personally difficult? She, of all people, should have understood what led him to the night that he'd thrown her to the floor and struck her with such force that her jaw had to be wired shut. She should have understood the rage and the need for power and control over his own fate that had made him rip at her clothes and force her legs apart with his knee.

She swallowed hard as she navigated through the dark streets. She breathed in deep, let the breath out slowly, and kept her speed just a fraction over the speed limit. Her heart beat fast as if Kyle was here now, watching her, waiting for another chance to hurt her; to take from her what had been taken away from him through years of abuse and neglect.

Hurting her wouldn't help him. And helping put Kyle behind bars hadn't helped her, either.

At the time, she'd argued that she was only looking for closure and that she'd only wanted Kyle someplace where he couldn't hurt her or someone else. In her heart, she knew it was a lie. She'd been furious. Her blood had been boiling. She had flown into rages at the least provocation. She had wanted him punished; she had wanted him hurt. She had wanted him to feel as powerless and small and vulnerable as she had, lying in the corner of her office, too hurt to even scream for help as she had watched him unzip his jeans, knowing what was about to happen and unable to make it stop.

Danny had made it stop. Danny, who had been impatient for her to meet him for drinks. Danny, who had called her cell phone and gotten no answer. Danny, who had come to her rescue, bursting into her office and throwing Kyle across the room.

And it had been on Danny that she had unleashed her rage next.

To everyone else, she'd managed to present a determined yet calm façade. Not to Danny. He was the one who was there when she'd hurled plates across the dining room. He was the one who saw the punched walls and uncontrollable weeping. He was the one who'd seen her half naked and bleeding—and Aimee had not been able to forgive him for it, even though he had been the one who saved her.

She had tried to pull it back together. She'd joined a women's running group in the hope that regular exercise would help her get back into control. It had helped some, but not enough and it had been too late. She'd damaged the relationship between them so much, had pushed Danny away so many times, had punished him so harshly for trying to help her, that sometimes she wondered if she'd *always* wanted to force him to walk out the door.

She pulled into the parking garage and sat for a few moments, resting her head against the steering wheel. Finally she pulled the key from the ignition and, after doing a quick scan of the garage, got out and locked the car behind her.

As always, her heart beat a little faster as she walked through the deserted garage. As always, she repeated to herself the security measures in the condo she had moved to after Danny had left the house they'd shared. As always, she reached the elevator with no one leaping out from behind a column or from the shadows behind a car. As always, the elevator arrived empty and unthreatening. She entered with a sigh of relief that she had arrived unscathed. The elevator doors swooshed smoothly shut and she pressed the button for the third floor.

She idly watched the numbers over the doors. When she stepped out onto her floor, something smelled bad. That was unusual, but garbage pickup wasn't until Tuesday; sometimes things got a little smelly at the end of the week. She turned the corridor to get to her condo . . . and froze.

The smell was coming from the pile of dirt and flesh and blood in front of her door. She gagged, fought back the vomit that burned the back of her throat, and ran for the stairs.

CHAPTER
19

Josh shot a grape into Dean's cage. Dean favored him with the slow flicker of an eye, but didn't pounce on the fruit. He'd have to go to the pet store tomorrow to get some crickets. Geckos did not live by grapes alone. Josh surveyed the remains of his own dinner. Perhaps someday he'd branch from his usual rare New York strip steak, baked potato, and salad washed down with a Dos Equis, but not tonight.

He knocked off the last of the beer and stood. The game had been over for a good hour. The A's had lost again, two runs short of a tie.

He felt a little that way himself.

Today every road he ran down had ended in a blind alley or taken an unexpected turn. Boyfriends with alibis. Nonexistent contractors. Disgruntled employees with uncles on the job.

Beautiful shrinks with fiancés.

He scraped his plate and put it in the dishwasher, then rinsed the beer bottle and put it by its fallen brothers to be taken out to the recycling tomorrow. It was nearly eleven; he might as well turn in.

He was headed toward his bedroom when the phone rang. The caller ID told him it was the station. Why the hell would they be calling him now? He sighed. Why the hell did he bother wondering? They called when they called; that was the way it went.

"Wolf here," he said into the phone.

"Hey, Josh."

He recognized the voice of Betsy Stewart, who worked in dispatch. That was odd.

"What's up, Betsy? How are the kids?" Betsy had two boys, one in junior high and one in high school. She complained about them endlessly, but obviously adored them both. She'd caught the oldest one smoking pot after school one afternoon and had asked Josh to have a little chat with him. He'd felt a little bad about scaring the kid quite that much, but he'd earned Betsy's undying gratitude by doing it.

"They're big and smelly," she said.

"I believe that's the natural state of the adolescent male until they discover girls."

"We got a call I thought might interest you," she said. "Wasn't the shrink you called in for a consult named Gannon?"

"Yeah."

"Well, she called in a disturbance at her condo. I thought you might want to know."

Josh left so fast, he didn't say good-bye.

Josh made it to Aimee's condo on L Street in less than fifteen minutes.

"What's up, Vu?" he asked the uniform in front.

Vu looked up, surprised. "What are you doing here, Wolf?"

"Dispatch buzzed me. Dr. Gannon's consulting on

my double homicide. I thought I'd come by and see what was up."

Vu nodded his head. "Oh, yeah. I wondered why the name sounded so familiar. Your consultant came home and found a dead puppy on her doorstep." He made a face.

Josh stared at him in disbelief. "What kind of freak puts a dead puppy on someone's doorstep?"

"Got me. By the smell of it, it's been dead a couple days, too." Vu shuddered a little.

How did a dead dog on a doorstep connect to the Dawkin case? Or did it? "Any note? Anything else? Any strange symbols scrawled on the walls?"

Vu shook his head. "Nope. Just a dead dog. Your friend freaked, took off for the garage, locked herself in her car, and called us."

That did not sound like the Aimee Gannon who faced him down at every opportunity. This must really have gotten to her. "Who's with her now?"

Vu shrugged. "Hance maybe. Possibly Bonnet."

"Who's dealing with the dead dog?" If there was a connection, it was critical that the evidence be collected correctly.

"Clyde's upstairs."

Excellent. Clyde might be a goofball, but he was a very competent goofball. Josh took the stairs two at a time. The dead dog might have nothing to do with his case, but it'd be foolish not to check it out. Coincidence made Josh uneasy; life was rarely as random as it looked.

The smell hit him the second he opened the door to the hallway.

Two uniformed cops kept the neighbors who were clumped in doorways up and down the hall from approaching, although nothing could stop their curious glances. Josh flashed his badge at the uniforms and they nodded him through toward Aimee's door. "Anybody talked to the neighbors yet?" he asked as he walked past them.

One of them nodded. "Yeah. You're going to be shocked. Nobody heard anything. Couple people noticed the smell and figured someone's garbage needed taking out."

"Any idea when the mess got dumped here?"

The shorter of the two flipped open his notebook. "Guy in Three-H came home around seven and didn't notice anything, but he didn't actually walk by the door. He's the opposite direction from the elevator. Still, he thought he would have noticed the smell. So, we figure after that and before when the lady got home at ten forty-five."

The other one said, "That would be a good time for something like this. If people were going out, they'd already be out, but they wouldn't be coming back just yet."

Josh nodded. Their reasoning seemed sound. "Security tapes?" he asked.

"We're getting them. We'll send 'em down to the lab and watch them as soon as we're done here."

Clyde was crouched over the nasty partially decomposed mess in front of Aimee's door. His saggy jeans had crept down, exposing a solid three inches of Bart Simpson boxer shorts.

Josh knelt down next to him. "What do you have?"

"Dead dog," Clyde replied.

"I can see that. Anything else? Maybe a fingerprint? A hair?"

Clyde didn't look up. "I've got all those. It's going to take a little while to figure out what's significant and what's not."

"Do we know how the dog died?"

Clyde sat back on his heels and gave Josh a baleful look. "Not yet, and I'm afraid the M.E. didn't feel like coming out on a Saturday night to determine a C.O.D. on a dead puppy."

"This could be connected to the Dawkin case," Josh said defensively. "I don't think it's outrageous to ask for a cause of death."

"I'm aware of the connection, Detective, even though it seems damned unlikely. It seems a lot more likely that one of your girlfriend's loony tune clients decided to leave her a special present. Maybe you want to go ask her about that." Clyde went back to what he was doing.

Josh stood up. "Fine. Where is she?"

"Down in the garage in her car. She hasn't been willing to come out of it yet. She made Hance show his badge, and she called the station to verify his badge number before she'd even roll down the window."

"She's staying locked in her car? Even now that we're here?"

Clyde nodded. "She freaked more than I would expect. I'd like her fingerprints for elimination pur-

poses. See if you can get her to come up here for that."
Clyde went back to his work.

Josh took the stairs down to the basement garage
since two of Clyde's fingerprint technicians were busy
with the elevator.

Sure enough, there was Aimee Gannon sitting in her
car. The door was open now, and Hance was crouched
down next to her.

She looked up as Josh walked to the car. He felt his
chest constrict as he met her eyes, but he'd gotten used
to that. He just wished it would stop happening: she
was taken.

"Detective Wolf, what are you doing here?" she
asked.

Hance stood up and shook hands with Josh. "Josh,"
he said, slightly wary.

"Dispatch recognized your name," Josh explained to
Aimee. "They thought I should be notified that something was going on here."

"This has nothing to do with Taylor," Aimee said.
"This is an entirely different matter."

Her hands were grasped tightly together in her lap,
and Josh could see them tremble. She was truly frightened.

"What kind of matter is it?" he asked, laying his arm
across the open car door.

"I think it's a former client of mine." Josh watched
the lovely line of her throat as she swallowed hard and
obviously schooled herself to keep her voice calm and
even. He wondered what it would take to make that
mellow voice rise in passion, and felt his stomach clench

at the thought. "He . . . he stalked me before. He's just recently been released from Vacaville. I'm guessing this has something to do with him."

Josh nodded. Stalkers were stalkers. Restraining orders and state-paid holidays in mental hospitals didn't change their nature. "You're talking about Kyle Porter."

She looked up again, eyes wide. "You know about him?"

He shrugged. "Elise looked it up. Your name rang a bell, so she did a little digging. How long has he been out?" Josh drummed his fingers on the car roof.

"A few weeks."

"Any contact from him before now?"

She took a deep breath and seemed about to say something, then let the breath out and looked down at her hands. "No. Nothing that I'm certain about, anyway."

Josh glanced over at Hance, who lifted one eyebrow and shrugged.

"Has there been contact that you've been uncertain about?" Josh asked, wondering what sense that made. Either the creep had been hanging around and she'd noticed, or he hadn't. People were never as slick as they thought they were, especially perps. They all thought they were criminal geniuses, but most of them couldn't find their asses with both hands.

Whether Aimee had noticed was a different matter. Most people walked through their lives oblivious to their own surroundings. After years of being a cop, noticing was what he did. Being aware of his environment could mean the difference between life and death someday.

Most people didn't seem to realize that it could make that kind of difference to them, too. He would have thought that after having been stalked once and knowing her stalker was on the loose again, Aimee would be aware though.

"I . . . I'm not sure," she said to her clasped hands.

Josh crouched down to eye level. Even braced for it, he still found the impact of her gaze powerful. "Dr. Gannon, is there something that happened that you weren't sure about, but that made you nervous somehow?"

She nodded, and words tumbled out of her in a rush. "Ever since Kyle attacked me and I found out how long he'd been stalking me, I've never felt safe. I constantly have the sensation that I'm being watched, or that something's out of place."

The pieces started to click together for Josh. Her caution. Her occasional stances of bravery. Aimee Gannon was afraid all the time, and she didn't think she had any right to be.

"I think we need to go over some of those sensations from the past few weeks and sort through them. If this isn't Kyle, it's somebody else." He stood up. Clyde should be finished upstairs, and the carcass should be cleaned up by now. It would take longer for the smell to go away, but there wasn't anything he could do about that. "Let's get you back to your condo now. Your fiancé is probably worried sick about you."

Aimee shook her head. "We split up almost a year ago, Detective. I don't have a fiancé."

Josh's broken engagement had left him devastated and he wouldn't wish that on anyone, but he couldn't help being happy that Aimee Gannon's fiancé was out of the picture. A million things raced through his head, from wondering what had gone wrong to wondering if he had a shot.

Aimee got out of the car and slung her purse over her shoulder. "I think I'm ready to go home now."

Kyle couldn't believe what he was seeing. What the hell was going on? The place was crawling with cops. What had Aimee done?

He crouched back farther into the alley between the travel agency and florist shop across the street. He'd been certain that she'd see the gift he'd left for her and come looking for him. Instead, minutes after she'd pulled into the garage, the first police car had come. And then another. And another.

And then *he'd* come. Kyle should have known the big Neanderthal was a cop. He had that swagger. Thought he was a big swinging dick, did he?

Kyle lit another cigarette and ducked down the alleyway to L Street. There were too many cops to try and find out what had gone wrong. He'd have to wait until he could teach Aimee a lesson about what happened when you called the cops.

Aimee walked through the hallway with her head held high, not looking at her whispering neighbors. The stench was still so bad that she pulled the neck of her shirt over her mouth to keep from gagging.

"You got any candles?" Detective Wolf asked.

She nodded, not wanting to open her mouth.

"It'll help. You should light some as soon as we get inside."

We. He clearly intended to come inside the condo with her. For a second, her knees felt weak with relief. The police had said there'd been no sign of anyone tampering with her lock, but they'd also said there was no sign of tampering with the locks on the front door of her "secure" building—and clearly someone had gotten in.

Tears filled her eyes. This condo had been her haven. She had left the house that she and Danny had shared six months ago, too tortured by the memories that assaulted her every time she turned around. The kitchen where he'd proposed over a truly fantastic Zinfandel and shrimp risotto they'd cooked together. The living room where they'd cuddled together on the couch under blankets and played Scrabble when the power had been knocked out by a storm. The bedroom, where Aimee had turned her back on her lover when the shame and humiliation of having him see her half-naked on the floor, bloody and helpless, had overwhelmed her. The dining room where she'd sat, looking at her folded hands, as he'd moved his belongings out.

She had come here to start over again and had felt safe here. Now Kyle had taken her sense of security once again, and she was powerless to do anything about it.

She couldn't stay in Sacramento; she was too easy a mark here. Forget packing, she'd just leave. She didn't care about the things in her apartment. Actually, she didn't care about much anymore. It was too hard to care. That was another thing that Kyle had managed to do to her.

The mess in front of her door had been cleared

away, but a stain remained on the carpet. Now *there* was a metaphor for what had happened to her life.

Josh nodded to the officer who stood outside her door. "You checked it out?"

The young man nodded. "All clear."

Josh looked down at Aimee. "You don't mind if I give it a once-over myself, do you?"

Mind? She couldn't be more relieved. She'd rather spend the night outside in the smelly hallway than walk in there by herself. The shame she felt at her own fear was nearly overwhelming. She felt her knees wobble and grabbed the doorframe. Josh steadied her, his arm encircling her, giving her balance and stability. She looked up at him, braced for the pity she knew would be reflected in his eyes.

She saw concern. She saw sympathy. But she didn't see pity.

She squared her shoulders, and they opened the door to her former sanctuary.

Aimee Gannon's fear had been nearly palpable as they walked down the hallway toward her door. Her jaws were clenched tight. Her shoulders were rigid. Josh had wanted to pull her close to him so she'd know she was safe and not alone, but he didn't dare. He had no idea how she'd react. Victims of crime sometimes needed to stand on their own.

Then she'd swayed at the doorway as if her knees were going to buckle. He'd steadied her and she'd looked up at him with those wide blue eyes, and he'd felt like his own knees had turned to water.

"Let me go in first," he said. "Just as a precaution."

She'd nodded and tried to smile.

Her condo was unexpectedly bland. He supposed all the beige was restful, but it made tapioca pudding look *muy caliente*. It didn't fit with the spark in her eyes when she'd been angry with him. It didn't fit with the passionate way she'd defended Taylor.

At least it would be easy to tell if anything had been disturbed. It'd be like looking for footprints in a newly raked sand garden.

"How many rooms?" he asked.

"Two bedrooms. One and a half baths," she said from the entryway. "I'll light some candles while you look around."

Josh checked each closet, behind each door, even under the bed. He came out to find she had arranged a series of candles on a silver platter that had seen better days. She struck a match and as she began to light the wicks, the golden light flickered over her face.

God, she was beautiful.

"This is probably going to smell even worse," she said, looking down at the platter. "One of my friends dragged me to a candle party. I bought a sampler, so each one of these is a different scent."

"I think it'll be okay," Josh said. Aimee had a lot bigger things to worry about than scented candles, but people often focused on some small detail so they didn't have to think about what was actually happening. "It doesn't look like anything's been disturbed. You might want to take a quick walk through to make sure."

She nodded but didn't move, staring down into

the flickering candlelight. "He was in the building. He wasn't supposed to be able to get into the building."

Josh rubbed the back of his neck. "People do stupid things. They hold the door open for someone who acts like they belong. Or they hit the buzzer to let someone in, even though they haven't heard the name clearly. They don't look behind them and someone ducks into the garage after they've pulled in. The truth is, if someone really wants in, they're probably going to get in."

She shivered and Josh felt bad for frightening her, but sugar-coating the truth wouldn't protect her.

"You're right," she said. "I should be relieved he didn't get in my condo—but even the hallway is too close for me."

"We'll pick him up in the morning. This will have violated his parole. He won't be coming back anytime soon."

She sank down into one of the chairs. "A fat lot of good that did me last time."

"Feel like telling me about last time?" Josh asked, sitting down in the chair across from her.

She straightened back up and shoved the hair off her forehead. "I'm not sure there's much to tell that you don't already know about, Detective. You've read the file."

"Please call me Josh. And I haven't gone over it myself."

Quiet stretched between them. Then Aimee asked, "Are you on duty, Josh?"

"No. Actually, I guess I'm not."

"Good. Would you like to have a drink with me?"

Aimee poured whiskey into two glasses and walked into the living room. She curled herself into a corner of the couch, pulled a throw over herself, and gestured to the other end of the couch. "Make yourself at home." She took a sip of whiskey and savored the trail of fire it left down her throat.

Josh filled the space, his long, strong legs stretched before him. Aimee could feel his heat from the other end of the couch.

"So this guy really got to you," he said, looking down into his glass.

"Yep. I guess you could say that." No matter how hard she fought it. "When a client turns violent and that violence is directed at you . . . it changes the way you view a lot of things."

"I can see that." He leaned back deeper into the cushions. "I can definitely see that."

"I still don't think Taylor killed her parents," she said quietly.

"Me neither," he said, his head tilted back and eyes gazing up toward the ceiling. "It doesn't feel right. I thought maybe the boyfriend and she might have done it together, but the little shit's alibi checks out."

That was good news. "You found Flick? What was he like?"

"Interestingly enough, Elise thinks that he looks like Sean Walter with a mohawk. I think he looks like a punk."

"That *is* interesting." Something niggled in the back of Aimee's brain, but it was gone in a flash. She took another sip of her whiskey. "You didn't let me talk to him."

He shrugged. "There wasn't an opportunity. The picture he painted of Taylor wasn't exactly a pretty one, by the way. Why is she so damn self-destructive? From the looks of things, she had it pretty good. What did she have to be so twisted up about?"

It was time to put her cards on the table. "I think Taylor might have been sexually abused."

Josh sat up a little straighter. "Do you think it was the father? Because if her father was raping her and her mother knew about it, it would be one hell of a motive for murder. She wouldn't be the first abuse victim to finally snap and take out her abuser."

Aimee shook her head. Abusers don't shell out a hundred and fifty dollars a session without much hope of an insurance reimbursement to a licensed professional intent on figuring out why their daughter has started listening to My Chemical Romance and cutting herself, when their only reward might be a jail sentence and complete estrangement from their family. "No. I don't, especially since I talked to them about the possibility that Taylor might have been molested."

Josh leaned toward her. She was intensely aware of how close he was, of his warmth and of the warm masculine smell of him. Her heart beat a little faster in her chest, spreading heat throughout her whole body.

"How did that go?"

Aimee took another sip of whiskey. "It could have gone worse. I went over everything that I could think of with them, anything that could have helped us pinpoint a time or a person. Nothing seemed to ring any bells with them."

"Did they have anything helpful at all? Any idea of what was going on with their own daughter?"

Aimee shot him a look. It was easy to judge someone else's parenting. Figuring out how to raise a teenage girl was a hell of a lot more difficult. "They were doing the best they knew how to do. She blindsided them, to be honest. For years she'd been quiet, well-behaved, clingy even. Especially with her mother. Then all of a sudden she was sneaking out of the house, stealing money from her mother's purse, dating a boy who was older and in so many ways inappropriate. Her parents had no idea what to do. At least they were trying to do something to help."

Josh held up his hands in surrender. "I give. So she was sweetness and light until six months ago. Is that when you think she was molested?"

Aimee shook her head. "I think it happened a long time ago."

"Why?"

"Taylor has very few memories from the time right

after her family moved to Sacramento, while her earlier recollections of Phoenix were really vivid."

Josh shrugged, making Aimee all the more aware of the muscles in his chest and shoulders through his thin T-shirt. "Yeah, well, it's not like I really remember third grade, either."

"No, but third grade was longer ago for you than it was for Taylor." She sat up more on the couch and leaned toward him. Big mistake. They were inches away from each other. At least she wasn't cold anymore.

"Ouch!" Josh clutched his chest in mock pain.

Aimee smiled. "You know what I mean. Besides, this was a definite gap with a specific beginning and ending. Even though she remembered things from after that summer, Taylor said she didn't remember that time period because Sacramento sucked and there wasn't much reason to remember anything that happened here. A lot of things sucked: geometry, sobriety, Hannah Montana, her parents—just to name a few."

"Sounds like a typical teenager."

"It does, but she was covering, maybe even from herself. A gap like that is a red flag to a therapist. Something happened at that time that Taylor didn't want to remember. There've been other things, too."

"Like what?"

"Like the fact that she had a big personality change a few months after they moved here. Her aunt said that before the move, Taylor had been an outgoing and friendly kid. Something changed. She got quiet and clingy. She reverted to a much earlier stage of her childhood."

"A kid having a personality change—even if you could possibly confirm that—doesn't mean much."

"It's not just the personality change, either. It's the way she's clutching the stuffed dog that she got as a present from her aunt at about that same time. It's something about the symbols she drew on that self-portrait, with her so small underneath them, and that she keeps drawing them again and again. It's all linked, Josh. I'm sure of it."

Josh shook his head. "I don't know." That would certainly make a nice neat little package out of this case, but Josh was inherently suspicious of neat little packages. They didn't occur naturally, and they almost never occurred in a homicide investigation. People were messy. Their lives were messy. Their emotions were messy. The way they killed was messy. "A pile of drawings doesn't mean the two things are related."

"There's something about the way she's turning back to the same time period in which she was molested that makes me feel like they're connected. I understand that one emotional trauma always, in some ways, connects to another. But why go back to that *particular* time, if they're not connected more strongly than that? If she was going to revert again, why not go back to the even earlier stage that she reverted to when she was molested? I think Taylor is trying to tell us something through her behavior, just like those symbols she drew are trying to tell us something."

Josh shook his head. "None of it's evidence you can take to court."

Aimee's hands flew up. "I'm not looking for evidence

to take to court. I'm looking for clues that will help me figure out what made Taylor break, so maybe I can help put her back together again."

Josh set his whiskey glass down. "Can't it be both?"

She stood up from the couch. "Of course it can! I'm just saying that my priority is—"

"I know what your priority is. I'm just saying what mine is." He stood and faced her.

Aimee's face was flushed and her eyes were bright. Josh wanted to feel that heat, and he wasn't going to deny himself any longer.

His hands slid up her arms, then he leaned down and his lips touched hers. They were soft and warm and he could taste the whiskey on them. He slid his arms around her waist and pulled her closer. Her hands slid up onto his chest, the pressure light but oh so tantalizing. He lifted his head and looked into her eyes. Her pupils were so dilated that they were nearly black, with only the thinnest rim of blue.

She looked back at him, eyes wide, then her arms slid around his neck and she pulled him down for another kiss. He relished the small moan she made as her lips opened beneath his. He swept his tongue in, tasting her, testing her, tangling with her, savoring her warm flavor as he nibbled on her full lower lip. She gasped and he pulled back, worried he'd shocked her. She blushed and ducked her head against his chest.

"You have no idea how long I've wanted to do that," he murmured into her hair.

"Longer than I've been waiting for you to do it?"

He chuckled. "Probably. You were kind of pissed at me that first night. I'm guessing you didn't want me to kiss you right then, but trust me, it was already on my mind."

"I *was* kind of pissed off, but that doesn't mean I was blind." Her hands reached up to tangle in his hair.

"I'll definitely want to hear more about that at some point. Possibly even some point soon." He kissed her forehead.

She brushed her lips against his.

"Aimee," he said gently, "I don't want to go."

She stiffened. "I don't want you to go, either, but I understand." She pulled away a fraction.

He pulled her back and brushed the hair from her forehead. "You *don't* understand. I want to stay here. I don't think Kyle will come back tonight, but I'm not keen on taking chances. And I'm afraid that now that I've kissed you, you won't let me stay."

"I don't want you to go," she said, her voice quiet but intense.

His heart did a somersault. He wanted her in his arms and in his bed.

He scooped her up and carried her into the bedroom, then he laid her on the bed. Her hands reached up and tangled in his hair again. He took them in his own hands and kissed her fingers, never taking his eyes from hers. He felt like he could dive in there and never surface. He released her hands and covered her with his body, then kissed her again.

She arched beneath him and kissed him back. Her fingers found the buttons on his shirt and undid them. He wanted to rip his shirt off, but allowed himself the delicious sensation of anticipation. Once his shirt was open, she ran her hands over his chest and he knew he'd made the right choice. The feel of her hands on him had been worth waiting for.

She sat up and he slid her top over her head, reached behind her and unclasped her bra, and laid her down on the bed again. As his flesh touched hers, she gasped into his kiss. Every place their skin touched felt electric and charged. He dipped his head to her breast and took the nipple in his mouth. She arched beneath him again, a small moan escaping from her throat. Her hands caressed his face and brought his lips to hers once again.

He settled himself between her legs. His erection pressed against her, and he felt her breath catch. He reached between them and unbuttoned her jeans. When he slid his hands down the silky skin of her stomach, she moaned again. He sat up and tugged the jeans from her long legs. For a moment, he simply looked at her and let the feeling of his heart tumbling inside his chest wash through him.

She lifted her hands to him. "Come back to me."

"I never left." *I never will, either.* He lowered himself to her again and caressed her through the lace of her panties, making her writhe.

"Oh, Josh!"

He slid her panties down her legs and his fingers curled in the damp curls between her legs. His eyes stayed on her face, now flushed with passion, and her eyes closed as she let the feeling wash over her, as over-whelmed as he was.

The scent of her arousal rose to meet him and his cock throbbed in response. He slid one finger inside her and she moaned. He slid a second finger inside her and she arched to meet him. He lowered his head to taste her and she gasped. As the wave of her fast orgasm shook her, she called his name. Quickly he stood and shucked off his jeans and boxers. He said a silent prayer of thanks that he had a condom in his wallet. He cov-ered himself and in moments he was over her again, the head of his cock pressed against the silky wet heat of her opening. "Look at me," he said, his voice hoarse and rough.

Her eyes flew open and, with their gazes locked, he slid inside her.

The room whirled around him like a kaleidoscope, with the constant center being Aimee's eyes. He moved slowly at first, until she met his rhythm with an urgency that mirrored his own. He matched her pace. As he heard her breath begin to come in small gasps and her eyes began to close, he changed his angle and her eyes flew open once again. He nearly laughed with the joy of it. He kissed her and his world rocked again as she flicked her tongue wickedly inside his mouth, invading him in turn.

He felt her clench around him as she began to climax again. He could hold back no longer, and together they rocked and shook while stars exploded in his brain.

Afterward, as she curled beside him, her head on his

chest, he pulled the blanket over them. She sighed and nestled closer. He kissed the top of her head and smiled, closed his eyes, and tried to let himself be content. But one thing still remained between them. He wasn't sure if it was the detective in him or the jilted fiancé, but he had to ask.

"So what happened to the fiancé?" He felt Aimee stiffen and he pulled her closer to him.

"I suppose Kyle happened," she said, not looking at him. "That's the short answer."

"I've got time. I could listen to the longer answer." She had allowed him to draw her closer, but she still had not relaxed. He knew he was treading on thin ice, but he needed to know. He wasn't entirely sure why it mattered to him. Aimee was not Holly. He was sure she had her reasons. Then again, it was entirely possible that some other guy had his arm around Holly right now and was figuring that she had her reasons, too. In all fairness, Josh supposed she had.

"You would think with the amount of time I've spent thinking about this and analyzing and trying to make it make sense, I'd have an answer to that question." She rubbed her forehead with her thumb and pushed away from Josh. "I think that after Kyle attacked me, both Danny and I thought that things would go back to the way they were before. Especially after the trial."

"And they didn't?" He wanted so much to pull her back to him again, but realized that she needed the space between them to explain.

She shook her head. "They most certainly did not."

"What was so different?" He turned onto his side and propped himself on his elbow to look more directly into her eyes.

"I was." Aimee sat up, pulled the sheet up over herself, crossed her legs and sat tailor-style facing him. "I was frightened. All the time. The slightest change in our routine, the least noise, anything could send me into a panic attack."

"That's normal after an experience like that. You needed some time." So the guy was a jerk. That was an explanation he could live with.

"That's what we both thought, and Danny did his best to give me that time and make me feel safe. We stopped going out to dinner or movies or to hear music. That probably sounds stupid, but Danny's the kind of guy who's always the life of party, in a good way. To stay in our little cocoon day after day, night after night, was killing him."

"He couldn't wait it out?" Josh was liking this guy less by the minute.

"He tried. I did, too. But after the trial, I realized that things were never going to go back to the way they were." She brushed the hair off his forehead. "I had changed too much."

"So he left?"

"Or I drove him out."

"And now?"

"In some ways, Danny leaving was what I needed to realize that I needed to get some therapy. To be honest, though, I don't think my life will ever be the way it was again."

Josh took Aimee's hands in his. They were freezing, and he rubbed them between his to warm them up. "Why not?"

"I don't trust my instincts the way I used to. I should have seen it coming. I should have seen how powerful his transference was becoming, and done something about it."

Josh looked into her eyes and saw how much that confession cost her. He could understand. How would he feel if he stopped trusting his own cop instincts? "How often do clients turn violent like that?"

"Almost never. But that doesn't mean I shouldn't have seen what direction Kyle was heading in. There's other stuff, too."

"What other stuff?"

"Why didn't I realize that he was stalking me? The signs were all there. There were so many little things that should have tipped me off, and I missed all of them until after the fact."

"I'm pretty sure that's why we have that saying about hindsight being twenty-twenty," Josh observed.

"I know. But the problem is, now I *always* think someone's watching me. I get this sensation at the base of my neck. The hair stands on end and I'm convinced there's someone behind me, watching and waiting and . . ." She shivered.

"Does it help that you were right some of the time? Kyle *was* watching you again."

"I wish it did, but I can't tell when I'm really in danger and when I'm not. No wonder Danny always looked at me like he felt sorry for me. I despise being a victim so much, and every time I looked into his eyes, it reminded me that that's what I was now: a victim."

"But that doesn't have to be all you are," Josh pointed out. "Being the victim of a violent crime does change people, but it doesn't have to take over your life forever. You're more than that. Any fool can see it."

"I'm not sure Danny could see it anymore. Every time he looked at me, I think he saw me broken and bleeding on the ground. Every time I looked at him, that's all I saw, too."

"Then he's an idiot." Josh smiled at her. "Which is fine by me, because my mama didn't raise no fools." He put his hand at the back of her neck and pulled her toward him for another deep kiss.

CHAPTER
21

It was very late when Aimee and Josh finally fell asleep, but Aimee still woke a few minutes before the alarm was set to go off. She shut it off before it could ring. Josh lay on his side, a possessive arm around her waist, pulling her close even in his sleep.

"You totally suck at sleeping in," he murmured into her hair. "Do you always wake up before the alarm?"

"A lot," she admitted. It felt so good to be held, to be sore in all the right places, to wake up with a man—this man—in her bed.

"Anything else I should know?"

"I eat cottage cheese out of the container, and leave my shoes all over the living room. What about you? Any confessions?"

"I sing in the shower." He kissed her neck in just the right spot and she shivered.

"Do you sing show tunes? Something embarrassing?" She turned so she was nose to nose with him and kissed him. The stubble on his chin scraped her cheek and a tingle ran down her spine.

"No, my tastes run to seventies rock 'n' roll. I do a fabulous rendition of 'American Pie.'" He kissed her back, sucking her lower lip between his teeth.

"The long version?" Aimee hooked her leg around him and pulled their hips together.

"Depends on how dirty I am." He rolled her onto her back, covered her body with his, and kissed her again.

They were busy long past the normal alarm time.

Josh was standing in her kitchen shirtless, making coffee. His wet hair gleamed and curled on the back of his neck, and she could smell his clean soap scent. Aimee let her gaze travel down the strong lines of his back, resting on the twin dimples just above the waistband of his jeans. "This looks like a scene from *Porn for Women*," she said.

He turned, coffee carafe in hand. "Excuse me?"

She laughed at his bewildered expression. "You know that book, the one with all the hot guys doing the dishes and taking out the garbage? It's been making the rounds."

"Not at the police station," he said, turning back to her coffee maker. "Am I doing this right?"

She came and stood next to him, loving the brush of his shoulder against hers and his heat. "Pretty much." She took the carafe from him and poured the water into the well and hit the buttons to start the machine. She turned to find him looking at her, a smile on his face. "What?"

"You think I'm hot." He chuckled.

She flushed. "Oh, the words that slip out of our mouths when we're not properly caffeinated. Go put a shirt on." She threw a dishtowel at him.

"In a minute." He pulled her to him for a long, slow kiss that had her whole body tingling.

Then the doorbell rang.

Josh released his grip on her a little. "Expecting someone?" he asked, his face serious.

She clunked herself on her forehead. "I forgot to call Simone. We run together almost every morning."

Josh frowned. "Does she always come at the same time?"

"Pretty much." Aimee started toward the door.

Josh took hold of her arm and pulled her behind him. "Let me answer it."

She looked at the grim set of his jaw. "Seriously, it's just Simone. She has the code for the security door downstairs."

"*Seriously*, if you have a routine that you do every day, it makes it very easy for anyone who's watching you. Kyle is clearly escalating things and may be looking for an opportunity to get a lot closer to you. Leaving your house at the same time every day is practically an invitation. Having someone let themselves in at the same time every day is an engraved invitation."

Aimee felt the blood leave her face. "I hadn't thought of that." She hadn't just endangered herself with her stupidity, she'd endangered Simone, too.

Josh brushed the hair off her face and kissed her forehead. "Varying your schedule should be one of the first things you do. We can talk more about it later. Now, please, let me get the door."

Aimee hovered behind Josh, feeling foolish and

afraid as he opened the door. It was almost worth it, though, to watch Simone's eyes open wide at the sight of shirtless Josh.

"Simone?" he said, looking back to Aimee for verification.

She nodded. "Simone."

"And you are?" Simone asked, stepping inside without taking her eyes off Josh.

Josh stuck out his hand. "Detective Josh Wolf. Sacramento PD."

Simone shoved past him to Aimee. "Are you all right? Did something happen?"

"Kyle left a calling card here last night. I found it when I got back from your place." Her throat clogged at the thought of the little decomposed body in front of her door.

"A calling card? What kind of calling card does a sick psycho stalker leave?" Simone asked.

"In this case, a dead puppy," Josh said.

Simone's face went white. "You poor thing! You should have called. I would have come right over."

"It was fine—I called the cops and they got here right away. On the plus side, I finally found a use for those candles Jane pushed me into buying."

"Don't joke. This is serious." Simone threw her hands up in the air in exasperation.

Aimee took Simone's hands. "I know it is, and it's under control. Josh is going to pick Kyle up today."

Simone turned to look Josh up and down one more time, then looked back at Aimee. "The Sacramento PD sends detectives to spend the night at your house?"

"It's the deluxe stalker service. You can sign up for it online," Aimee said.

"I'll go gather my things," Josh said, and slipped past them to the living room, gently brushing Aimee's shoulder as he went past.

Simone followed Aimee into the kitchen. "Detective Hot Stuff really spent the night here?" she asked in a whisper.

"Detective Hot Stuff?"

"What do you want me to call him? Officer Cutie? Sergeant Honey Buns?" Simone plopped down in a kitchen chair.

"How about Detective Wolf? Or even Josh?" Aimee poured a cup of coffee for Simone and got the half-and-half out of the refrigerator.

Simone shook her head sadly. "You have no imagination. Did he spend the night here?"

Aimee smiled and didn't say anything.

"You dog! You've totally been holding out on me!"

Josh came back into the kitchen, shirt on. "So what exactly do you ladies have planned for this morning?"

"The usual," Simone said. "Five miles through Capitol Park."

"Any chance I could talk you into taking a different route or going to a gym?" Josh asked.

"Neither of us belongs to a gym," Aimee said, sitting down next to Simone.

"We could go back to my place and run that route in the park that we've been meaning to try," Simone offered, sipping her coffee.

"Sounds like a good plan," Josh said. "And after that?"

Aimee frowned. "Probably some more time with Taylor's file. I need to figure out what that pattern means."

"Have you considered that it could be nothing more than that? Just a random pattern that she draws? Elise draws spirals on everything." Josh sat down next to her.

Aimee shook her head. "It's got to be more than that, just like Elise's spirals are probably more than that."

"Like what, besides the fact that she gets bored easily?"

"Spirals mean advancement, progress. I'm guessing Elise is an ambitious woman." Aimee smiled at him.

"You'd be right about that." He got up from the table. "Okay. Look into the symbols, but try to stay out of trouble, okay?"

"Hey, Sean." Sarah smiled up at him as he walked into the kitchen. She was sitting at the table, drinking coffee and working on her daily Sudoku.

"Hey, yourself," he said, grabbing a mug from the cupboard and pouring himself a cup. He looked out the kitchen window. The sky was blue, the trees waved a little in the breeze; all in all, it was pretty much a perfect spring day. He'd had a good meeting the night before. He'd also tossed those blood-spattered shoes into a Dumpster behind a busy Starbucks. Maybe he could put the ugliness of what had happened to Stacey and Orrin behind him. Maybe there would be no more nasty little surprises waiting in closets or garages or under bushes. Maybe he could move on.

There was still Taylor to consider, but he'd find some way to make amends to her. She'd need help now that her parents were gone. Maybe he could help her. Maybe she'd be grateful enough to keep what she knew to herself. That wasn't so far-fetched.

He sat down across from Sarah and took the front section of the newspaper.

"Have you been outside yet?" Sarah asked.

"Nope, I just got up. It looks gorgeous out."

"It is, but . . ."

Sean looked up. She was biting her lower lip, something she did when she was nervous.

"What's wrong?"

"You know that tree you planted for me? The crape thing?"

Sean nodded. "The crape myrtle. Did I put it in the wrong place? I can still move it, or get you a second one."

"No, it's great where it is. Or was. Someone dug it up last night."

Sean set his coffee mug down with great care. Keeping his voice calm, he asked, "Why would someone do that?"

She shook her head, her big caramel-colored eyes wide. "I have no idea. They didn't even take the tree. They left it lying there next to the hole."

"Was there anything in the hole?" Sean asked. *Easy. Don't sound concerned. Breathe. Once. Twice. Again.*

Sarah's brow furrowed. "Just dirt. I didn't look all

that close. Do you think we ought to call the police? I mean, people shouldn't be allowed to come on someone else's property and dig up their trees."

Sean swallowed hard. "Oh, it was probably some neighborhood kids playing a prank."

"What kind of prank is digging up a tree?" Sarah still looked confused.

Honestly, that was her natural state. She was sweet, but not the brightest bulb in the chandelier. She didn't need to be. Not for Dad.

"A stupid prank." Sean bit the inside of his cheek. Had someone seen him when he'd planted the tree? Had they seen what he'd left in there? Oh, Jesus. Had his father seen? "What did Dad say when you told him about it?"

"I haven't told him yet. He'd already left for the gym when I saw it. I figured I'd tell him when he got home."

Sean's mind raced. There was still a way out of this. "Let's not bother him. You know how stuff like this upsets him, and he's got so much on his mind right now, trying to figure out what to do with the business now that Orrin's gone. I'll replant the tree. He'll never even have to know that it happened."

Sarah frowned for a minute and then nodded. "I don't like to lie to your dad, but not saying something isn't exactly lying. Maybe it *would* be best not to get him all riled up. Thank you, Sean. I never know what to do about stuff like this. You and Carl are so good at knowing what to do, and taking care of it." She reached across the table and put her hand over Sean's. "I feel so lucky."

Sean forced himself to smile back at her. "Me too."

He fled the kitchen as soon as he could without arousing any suspicion. Although what it would take to arouse Sarah's suspicion, he couldn't say. She was trusting to an extreme, and took everything at face value.

The only person who could possibly have known what was under that tree was his father. But why would he have dug it up? Why would he take that kind of chance? And if he had, what had he done with it?

Sean sat on his bed and bumped his head against the wall softly, as if it would help him think. Who else could have seen him? Surely not Thomas. Besides, the little guy couldn't dig the damn tree up. And definitely not Sarah.

Which brought him back to his father. If there was anyone who wouldn't want to expose what Sean had buried there, it would be Carl. They hadn't spoken of it. Years of shared secrets tied them together. This was just one more—but one that could unravel their lives if someone picked too hard at it.

It was okay. He'd had his father's backing before and he had it now. He might not always understand his dad, but he loved him.

So it must have been an outsider. The idea that someone had watched him and unburied his secret made Sean's stomach heave. Who could have done such a thing?

One thing was clear: whoever it was had to be as sick and twisted as Sean was.

The poor bastard.

———

Josh called Elise on his way to the station and filled her in on the dead puppy, and on Aimee's suspicions that Taylor had been sexually assaulted and that it was all tied together. He did not tell her about where he'd spent the night.

But Elise was nobody's fool. Outside the station, she looked him over, sniffed, and said, "That's the same shirt you wore yesterday, isn't it?"

"I haven't had time to do laundry."

She sniffed again. "And that isn't your usual shampoo I smell, either."

"I like to try new things." He opened the car door for her. "Can we go show this photo lineup around now? Or do you want to check to see if I have on clean underwear?"

"Far be it for me to advise you on matters of personal hygiene." Elise slid into the car. "But a woman notices these things. I'm just telling you."

When he got in the driver's side, she asked, "Where are we starting with your lineup?"

"I figure we can start around Aimee's office building, then its parking garage." Josh started the engine and reversed out of the parking space.

"Aimee?" Elise asked. She hummed a little tune to herself.

Josh ignored her and pulled onto Freeport.

"What?" he finally asked.

"Yesterday she was Dr. Gannon. Now she's Aimee all of a sudden. I had no idea that a dead dog was the way to your heart. I would have told Jane Burton that months ago."

"Who's Jane Burton?"

"The blonde with the overbite over in dispatch. She was asking if you were single, and I don't think she was looking to help you fill out your W-2, if you know what I mean."

Josh cast his mind through the women over in dispatch and tried to remember a blonde with an overbite. "Do you mean the one with the crossed eyes? Who looks like a Siamese cat?"

Elise considered for a moment and then snorted. "She does look a little like a Siamese. Kind of whines like one, too, doesn't she?"

"Tell her I'm gay," he said. "Please."

"Should I tell Aimee Gannon that you're gay, too? Or does she already have proof that you're not?" Elise teased.

Josh scowled at her.

"Come on," she wheedled. "How'd she go from Dr. Gannon to Aimee in one night?"

"We talked. She's not so bad." Josh felt the corners of his mouth quirking up, and fought it. Aimee was way better than "not so bad." She was smart, compassionate, and her legs practically went all the way to her neck.

"Not so bad? Is that some kind of guy euphemism?" Elise pressed.

Josh opted not to answer.

Elise settled back in her seat. "Fine. Be that way, but that's the last time I spill my guts to you about my love life."

"Thank God for that," Josh muttered under his breath.

Forty-five minutes later, he held a set of photos out for the rent-a-cop at the parking garage attached to Aimee's office. Security at her office was nonexistent. That had become clear pretty quickly. Both Josh and Elise had shaken their heads at each other over the lack of a doorman or anything else. At least the garage had someone walking patrol. "You seen any of these guys around?"

The kid couldn't be more than twenty years old. He still had acne, for Christ's sake, and he gulped nervously as he talked to Josh. He wouldn't make eye contact with Elise at all, and she wasn't even wearing her Angry Black Woman face this morning.

Chris McBride hitched up his uniform pants and squinted down at the photos. He hesitated only for a moment and then pointed to the photo of Kyle. "I seen him around here a couple times in the past month or so. I kicked him out of one of the stairwells. I didn't think he was a stalker, though. Maybe a homeless kid or something. He was just sitting there and smoking. You want me to find him on the security tapes? I could probably find him if you give me an hour."

"Yes. Thank you." Josh turned to Elise. "You think that will be enough for a warrant for Leal?" Getting a search warrant from that judge was like getting a bone from a dog. It took a hell of a lot of pulling, and you were likely to get bitten a couple of times in the process.

"I sure hope so," Elise said. "I'm never sure what he wants. A signed confession, maybe?"

"He just likes to watch us squirm, to make us jump through hoops," Josh groused.

"And what's with the way he walks?" Elise asked, adjusting her shoulder holster. "It's like he's trying to carry quarters between his butt cheeks."

Josh snorted. "Great. Now I'm going to have that image every time I talk to him. I'll never be able to keep a straight face."

Elise smiled. "Then my work here is done."

So was Chris McBride's. He came jogging over to where Elise and Josh waited with a VHS tape in his hand. "I got it. I remembered that the day I booted him for smoking in the stairwell was the day I had my tooth pulled. That was why I noticed him. I was kind of sick to my stomach, and the cigarette smell almost made me puke. Anyway, he's on here."

"Thanks, man." Josh clapped the boy on the back and the kid's chest puffed out like he'd received the Congressional Medal of Honor. "Excellent work."

"You're welcome. Anything I can do to help." Chris paused. "Can I ask what he did?"

"He left a dead dog on a woman's doorstep," Elise said.

Josh shot her a look and turned back to Chris. "The guy's a stalker. This is just what we need to pick him up."

"I'm glad I could help," the boy said.

"You thinking about a career in law enforcement?" Josh asked.

The boy flushed. "Yeah. I'm thinking about it."

Josh pulled a card from his jacket. "Give me a call. I'll give you some pointers."

They walked away. When they were out of earshot, Elise finally said, "So you clearly got laid last night."

Josh shot her a look.

She whistled. "She must be damn good if she can put you in this sweet a mood."

"Shut up," he said, unlocking the car and tossing her the keys. "It's your turn to drive."

She snatched the keys out of the air without even looking. "Did you just tell me to shut up?"

"I did."

She shook her head. "Then it *is* serious. You haven't told me to shut up since Holly."

Josh got in the car and waited until Elise slid into the driver seat. "Aimee is not Holly."

"We can thank the good lord for that." She started the car. "Now let's go pay a happy Sunday morning visit to Judge Leal."

CHAPTER
22

When Aimee had gotten home from her run with Simone, there'd been a message from Dr. Brenner. He was ready to allow her access to Taylor again. He was not, however, ready to have Aimee give Taylor the CD that Sean had brought for her. He'd asked if Aimee would bring it to him to listen to first.

"Dr. Gannon to see Dr. Brenner," she told the woman behind the glassed-in desk.

"Just a moment, please." The woman buzzed her through after a quick check of the approved visitor list.

"I know my way," Aimee said, and walked through the atrium to the stairs that led to Brenner's office.

"Dr. Gannon." He stood and extended his hand.

She shook it and sat down. "Tell me what's going on with Taylor."

He shrugged. "She still hasn't spoken, but she seems somewhat more responsive. She's not rocking herself as much and she's looking at people more. I think she's making some real progress. I'm going to restrict her visitor's list to you and the aunt for now. At least until she can tell us a little more about what upset her so much."

That sounded reasonable. A parade of visitors was too intense for a girl fighting her way out of her emotional pit. She pulled the CD Sean had given her out of her purse. "This is the CD I was telling you about. The young man whose father was Taylor's father's business partner wanted me to give it to her." She handed it over to Brenner.

He flipped it over in his hands. "Aerosmith. That takes you back, doesn't it?"

Aimee smiled and nodded. She doubted that Brenner had been out of grade school when *Pump* was released; she'd been in high school. "I haven't listened to it for years. Let me know if you think it's all right for Taylor to have it."

"I'll listen to it in my car on the way home—if I ever get out of here tonight." He gestured at the piles of papers.

She said good-bye and walked through the corridors to Taylor's ward. Once again, she was buzzed through and directed to the common room. Taylor was sitting with her aunt.

"Hi, Marian," Aimee said.

Since it was the weekend, the place was more crowded than usual with family members visiting. These weren't joyous get-togethers, however. Silent people sat with drawn faces, clumped around tables, their unresponsive or too-animated loved ones chattering at them or ignoring them entirely. Aimee couldn't see one "normal" family interaction taking place. Of course, if any of these people were capable of "normal," they probably wouldn't be here.

Marian Phillips sat with Taylor at the end of one of the long tables. The other end of the table was occupied by an older man in a gray sweat suit. A pale, tense young woman in faded jeans sat next to him. When he reached out to take her hand, she pulled it away and then began to quietly weep.

Aimee wished she could help all of them. She wished she could help them break through the traumas from their pasts that held them apart or made them dependent on alcohol or drugs as a way to cope. But she couldn't. There was simply too much pain here for one woman to handle.

Aimee focused on Taylor and sat down next to her and Marian.

"Hello, Taylor," she said.

Taylor said nothing, but did give Aimee a sidelong glance. Marian smiled and gave a little shrug. Aimee set her hand next to Taylor's on the table, hoping Taylor would take her hand again, as she had when Sean Walter was visiting. She didn't, but she didn't move it away, either.

"How are you today?" she asked, but got no answer. Aimee looked over at Marian.

"I think we're making progress," Marian answered for Taylor.

"That's great," Aimee said. She hoped that some of the things she was going to ask today wouldn't set Taylor back further, but her instincts said it was time to forge ahead. Taylor had been trying to communicate. Those efforts had frightened her. She needed to be encouraged to move forward.

"Taylor," Aimee said, placing her hand on Taylor's back. "I'd like to talk to you about your drawings."

Josh pounded on Kyle Porter's apartment door and roared, "Police! Open up!"

The building was an old faded Victorian that had been divided into six tiny apartments. Kyle's was on the second floor.

Josh's voice was so loud Elise could see people two doors down the street opening their doors. Her partner's jaw was clenched and his patience was gone, thanks to Judge Leal.

Leal was a small man, and Josh was nearly six foot three. Call it a Napoleon complex. Call it Short Man Syndrome. Hell, call it George and take it home to meet your mother. She'd seen it too many times. It took a big man on the inside not to be bothered by small stature on the outside. Give a little guy power to wield over a big one, and things could get ugly—which they almost had.

Her own presence hadn't helped. Elise didn't know if it was the color of her skin or the fact that she was a woman that made Leal act like she was an idiot, but it wasn't pretty either way. Elise was used to it. You didn't go into law enforcement as a woman and not expect some roadblocks. Leal wasn't the first and he wouldn't be the last. Sure, it was irritating, but she and Josh had always taken boneheaded tight-assed women-haters in stride.

But not this time. Not Josh.

He pounded on the door again. "You've got one minute to open this goddamn door, Porter. Then I'm coming in."

He glanced at her and nodded. She checked her watch. She'd give him the nod at fifty-five seconds. Josh had at least sixty pounds on her, so he'd kick the door in. Then she'd go in low, he'd go in high, and they'd probably find Kyle Porter in the corner of his closet shitting himself. It had worked that way a hundred times. This case wouldn't be any different.

Even if everything on her partner's face said that this time, it was different. It had become personal.

Elise hoped the idiot would open the door. The dude was in there; they'd heard noises inside that stopped after Josh's first hard knock. Did he honestly think that if he hid, the police would go away?

There were the occasional smart-asses who tried to make a break for it down a fire escape or out a back door. It almost never worked. At this very moment, two uniforms were at the bottom of Kyle's fire escape and there was no back door. The average police officer might not have a Ph.D., but he wasn't stupid.

Ten more seconds. Josh glanced at her. He hardly needed a watch; his brain was like a stopwatch. She shrugged. What was five seconds, give or take? She nodded. His foot came up and the door never stood a chance.

It took approximately ten seconds to find Kyle behind a mound of dirty clothes in the closet. And if Elise's nose wasn't fooling her, he had shit himself.

She looked down at the sniveling man and said, "You are *so* not riding in my car."

Taylor had started to rock herself again. Marian Phillips licked her lips nervously. "Maybe we shouldn't do this, Aimee. Maybe it's too soon."

Aimee shook her head, still keeping her hand on Taylor's back. "I don't think so. I know this is going to be difficult for Taylor, but I think if we can get through this together, Taylor can really start to heal."

Marian shifted in her chair uncomfortably. "If you really think so."

"I do, Marian. I think her drawings convey something she wants to tell us about it, but saying it out loud is too hard. Unfortunately, we haven't been able to figure out what it is. She's going to have help us a little bit more."

Aimee could feel Taylor begin to tremble. She gave Taylor's back a reassuring pat, then pulled out the drawings from her briefcase and spread them out on the table.

Taylor began to rock faster.

"All of these are drawings that you've made since you came to Whispering Pines," Aimee said, keeping her voice calm. "Can you tell me what they mean, Taylor?"

Taylor continued to rock.

"What about the drawing you did back in my office, Taylor? The one I brought the other day?"

Taylor began to whimper. The man at the other end of their table and his daughter looked up at them.

"It's okay, Taylor. You're safe here. You can tell me what the drawings mean to you. You can tell me if what happened to your parents is connected to what happened to you."

Taylor covered her face with her hands and began to cry. Marian Phillips got up from her chair and wrapped her arms around the girl.

Aimee kept her gaze firmly on Taylor as conversations around them came to a halt. "I know they mean something important, Taylor. You wouldn't keep drawing them otherwise. You certainly wouldn't have drawn them on the wall if they didn't mean something to you. Or if you didn't want us to notice them. I think you *want* us to know what they mean. I've tried to figure it out, but I can't. I need you to help me, Taylor. Please. I need you to help me help *you*."

A horrible noise came out of Taylor's throat, between a wail and a howl. Everyone else in the common room was looking at Taylor and Aimee and Marian as they huddled around Taylor's drawings. Over in the corner, a hollow-eyed woman began to bang her head against the wall.

"Taylor, were you trying to use these drawings to tell me about something or someone that hurt you?" A nurse came into the room and started toward Taylor and Aimee; Aimee held her hand up like a traffic cop to hold her at bay. "Did someone do something to you, Taylor? A long time ago? Back when you first moved to California? Did that same person hurt your parents, Taylor?"

Taylor shoved Marian away from her, knocking her onto the floor. She grabbed the drawings from the table and tore at them. Her eyes were wide and wild, spittle flung from her mouth, and she continued to emit a terrible anguished cry like a wounded animal.

Aimee's restraining hand was no longer enough to keep the nurse at bay. She grabbed Taylor. Two orderlies were right behind her. They hustled Taylor out of the room, leaving Marian and Aimee facing each other over the torn bits of paper.

"How could you?" Marian whispered, her face a mask of horror. "How could you have done that to her? She was getting better."

Aimee reached her hand out to Marian. "It needed to come out, Marian. It's like a splinter that's festering. It hurts, but it has to come out before Taylor can start to heal."

"She wasn't ready." Marian shook her head. "She needed more time."

"There *isn't* a lot more time. This is all connected, Marian. Someone out there has hurt your family. Someone out there did something terrible to Taylor, and I think that same person might have murdered your sister and your brother-in-law. Taylor knows who did this, Marian. She *knows*. Don't you want to find who did this and punish them?"

"Do you think that will bring my sister back to me?" Marian's voice began to grow loud now. "Do you think pushing Taylor until she ends up nothing but a drooling vegetable will make me feel better?"

Aimee briefly shut her eyes. "No. I know that it won't. I also know that this has to be done—and the sooner the better."

"Why? Hasn't that poor child suffered enough?"

Marian's hands balled into fists. "Get out of here, Dr. Gannon. And don't come back."

"I'm not the sicko." Kyle looked down at his hands, cuffed in front of him on the table of the interrogation room. "I'm not the one with the problem."

Josh worked to keep his own hands by his side and off of Kyle Porter's throat.

"Really," Elise said. "You leave a dead dog on a nice lady's doorstep and you don't think you have a problem?"

"I didn't *want* to do that, but I needed to warn Aimee. I needed to send her a message." Kyle smiled at Elise.

"Well, you sent it all right. Now we're going to send you away again." Elise smiled back.

Kyle paled. "No. That's not fair. I'm trying to protect Aimee. I'm telling you, I'm not the sicko. I didn't kill that puppy. I didn't bury it. I *un*buried it. I brought it into the open so she could see it. She needed to *know*."

"So who is the sicko, Kyle?" Josh sat down next to Elise, across the table from Kyle. "Who were you trying to warn Aimee about? Who killed the puppy and buried it?"

Kyle glared at Josh. "I'm not telling you anything."

Elise said, "Tell me. Who were you trying to warn Aimee about? If you give us a name, we'll give her your message."

Kyle's mouth twisted down. "This doesn't involve you. This is between Aimee and me."

"Dr. Gannon is not your girlfriend," Josh said. "She

was your doctor, and she's not even that anymore. You're too screwed up for even your psychologist, Kyle."

Kyle's jaw clenched. "That's not true."

"I'm pretty sure it is, Kyle." Josh cocked his head to one side and smiled. "I'm pretty sure she made that clear to the whole world when she testified against you at your trial."

"They made her do that," Kyle screamed, up out of his chair, leaning across the table.

Josh leaned forward slowly. "Sit down, Kyle. You're not going anywhere. Nobody made her testify against you. She wanted to. She couldn't wait to tell them what a sicko you were. I bet she even laughed about it later."

Kyle sat down, his whole body trembling now. "She didn't laugh."

Josh shrugged. "Maybe she did. Maybe she didn't. Personally, I think it's kind of funny."

Kyle's chin quivered. "What's so funny about it?"

Josh leaned back. "That a twisted little psycho like you could think that someone like Dr. Gannon would think of you as anything but a boring case to be tolerated. That's funny."

"I was more than that. I *am* more than that! She loves me—I know she does. We were meant to be together. She just hasn't seen it yet. I can show her, though. I can!" Spittle flew from his lips as he shrieked at Josh.

"By leaving her dead dogs?" Josh laughed. "It wasn't even your dog, was it?"

Kyle's eyes turned sly. "That's right. It wasn't my dog."

Elise leaned forward. "Whose dog was it, Kyle?

Whose dog did you kill, and why is it a message for Dr. Gannon?"

Kyle crossed his arms over his chest, and pressed his lips together. "Get her in here and I'll tell her. You two can go fuck yourselves."

"No, Kyle. I'm pretty sure you're the one who's going to get fucked now. New fish like you? They're going to be *so* happy to see you in lock-up. Why, I bet you'll be the belle of the ball." Josh stood up from the table.

"You're going to send me into the general population? No way! I'll go back to Vacaville, back to the hospital."

"I sincerely doubt that, Kyle. You're a parole violator now, and I think you're going to do time like a big boy. I think you're going to see what it really means to be locked up." Josh pulled his cell phone out of his pocket as he walked out of the room.

Once they were outside, he said to Elise, "I'm going to call Clyde and see if there's any way he can find out whose damn dog it is."

Aimee let herself back into the condo, wondering who else might be able to cast some light on Taylor's drawings. Marian Phillips hadn't had any idea what they meant. Carl Walter had known Taylor for years; maybe he'd have some idea what the pattern could represent.

Aimee dug in her purse and found the card he'd given her at Whispering Pines. His cell phone number was at the bottom. She felt a moment of unease. He was another adult male who'd had access to Taylor. Could he be the person who molested Taylor all those years ago? It didn't seem right. When a victim lives near the abuser, it's rare that the abuse happens only once. Everything pointed to something traumatic happening to Taylor around the time her family moved to Sacramento, not an ongoing cycle of abuse.

She picked up the phone and dialed.

"Carl Walter," he said, his baritone voice strong.

"Mr. Walter, this is Aimee Gannon. I'm the psychologist who's helping Taylor. We met at Whispering Pines the other day when you were visiting her."

"Of course," he said. "How are you? What can I do for you?"

"I'm fine, thanks. I was hoping you could look at

something. Taylor keeps drawing the same pattern over and over again. I was wondering if you'd have a few minutes to take a look at one of her drawings and tell me if it means anything to you. I think figuring out what the drawing is about could be a huge step in helping her."

"I'm happy to do anything that might help Taylor."

Excellent. "Would you be free today? I could bring the drawing to you."

"Sure. How about this afternoon around three?"

Aimee jotted down Carl Walter's home address, and hung up feeling like she was finally starting to tie up the loose ends.

"It's got a microchip in its shoulder," Clyde told Josh when the tech called to report on Kyle's "gift" to Aimee.

"One of those chips people implant in their pets so that they can be tracked?"

"Yep." Clyde sounded deeply satisfied with himself.

Josh rolled his shoulders, trying to release some of the tension in them. "So whose dog was it?"

"I don't know, dude. It's not a database I normally need access to. I don't have any of the codes. I called the company that made the chip, but their customer service line is closed on the weekends. I can't hack into it."

Someone had to know how to get into the database. "Who would have access?"

"I dunno. Veterinarians, I suppose."

"I'll come pick up the chip in about half an hour. Have it ready for me," he said as he pulled out the

Yellow Pages and began looking for a twenty-four-hour veterinary service.

The Walter home was very nice. Perhaps even a shade nicer than Orrin and Stacey Dawkin's home. It was a two-story Meditteranean with a red tile roof and a veranda that ran across the front of the house in Land Park. There was a detached garage with a granny apartment over it in back, and a front patio with a stucco wall that matched the exterior of the house. Through the wrought iron gate that secured the driveway, Aimee could see a basketball hoop attached to the garage and glimpsed a swingset in the backyard. It was exactly the kind of house Aimee had grown up in and she knew that appearances like these could be very deceiving.

Of course, sometimes a cigar was just a cigar, and placid exteriors hid nothing dark inside.

She parked behind the silver Honda Odyssey in the driveway, then walked through the container garden in the front patio and rang the doorbell. A petite blond woman with a heart-shaped face opened the door. She had on jeans and a white blouse and white sneakers. She smiled. "You must be Dr. Gannon. Carl said you were coming at three. Come in, please."

Aimee followed the woman into the house.

She turned. "I'm Sarah, Carl's fiancée."

Understanding dawned for Aimee. Sarah must be the mother of Sean's new stepbrother. Aimee put out her hand. "Thank you for letting me disturb your Sunday afternoon."

"Oh, it's no problem. Carl said it was important.

He said he might be able to help Taylor." Sarah's open, sunny face clouded a bit. "I didn't know Taylor all that well. You know how teenagers are. They don't want to hang out with grownups, but I knew Stacey and Orrin. It just breaks my heart. Who would do such a thing?"

"I wish I knew," Aimee said. Sarah stood and shook her head, but made no move to get Carl. The silence stretched and began to feel awkward. Finally, Aimee asked, "Is Carl here?"

Sarah looked startled. "Oh, of course. I'll go get him. Do you want something to drink? A soda or something?"

Aimee shook her head. "No, thank you. I'm fine."

Sarah headed off down a hallway calling, "Carl!" and Aimee sat down on the sofa in the living room. The room was immaculate and sun-filled. There were no shoes lying on the floor, no magazines on the coffee table, and no dust anywhere—a feat in Sacramento. Aimee pulled the file with Taylor's drawings out of her briefcase and set it on her lap.

Carl came down the hallway, followed by Sarah. "Dr. Gannon," he said, extending his hand. "It's good to see you again."

He sat down on the other side of the coffee table in an overstuffed chair. Sarah stood behind him, clasping her hands. Carl followed Aimee's glance behind him and said, "Thanks, Sarah. I've got this."

She nodded and left the room. Aimee couldn't help but get the impression that she had been waiting for orders and was relieved to have been dismissed.

"Now, what is it that you wanted to show me?" Carl asked.

Aimee had been thinking of how to introduce the topic. "I'm not sure how much detail you have about what the police found at Orrin and Stacey's home."

Carl leaned forward and braced his elbows on his knees. His lightweight sweater bunched around his biceps and outlined the breadth of his shoulders. His brow creased and he glanced downward. "I'm afraid I haven't wanted to delve too deeply into that. Losing Orrin has been so painful." His head came up and he looked directly into Aimee's eyes.

"I can only guess at how difficult this is for you. It's been hard enough on me, and I barely knew them. Are you sure you feel up to this?" she asked.

He nodded, his thick sandy brown hair falling forward over his forehead. "Anything to help. Anything at all. One of the most difficult things is how powerless I feel in this situation. I want so much to do something to help, and there doesn't seem to be anything at all."

"I know what you mean. I feel as if I'm grasping at straws myself." Aimee opened the file. "Taylor apparently drew a set of symbols on the wall of the living room after she found her parents." Aimee opted to leave out the fact that Taylor had used her own blood to do so.

"Really?" Carl asked. "Do the police think it's a clue?"

Aimee smiled ruefully. "Not really, but I think it has to mean something. I'm not certain if it has to do with what Taylor saw that night, or something else entirely. I just know it seems to be important to her.

She's continued including the symbol in her drawings at Whispering Pines. I'm hoping that if I can figure out what the symbols mean, then I'll be able to help her. At the very least, I'm hoping that we can help her come out of the catatonic state the shock of finding her parents has put her into."

"I see," Carl said, nodding his head. "Do the police think she saw something that night?"

Aimee shook her head. "At this point, I think they're more likely to consider her a suspect than a witness. They haven't ruled out the idea that she might be involved somehow."

"Sean," Carl said, standing. "Come on in. Maybe you can help with this, too."

Aimee turned to look behind her. Sean Walter had come into the living room from the same hallway that Carl had emerged from a few minutes before. The resemblance between father and son was remarkable. "Hey, Sean," she said.

Sean smiled at her nervously. "Dr. Gannon, what are you doing here? What is it that I can help with?"

"Dr. Gannon has brought some drawings that Taylor made," Carl said before Aimee had a chance to answer. "She was hoping I could tell her if they mean anything to me. She thinks they hold some kind of key to Taylor's behavior."

"Really?" Sean said. Aimee could swear his face went a little bit pale.

Apparently Carl noticed as well. "It's okay, son. Sit down. We'll look at them together. It'll make it easier if we have each other here." He turned to Aimee. "Sean had been working very closely with Orrin at Dawkin-Walter Consulting since he came back to California. They'd become quite close over the past six months. I know this has been a huge blow to him, as well."

Sean nodded, his Adam's apple bobbing up and down for a moment. "Orrin was a great guy. I was learning a lot from him. There's nothing like having a mentor in the real world to show you the ropes. I really miss him."

"I'm so sorry. I know it's hard, but I'd be very grateful if you would take a look at these drawings, too. You're closer to Taylor's age. Maybe there's some reference here that you'll grasp that we old folks will miss." Aimee smiled at him.

Sean smiled back and sat down in the matching chair next to his father's.

Aimee pulled Taylor's drawings out and spread them across the coffee table in front of the two men, then looked from Carl to Sean. Carl steepled his fingers and looked from one drawing to the next. "She's nothing if not consistent, isn't she?" he murmured.

Aimee nodded. "It's part of what makes me think it means something important to her. She drew it the night of her parents' murder, and as soon as she began to draw at Whispering Pines, it turned up again and again. I found it in a drawing she did for me months ago, too."

"I see." Carl shook his head. "I'm sorry. I don't see anything there that I recognize. Could it be some kind of code or something?"

"Maybe, but if it is, I don't know how to break it."

Aimee looked over at Sean and was surprised to see him shoved back into his chair, fingers gripping the arms so tight that his knuckles had turned white.

"Sean," she said, "are you all right?"

He nodded, but didn't speak.

"Do you recognize something?" Carl turned to his son and laid his hand on Sean's knee. "Is there something you see there that you want to tell Dr. Gannon about?"

Sean's head turned slowly toward his father. He stared at him for a moment and shook his head. "N-n-no, Dad." He swallowed hard. "Sorry. I can't help but think about how horrible that night must have been for Taylor. I keep imagining her coming in and finding Orrin and Stacey. I keep wondering what I would feel like in her shoes."

Orrin clapped Sean on the knee and said, "You've always been a kid with a big imagination. This might be one of those times you might want to turn it off. There's no point in tormenting yourself about it. It's a tragedy, but we can't change it now."

Sean's gaze did not leave his father's face. He simply nodded his head up and down once, then again. He looked almost as if he'd been hypnotized. "Of course. You're absolutely right." He looked back at the drawings.

"Does it ring any bells at all?" Aimee asked.

Sean chewed his lower lip. "I'm sorry. I can't think of anything. Are you sure they mean something? Maybe they're just . . . I don't know . . . drawings?"

Aimee smiled. "I suppose they could be. It's certainly

what the police think. I just can't seem to let go of them, though. I feel like there must be a reason for her to draw them so often."

"What were you hoping they meant?" Carl asked, his head cocked to one side.

Aimee shivered. There was something almost predatory in his stare, like a hawk gazing down on a field mouse. "I thought maybe they might be windows from a certain room. Or a decoration from something that might indicate a certain time or a place. I'm not sure what else to consider."

The front door banged open and a little boy, all elbows and freckles, came rushing in. He saw Carl and screeched to a halt. Carefully, he sat down on the floor, took off his shoes, and put them in the shoe rack by the door.

Aimee stared. She'd seen Simone's boys come in from playing outside. They were a rolling, tumbling stream of dirt and chaos. This child looked like he'd be more likely to eat his shoes than get dirt on the Berber.

"Hey, Thomas," Carl said.

"Hey, Dad," the boy said, walking into the living room. Then he grinned and said, "Hi, Sean."

"Hey, buddy, what's up?" Sean stood up and walked over to Thomas.

"The sky." Thomas grinned up at him.

They high-fived.

"Thomas, I'd like you to meet Dr. Gannon," Carl said.

Thomas's face went serious and he stuck out his

hand. "Hello, Dr. Gannon. It's nice to meet you. My name is Thomas."

Aimee smiled. "It's nice to meet you, too. Have you been out playing?"

"I've been out looking for Bingo. We can't find him."

"Who's Bingo?" Aimee asked.

"He's my dog. I'm real worried about him."

Aimee looked from Sean to Carl. She could have sworn she saw a bead of sweat on Sean's upper lip.

"Hey, champ. I'll go out and help you look later, okay?" he said.

"Will you? I don't know where he's hiding. I've looked everywhere." Thomas's lower lip quivered.

Sean put his hand on the boy's back. "Maybe I can think of a few more places to look."

"Thanks. Is Mom in the kitchen?" Thomas looked up at him.

"Yep."

As he walked past, Carl grabbed the boy, turned him upside down, and tickled him. Thomas squealed and kicked.

Aimee turned to say something to Sean, and saw the strangest look on his face. For a moment, it looked as if he was going to cry.

"I really appreciate you helping out like this, Crystal," Josh said, leaning over the counter and giving the round little veterinary assistant at Emergency Vet Services a big smile.

Crystal's pale skin flushed pink right up to the dark

roots of her limp blond hair. "It's not a problem. Plus it's kind of cool to say I assisted the police. I mean, we do a lot of good stuff here. We save animals every day. But helping in a homicide case? That's not something that goes on all the time." She shoved her black-framed glasses up her nose.

Crystal couldn't pull off the cute nerd look as well as Aimee did. The glasses were the same, but Crystal's face was round and undefined. She didn't have Aimee's aquiline nose or high cheekbones or that wide lush mouth that Josh could kiss for hours. Still, Josh was feeling quite kindly to Crystal at the moment since she'd scanned the mystery microchip. She'd gotten the serial number in seconds; now she was calling the business that had registered the microchip. From there, it should be only a few minutes until Josh and Elise had a name, address, and phone number for the dog's owner.

Crystal pushed a few more buttons on her computer. "Got it. Ohhhhh," she said sadly.

"What's wrong?" Elise asked from behind Josh.

"He was just a puppy. His name was Bingo and he belonged to a Thomas Barlow in . . . I think Land Park. I'll write down the address for you."

This was not good. Oh, no. This was not good at all. He didn't like the doctor nosing around with those drawings one bit. Who else had she shown them to? Who else might figure out what they meant? Thank God the police weren't taking her seriously.

Still, she was persistent and that could end up being a problem. A huge problem. And now there was the girl to consider. Damn it all to hell. What had she seen that night? He'd been so sure that he'd been long gone before she'd come home. How could she have seen him?

His heart began to pound as he considered the ramifications. How long would she stay in her silent world? She'd already shown signs of coming out of it. That could no longer be tolerated. Taylor was going to have to be silenced permanently. He had a little time before he had to deal with her, but the psychologist had to be dealt with right away.

Christ, he felt dizzy and it was getting hard to breathe.

All right. This was bad, but not nearly as bad as it could have been. He'd been warned now, and he could do something about it.

He fingered the cord that he carried in his pocket, stroking it with his thumb. The doctor's neck was so long and slender. It was easy to imagine the cord wrapped tight around it. His breathing became heavier, and his cock began to swell in his pants.

He imagined the way the doctor's eyes would glaze over. Yes, he could take care of her with pleasure.

Then he'd figure out what to do about Taylor.

CHAPTER
24

Aimee glanced up at her office clock. It was nearly seven. She'd spent the last few hours entering billing codes and sending follow-up e-mails. She'd gotten behind in the past week and it was time to catch up. Her cell phone rang in her purse. She fished it out. "Aimee Gannon," she said.

"Josh Wolf," he replied.

Aimee felt the blood rush to her cheeks, happy to hear his voice on the other end of the line. "Hey. How are you?"

"I'm fine. I was calling to find out the same about you. Where are you?"

"At my office. I needed to get some paperwork out of the way."

"Are you almost done?"

"I just finished up. Why? Are you checking up on me?"

"I don't need to check up on you. I got the guy who's been bothering you in custody."

"Great! Then why are you calling?"

There was a pause. "I was, uh, wondering . . ."

"Wondering what?"

"I was wondering if you'd like to have dinner with me tonight," he said.

"I would love to," she said immediately.

There was a sigh, as if he'd been holding his breath. "Great," he said. "Do you want me to pick you up at your office?"

Aimee looked down her plain black skirt and sweater. "No. I want to go home and change first. Pick me up there?"

"Sure. How about seven? That'll give me time to stop at home and feed Dean."

"Dean?"

"My gecko."

"You have a gecko? As a pet?"

"Wanna make something of it?"

She laughed. "I'll reserve judgment until after I meet Dean."

"I'll check his schedule and see if I can arrange it." He paused. "Aimee, are you sure you feel okay going home alone? I know it's got to be a little weird right now."

She leaned her head back on the chair again, relieved that he understood without her having to explain it. "I'm okay. With Kyle in custody, what's there to be afraid of?"

"She said yes, didn't she?" Elise plopped down on Josh's desk with a big smile.

"Were you eavesdropping?"

"It's hardly eavesdropping. I can hear everything you say over the top of these cubicle walls. It'd be more work to try and *not* listen. Then I'd be costing the good taxpayers of the city of Sacramento even more money, so it would be downright unpatriotic to not listen in on your conversations."

"You can rationalize anything, can't you?"

"Pretty much. I'm still having trouble with the idea of miniskirts and Uggs at the same time, but other than that, I'm good. Where are you going to take her?"

"I have no idea."

"How about the Firehouse?"

"A little pricey for a first date, don't you think?" And not exactly in a police officer's day-to-day budget either.

"Does it really count as a first date when you've already spent the night together?" Elise asked with a wicked grin.

Josh shook his finger at her. "I am not discussing that."

"If you didn't spend the night, then we need to have a chat about your personal hygiene. It is not okay to wear the same shirt two days in a row." Elise plopped down on his desk.

Josh leaned his elbows on his desk and looked up at his partner. "This is different. It's special. I don't want to joke about it."

"Josh, that's so . . ."

"Boneheaded?"

"No, sweet. If you don't cut that shit out she'll start to expect it all the time, and I don't know how long you can keep it up, partner. Although I have to say that it suits you."

Aimee walked through the empty garage. Not many people came to the office on Sunday. As she came out of the stairwell, she got that creepy sensation of being watched again. Frowning, she rubbed the spot on the back of her neck where the hairs stood up.

Kyle was in custody, and the Subaru was only a few steps away. She'd be there in seconds. She opened her bag to fish out her keys. She'd just found them when she heard running footsteps behind her.

Her mind screamed. *Run! Scream! Fight!* But her body froze, like a deer in the headlights. She finally broke free and started to turn to face whoever was coming—

Too late. A cord slid around her neck and she was yanked backward, almost off her feet.

Her hands flew up to clutch at the cord, but it already dug too deep into her throat. Her keys and purse fell to the ground as she frantically tried to get loose from the cord that was cutting off her air.

The edges of her vision began to blur. She was yanked back even harder. Whoever was behind her was big. He'd reached over her head and pulled her back against a broad chest. She could hear his harsh breath in her ear as he panted with exertion or excitement, then she registered the feel of his erection pressed against her back.

No! Not again! She *wouldn't* be a victim again.

As the darkness at the edges of her vision spread, she stamped around her with her foot, hoping to connect with the keys. She felt her heel crunch on plastic, then her car alarm blared.

The man's grip loosened for a second, and Aimee instantly got her hands under the cord and pulled it away from her neck. Oxygen rushed into her lungs. Over the rushing in her ears, she heard someone shout, "Hey! What's going on here?"

The man released her and Aimee sank to the floor, gasping for breath as she heard him race away.

The skinny security guard was by her side in seconds. "Ma'am, ma'am, are you all right? Are you okay? Do you need an ambulance?"

She shook her head and turned. Her attacker was gone.

"Should I call nine-one-one?" the security guard asked.

Aimee pulled Josh's card out of her purse. "Call him," she croaked.

Josh hung up the phone, ran out his door, and called the attack in as he locked up. He wanted people out looking for this creep as soon as possible. He just wished he knew which creep it was.

He called the jail. "Hey, Vasquez Reed. Josh Wolfe here. Do you still have Kyle Porter in custody?"

"Yeah. Why?"

"Do me a favor. Double-check. Lay your eyes on him. I'll hold."

There was a pause. "Why you want me to do that, Wolf? I'm comfy here at the desk."

"Just *do* it." Something in his tone must have come through, because Vasquez told him to hold.

Not wanting to lose his connection to Vasquez if he got in the elevator, Josh ran down the six flights, two stairs at a time. He was headed out the door by the time Vasquez came back on the line. "He's there. You want me to take him a snack? Maybe give him a manicure?"

"I just needed to know for sure. Thanks, man. I owe you one."

Who the hell could Aimee's attacker be? Whose button had she pushed? What did she know that had put her in danger? The security guard had said that someone had tried to choke Aimee. A vision of Stacey Dawkin on a cold slab in the morgue flashed into Josh's brain. Could this be connected? How could it not be? Josh gritted his teeth in frustration as he navigated his way through Sunday afternoon traffic. He needed to get to her. He needed to see she was safe. Then he could ask all the questions he wanted.

By the time he got to the garage, three squad cars and an ambulance were at the scene. He flashed his badge to the officer at the entrance to the garage and ran through. He found Aimee sitting in the back of the ambulance, an ice pack to her throat.

"Hey," he said. "I got here as fast as I could."

She smiled and took his hand.

The paramedic said, "She's having some trouble speaking. I'm pretty sure it's temporary. I want to take her over to the hospital to check it out for certain, but she's not so keen on the idea."

"Where do you want to take her?" Josh asked.

"Mercy. She'd probably get through their ER faster than at the Med Center." The paramedic folded up the blood pressure cuff he'd taken off Aimee's arm.

Josh smiled down at Aimee. "It'll be like old times. Just like the night we met."

Aimee rolled her eyes and croaked, "I'd rather go home."

"And you will. We'll make this one stop first. I'll be there with you." *And then I'm going to catch the son of a bitch who hurt you.*

She squeezed his hand, then scowled.

"What's wrong?"

"I didn't get to use my pepper spray," she whispered.

In the emergency room, the nurse had Aimee stand with her chin lifted as far as possible and aimed a huge camera at her throat.

Josh's first instinct was to look away. The deep red gouges were enough to send him over the edge. The way she held her shoulders and head high, despite the way her hands were shaking, made him feel like he was falling off a cliff. He wanted to find the bastard who had done this to her and pound his face in.

Instead, he'd find the bastard who did this and put him behind bars, preferably for life. To do that, he needed every shred of evidence he could gather. He forced himself to look at the photographs as they slid out. What he saw didn't surprise him.

"Hey, Elise—come take a look at these."

Elise walked over. "What do you have? Something good?"

"Something seriously bad. Look at those, and tell me if Aimee's wounds don't remind you of something."

Elise looked down at the photographs and then back at Josh. "Holy shit."

"My sentiments exactly," Josh said.

It had been hard to see the details of the ligature marks on Aimee's throat. Living flesh doesn't always take a mold the way dead flesh can. Once the camera had magnified the marks, though, the long, ridged line in the middle of the ligature mark was clear. The same long thin line that had made Doc Halpern decide that Stacey Dawkin had been strangled with an electrical cord.

"If not Kyle, who?" Elise asked quietly as they sat in the waiting room. Aimee had gone up to X-ray a while ago. The hospital staff wouldn't let Josh stay with her, and no amount of badge flashing or glowering had changed their minds.

"I have no idea," he said. "It's been close to a week and we've got *nothing*." He couldn't think of another case where he'd followed more leads and come up with less.

A nurse wheeled Aimee past the waiting room and back toward the emergency room. Josh and Elise stood up and followed.

"The patient needs to rest," the nurse said.

"We're not going to keep her from resting," Josh promised.

The nurse didn't even glance at him. "Ms. Gannon has been through a traumatic experience. She can talk to you later. She needs to go home and rest."

"Dr. Gannon is perfectly capable of telling me to leave whenever she wishes to do so," Josh told her. "I'm not going to make her talk. Besides, I'm her ride home."

The nurse did give him a glance now, then asked Aimee, "Is that so?"

Aimee nodded.

The nurse helped Aimee transfer from the wheelchair to the hospital bed. "I'll be back in forty-five minutes to check Dr. Gannon's vitals. If everything's stable, she can go home. If you upset her, she might have to spend the night."

"I won't upset her. I promise." Josh pulled the visitor's chair up to Aimee's bed. She looked tired. The circles under her eyes were deep and dark, like bruises against her pale skin. The ligatures across her next were angry and red. He wondered how many times the bastard would have choked her and released her if she hadn't gotten away, and he clenched his fists.

Elise stood up. "I'm heading home. See you in the morning?"

Josh nodded.

Elise turned to Aimee. "I'm going to have a lot of questions for you tomorrow, but now you need to rest. Let Josh take care of you tonight. He's probably crappy at it, but he's got to start somewhere." She gave Aimee's hand a squeeze and left.

Aimee looked at Josh. Her voice was barely above

a whisper. "I didn't see anything. He came at me from behind. I wasn't . . ." She hesitated. "I knew that Kyle was in custody. I thought that I was safe."

Josh's gut twisted with guilt. He was the one who'd told her she was safe. He had been the one who made her think she could let her guard down.

"I'm so sorry," he said, lowering his head onto his hands.

"It's not your fault." Aimee put her hand on his shoulder.

"Whose fault would it be then?"

"The bastard who tried to choke me."

CHAPTER
25

They rode to the condo in silence. Aimee's throat hurt and talking was a strain for her, so Josh put his hand over hers as he drove. She looked over at him, smiled, and let her head lie back against the headrest. Josh felt something unspool inside him, some tightness that he'd held on to for so long that it had become a part of him.

Aimee directed him into her spot in the underground garage and they rode the elevator, in silence. He put his arm around her. She leaned her head against his shoulder and he felt as if he might stop breathing.

Inside her condo, she locked the door, then turned to him, put her arms around his neck, and looked up into his eyes.

The pull that Josh had felt in his gut the first time he'd looked into Aimee's eyes moved to his chest. He knew that he would kiss her. He would kiss her because he wanted to kiss her more than he wanted to solve this case, more than he wanted to be a cop, maybe more than he wanted to breathe. He dipped his head and his lips met hers.

Aimee angled her head back and her body molded against his. The heat in his chest threatened to turn into an inferno, and he kissed her until he thought his lips might catch on fire.

She put her hands against his chest and pushed him away, but only to take his hand and lead him to her bedroom. There she stopped in the doorway and kissed him again.

Damn. What that woman could do with her lips.

"I thought you were tired," he said. His throat felt tight. His heart pounded in his chest.

Aimee reached up and brushed his hair off his forehead. "I almost died tonight, Josh. I got lucky, and it's not the first time. I want this, Josh. I want *you*. I don't want to miss a second more of my life." Her voice was a husky whisper.

At the foot of her bed, Aimee undid the buttons of his shirt one by one, caressing his chest as she went. Her fingers were tantalizing and light as they brushed through his chest hair, down to the waistband of his jeans.

She slid the shirt off his shoulders, running her hands up and down his arms, tracing the muscles of his biceps. He bent to kiss her and her mouth, wet and hot, opened to him. Her tongue swept his and he pulled her tighter against him, his erection against her belly.

Last night she had been so sweet and soft, he'd felt like he was melting against her. Tonight she was setting his blood on fire.

Aimee broke the kiss to unbuckle his belt, sliding her hand down to cup him through his jeans. He closed his eyes, savoring the warmth, wanting more. She flicked her tongue against his nipples and he hissed at the jolt to his loins.

He fumbled with her top, pulling it over her head. His hands brushed over the smooth skin of her stomach and she moaned.

Her fingers were at his zipper now, releasing him. His cock sprang free and into her hand and she stroked him. Once, twice, her fingers cool against his heat. Then she slowly sank to her knees, slid his boxers aside, and flicked his tip with her tongue.

He tried to retain some control as the heat raged through him. His fingers twined into her thick hair, urging her on as she closed her mouth over him. She slid his length in and out of her hot, wet mouth and he thought he might explode. His hands roamed down her back, finding the clasp of her bra and releasing it. As her bra fell to the floor, he lifted her to her feet and relished the feel of her hard nipples as they brushed against his skin.

He kissed her lips once more before he laid her back on the bed and slid her jeans and panties off her slender legs. Her hands reached up to him, her arms pale in the dim bedroom. He kicked his own jeans aside and knelt between her legs.

She was hot and wet and slick with desire. He slid one finger inside her and she ground down against his hand in response. And then he lowered his head to taste her.

Aimee arched her back and almost screamed, the sensation that raced through her was that strong. Her desire spiraled down inside her, focusing in on Josh's hands, Josh's lips, Josh's tongue. She gasped his name. He urged her on, first one finger and then two inside her, his tongue swirling across her clit. She climbed higher and higher until the lights burst behind her eyes and she plunged over the cliff of desire, free-falling.

She was still shuddering when he entered her, rocking her in the same rhythm that he'd used to bring her to orgasm. Before the shock waves of the last climax completely faded, she came again. He stilled for a moment, letting her catch her breath, kissing her forehead, her eyes, her mouth.

She ran her hands up his arms, caressing his biceps and his shoulders, loving the feel of his hard muscles under her hands, knowing he wanted her as much as she wanted him. She rocked her hips against him, and he let out a low growl that made her smile.

She did it again.

His face was tense, and a sheen of sweat covered his shoulders as he slid out of her and plunged in again. She arched to meet him, urging him on. She caressed his back, her hands roaming down to cup his ass and pull him more fully against her.

He plunged into her again, sending shivers to her very core. Her hands found his hips as he found his tempo, rocking hard and fast until he released inside her in a hot rush.

Josh collapsed against her, murmuring her name.

He sat in the car and wrapped the cord so tight around his wrist that his hand began to turn purple. He had failed. Failed! How could it have happened?

Granted, he hadn't time to plan, but that hadn't stopped him before. With Orrin and Stacey, he'd only had seconds to make his decision and act. If he hadn't made his move precisely when he had in the precise way he had, it would never have worked.

So what had gone wrong this time?

That damn psychologist continued to ruin everything. It was her meddling that had made everything fall apart. It was actually *her* fault that he'd had to kill Orrin and then Stacey.

If she hadn't been pressing Orrin to think about something that had happened to Taylor years before, Orrin might never have put those pieces together.

Orrin wouldn't have had anything to hold over his head when confronted about the fake subcontractors and the missing money. He couldn't let Orrin continue to bleed the company dry to cover his idiotic investing schemes. Nor could he let Orrin tell the world what had happened to his daughter all those years ago. Neither option was tenable.

It had taken only a split second to come up with a third option that night, and less than that to put it into action. It had all gone beautifully.

And then Aimee Gannon had shown up with Taylor's drawings.

He knew what those drawings meant. He knew what Taylor had seen. He even had an inkling of how it all tied together, just the way Dr. Gannon suspected. Once she figured out what the drawings meant, everything would come crashing down.

But when he'd tried to stop her, it had all gone wrong. She'd managed to make her car alarm go off, and the rent-a-cop with the pimply face had come running around the corner. Good thing he'd worn the balaclava. He could have been recognized by the little creep.

He wrapped the cord tighter around his wrist. Running it through his fingers no longer soothed him the way it had right after he'd killed Stacey. Maybe it was time to get rid of it.

But not yet. It still held power. He could feel it surge through him every time he ran it through his hands, smooth and strong and flexible. He'd keep it for a little while longer.

Aimee opened her eyes and for a moment had no idea where she was. Waking up with Josh beside her totally changed her perspective on her bedroom. When had she made everything in here so bland? It needed some color, some life.

She'd almost lost her own life last night, and that had shown her that she hadn't really been living it. *That* had certainly changed. She had never felt more alive than when she was making love to Josh. She struggled to sit up, her neck throbbing with pain. He was there next to her. She was safe.

"Good morning, sunshine." He opened one eye. He looked rumpled and exhausted, and Aimee wasn't sure she'd ever seen anyone look better to her.

"Back atcha," she croaked. Her voice was a little stronger than it had been last night, but not much.

"You okay?" he asked, reaching out to caress her arm.

She nodded, her hand straying to her throat. "Still a little sore, but not too bad."

"We need to figure out what you said or did that scared someone enough to attack you." He caressed her thigh and sent a shiver running through her.

She put her hand over his. "After a shower and some coffee?"

He smiled and pulled her toward him. "Sure. Later."

She let herself be pulled into his arms and settled her cheek against his chest. She listened to the reassuring measured thump of his heart in his chest and snuggled in closer, hoping to hold on to that feeling of safety.

While Aimee was in the shower, Josh lay in her bed, savoring her smell and remembering the feel of her in his arms. His feeling of contentment was shattered when his cell phone buzzed in his pants pocket.

He fished his pants up off the floor, grinning as he thought of how fast he'd shucked them off and the urgency that Aimee had clearly felt as he'd kicked them away.

"Wolf." He looked over at the clock: eight-thirty. Shit, he should have been in the office half an hour ago.

"Wanna know why the name Thomas Barlow was so familiar?" Elise asked. "The kid whose dead puppy Kyle Porter was toting around town?"

"Lay it on me."

"He's Sean Walter's stepbrother-to-be. Somehow Kyle Porter got hold of a dead puppy from the Walter place, and left it on Aimee Gannon's doorstep."

Josh sat bolt upright. A connection between Porter

and Walter? Where the hell had that come from? "What does Porter say about it? Did he kill their dog?"

"Porter says he's not saying another word to anyone but Aimee."

"That's not going to happen." There was no way he was going to let Kyle Porter anywhere near Aimee. Josh sat up and set his feet on the floor.

"Careful before you say never, partner. One conversation with her, and we could know how Kyle even knew the Walters existed. It could take us days to figure it out without her help, and based on what happened to her last night, we don't have days. I think this thing's breaking loose. If we don't figure out how to catch all the pieces, we could end up looking like idiots."

Everything Elise said was true. Josh didn't care. "I said no."

"Who are you saying no to, and about what?" Aimee asked from behind him.

"It was Bingo?" Aimee blinked back tears. She didn't know why. She barely knew Thomas Barlow, but all she could think of was the little boy coming in from another fruitless morning searching for his dead puppy. It broke her heart.

Josh stared at her over his coffee cup. "How did you know the dog's name?"

"I was at the Walters' yesterday. I wanted Carl to look at Taylor's drawings."

Josh set his cup down so gently that it didn't make a sound. His deep chocolate brown eyes went wide for a moment and then his gaze settled on her, steady and even. "You were where?"

Aimee didn't understand his reaction. "I took some of Taylor's drawings over to Carl Walter's house. I thought maybe he would have a clue as to what they meant and why she might have drawn that symbol on the walls. I'm sure the murders are connected with what happened to her when she was just a kid. Carl is one of the few people who knew her as a child that I hadn't asked."

Josh closed his eyes, breathed in deeply, and asked, "What time did you decide to go to see Carl Walter?"

"After I stopped by Whispering Pines and Marian Phillips threw me out." Aimee didn't want to look at his face, but she made herself.

His eyes flew open. "Marian Phillips threw you out of Whispering Pines? For what?"

"For trying to press Taylor about her drawings. She wants to talk to us, she just needs some encouragement."

Josh shoved his chair back and looked her up and down. "What happened to staying out of trouble?"

Keeping busy had been her antidote to the fear that Kyle had brought back into her life. "I was trying to help my client." *And me*.

Josh got up and started pacing the kitchen. "Was Carl Walter the only person you saw at the house?"

"No, the whole family was there. Sean, the fiancée, and the stepson. I don't think the little boy saw the drawings, but Sean and Sarah both did."

"Did anybody have any clue what they meant?"

She shook her head. "No such luck. Did Kyle say how he got Thomas's dog? Or why?"

He sat down again across from her and took his hands in hers.

"The only thing that Kyle Porter will say is that he won't talk to anybody but you."

Aimee sighed, then shoved her chair back. "So why the hell are we sitting around here?"

As they stood outside the interrogation room, Josh couldn't stand it. "You don't have to do this if you don't want to. You can walk away right now and never see this sick bastard again."

"That's about the fifteenth time you've told me that," she pointed out. "Josh, I *need* to do this."

He loved her for being so determined, but the thought of her forcing herself to confront Porter made his teeth clench. "We can get Kyle to talk some other way," he tried.

"This will be faster. I'm a big girl, Josh. I can handle this." She turned to Elise. "Can you get him to shut up and get out of the way?"

Elise smiled. "Rarely."

Josh held up his hands in surrender. "Okay, okay." He opened the door to the interrogation room, and Aimee walked through it to face Kyle Porter directly for the first time since the day he'd been sentenced.

Kyle shot to his feet the second Aimee walked in, and it took all of Josh's will power not to backhand him into the wall.

"Aimee," Kyle breathed. "You came."

Aimee sat down in the chair across from Kyle and folded her hands in her lap. Josh's heart nearly broke. He knew why she did that, and he wanted more than anything to take her hands in his to stop their shaking.

"Hello, Kyle," she said. "What is it you needed to say to me?"

Kyle sank down into his chair across from Aimee. "It's been so long. I didn't know if I'd ever see you again. I had to talk to you. I had to explain."

"Is that why you left that poor dead puppy at my door, Kyle? So I'd come to see you?" Aimee leaned slightly forward, her eyes intent on Kyle.

Kyle laughed. "I knew you'd understand! I knew it!" He looked at Elise and Josh. "See, she knew all along."

"No, Kyle," Aimee said. "I *don't* see. I don't see why you killed that dog, buried it, dug it up, and then left it on my doorstep."

Kyle pushed away from the table and shook his head. "No. No! I didn't do that. I dug it up, and left it at your door, but I didn't kill it or bury it."

"Who did, Kyle? Who killed that dog?"

Kyle looked down. "I don't know who killed it. I didn't see that part. It was dead already when I saw him bury it. You had to know the truth about him. I saw the way he looked at you, I couldn't let you be fooled. I had to make sure you knew the truth about him."

"The truth about who, Kyle? Who did you see looking at me?"

"That pretty boy. They call him Sean."

CHAPTER
26

"Sean Walter moved back to California about six months ago," Josh said, his voice quiet and even, his eyes black. He'd practically dragged Aimee out of the interview room the second they had what they needed from Kyle.

She nodded. So much started making sense. Taylor had admired Sean and trusted him when she was a kid. He'd been around when she'd had her first personality shift at age eight, and then he'd gone from her life for years. His reemergence in her life had corresponded to when she'd begun acting out again. Her sudden setback at Whispering Pines had happened right after one of Sean's visits. If, like many victims, she had been trying to re-create the relationship with her abuser, Brent Mullen was a perfect answer. He was arrogant, selfish, and looked enough like Sean Walter to be his brother.

And there was something more to consider. "Josh, it's rare that an abuser stops with one victim. There are often chains of victims that go back for years, and if an abuser isn't stopped, those chains can stretch into the future."

"I know," Josh said. "Do you think we could get someone else to corroborate Taylor's testimony? Assuming she's ever able to testify?"

"That's not what I'm worried about. There's a little boy in that house: Sean's new stepbrother, Thomas. That child is in danger. If Sean hasn't already begun to abuse him, I'd bet that it's just a matter of time." Marian Phillips's friendly chatter about how Sean doted on Thomas now made Aimee's stomach churn.

"Everything here is circumstantial, Aimee. It's going to take time to get a search warrant, but I'll get it as fast as is humanly possible."

"We don't need a search warrant to protect that child. I'll go talk to his mother and get her to take the boy out of that house. Or to kick Sean out—it doesn't matter which. All that matters is that he not be allowed any contact with Thomas."

"And tip him off that we're looking at him for the murder? What you've figured out about Sean is important, but I'm pretty sure he also murdered two people, and he needs to be stopped. Now we can search the house for evidence to link him to the murders. Even the most careful murderer takes something away from the scene that can end up incriminating him." Josh crossed his arms over his chest.

Aimee shook her head. This was too much information, too fast. "Wait. Why would he have murdered Stacey and Orrin? I don't understand that."

Elise put in her two cents' worth. "Try this on for size: Sean was helping Orrin with the books for the consulting firm. He knew the names of at least two of the phony subcontractors Orrin was using as fronts to embezzle money from the firm. He'd be able to follow the money trail. What if he confronted Orrin with that information that night, and Orrin countered with the information that he knew Sean had molested Taylor? What if that confrontation escalated and ended up with a man dead on the floor?"

"Do you think Orrin *knew* Sean had raped Taylor? Do you think he knew that and kept it to himself?" Aimee wondered, what kind of father would keep that kind of information to himself? Worse yet, what kind of father would use that information to protect himself?

"It's hard to conceive of a mind that would work like that," Josh admitted. "My first reaction would be to pound the guy's face in, but these people don't think like you and me."

Aimee thought back to her first meetings with the Dawkins. Could Orrin be that much of a monster? She thought over everything that she knew about sociopaths, and the information she had about Orrin Dawkin swirled like pieces in a kaleidoscope to form an entirely new picture of him.

The daredevil behavior. The chilliness. The emotional separation from his family. Stacey Dawkin's depression. The possible sexual harassment at his office. Had there been something about him that wasn't quite right? If he had been a sociopath, he would abuse his family and everyone around him in little ways all the time. Using information to blackmail someone else into silence wouldn't be that big a step.

"It fits with the things you told me about his office." Aimee chewed on her lower lip. "I don't want this to be true, Josh."

"You have no idea how often I think that." He leaned back in his chair and stretched. "I'll start pushing the search warrant through right now. Meanwhile, I'm going to pick up Sean Walter for questioning."

"How long do you think the warrant will take?" Even one more night with a potential molester was too long to leave a little boy unprotected. Aimee shuddered.

"If Judge Leal decides to make my life difficult, it could be a day or two."

"That's unacceptable, Josh. That little boy is in danger!" Aimee stood.

"And has been for the past six months. I hate to say it this way, Aimee, but if the worst has already happened, I doubt another day or two is going to make a difference," he said with a pained expression.

Aimee was livid. "And if it hasn't? If that child hasn't been raped yet? *Then* what?"

"Then what's to say he's going to be raped now? Aimee, this *has* to go forward by the book. I will not screw up a potential conviction for a brutal double homicide because I wasn't willing to take this step by step." He tried to take her hand, but she snatched it away.

Aimee gritted her teeth. They had come so far, yet they were essentially exactly where they were the night they'd met in the emergency room of Mercy Hospital. "Would you be willing to screw up a potential conviction to save a child's life?"

"Of course I would. Exigent circumstances will always trump anything else." Josh brought the front legs of his chair down with a thump.

"That's what this *is*, Josh. You don't see what I see each day. You don't see the damage that goes on for decade after decade in people's lives. Abusers steal everything from these children. They steal their trust. They steal their innocence. They steal their ability to have relationships later. They steal everything before these children even know what is being taken from them.

"None of it can ever be given back fully. Those things are gone forever. Even the ones who manage to heal, bear the scars of those betrayals until the day they die. Even worse, many of them then turn around and perpetrate those same abuses on someone else. Saving Thomas could be the first step in saving a long line of little boys and girls. Isn't that worth stepping outside the lines?"

Josh's eyes flashed. "You may be there mopping up the mess years later, Aimee, but I'm there first on the scene. Don't tell *me* about what kind of pain these sick assholes cause. I'm the one who's there when the blood is still wet and running.

"If that child molester goes free because we can't get Taylor to talk, and I've compromised my chances of nailing the bastard for killing two people, what happens then? How does that safeguard that long line of little boys and girls, Aimee?

"You have to step back and look at the bigger picture. The system isn't perfect, but it's the only system we've got."

"I don't care about the system. I care about that little boy. I care about Taylor."

"And I care about all the other little boys and all

the other Taylors out there. Let me stop the monster who's hurting them, Aimee. Give me the chance to do that."

Aimee bowed her head in defeat. She didn't know how to argue with him. What he said wasn't wrong; there was simply another side to it.

Josh turned to Elise. "We need to get a search warrant for Carl Walter's home and we need it pronto."

Elise nodded. "I'll start the paperwork. But we've still got Leal for a judge, so we're not going to get anything pronto."

"I'll run an ANI. I want everything on the warrant, including all their cars." All Name Index would give them the makes, models, and years of all vehicles owned by Sean Walter.

"Make sure you toss his father and stepmother in there. The kid could be using their cars," Elise pointed out.

"I doubt he bought that Saab he's driving with his graduation money," Aimee observed.

Josh grinned. "Good point. I didn't take you for a car person."

She shrugged. "I have hidden depths."

More than he knew. While he and Elise acted on their plans, Aimee was making one of her own.

A few minutes later, Elise stood up and peered over the top of his cubicle wall. "You about done there, cowboy?"

"I've got things moving, but it'll be another hour or so." He looked up at her. "What do you think we should do in the meantime?"

"I'm considering taking up crocheting. How about you?"

"I'm going to follow Aimee back to her apartment and listen outside the door while she turns all the locks. Then I'm going to come back here and bust that bastard."

Aimee pulled up in front of Carl Walter's home. After Josh had brought her back to her condo, she'd called to make sure that neither Carl nor Sean was at home. Then she'd wrapped a scarf around her mauled neck and driven over here before her nerve left her.

Even with the lowering gray sky above it, the Mediterannean-style house looked picture perfect, inviting and comforting.

She walked up the path and rang the doorbell. Sarah Barlow opened the door. "Hello, Dr. Gannon."

Aimee held out her hand. "Hello, Sarah, do you have a minute to talk?"

"Carl's not here." She glanced behind her into the house as if he might suddenly appear. Aimee wasn't sure if it was out of fear, or if Sarah was looking for guidance. Either way, it spoke volumes about their relationship.

"That's okay. I'd really like to talk to you first." Aimee had no idea how Carl might react to the idea that his son was a pedophile. Carl was a powerful enough personality that if he chose to protect his biological son from charges like these over the safety of his stepson—another man's child—she might not be able to convince Sarah that Thomas was in danger. *Unacceptable.*

"I really don't see how I can be of much help. I didn't know Taylor that well, and I didn't know Orrin and Stacey anywhere near as well as Carl did. Anything I know, Carl will know, plus a bunch of other stuff." She smiled. "He's really smart."

"He is, and I'm guessing he wouldn't want to marry a stupid woman. I'm sure you have plenty to offer that would be helpful to me right now." Aimee hesitated. She didn't want to lay it on too thick. Or to scare Sarah. "And I think I might have some information that would be helpful to you. If I can come in, I'll explain everything."

Sarah thought for a second, then stood aside to let Aimee enter.

"I've got the vehicles." Elise waved a piece of paper at Josh.

"Let's add 'em to the warrant. What's he got?"

Elise peered down at the list and then held it out with her arm. "I swear the type is getting smaller every month."

"You're just too vain to get bifocals." Josh took the paper from her. "You ready to type?"

She nodded.

"They've got a new Toyota Highlander hybrid."

"Nice," Elise said. "Those are snazzy."

"They've got a BMW 350i."

"Also quite nice." Elise kept on typing.

Josh stopped talking and stared at the piece of paper. "Holy *shit*."

"They've got something even better than the

Beemer? What the hell is it?" Elise stood up and looked over Josh's shoulder.

"Carl Walter owns a 1968 Mercury Cougar." Josh stared at Elise.

"So he likes classic cars. What's the big deal?"

"Have you ever seen the taillights on a sixty-eight Cougar? They're very distinctive." It had never even occurred to him. It was right there in front of him, and he hadn't seen it.

"Yeah? How?"

"The taillights are long rectangles divided into three, with a center brake light." Josh grabbed the pen from Elise's hand and scribbled a quick sketch on the back of an envelope. "Look familiar?"

"Holy shit." Elise sat down.

"Exactly." Josh felt like he'd been punched in the gut.

"You think this is what Taylor is trying to tell us? Do you think Taylor saw him at the scene?" Elise looked as poleaxed as Josh felt.

"At the very least, she saw his car. He could have been leaving just as she got home from Jenna Norchester's house." Would the timing have been right? It could be.

Sean could have been driving his father's car. Taylor had seen Sean leaving her house, then had walked in and found her parents dead on her living room floor. She'd been trying to tell them what she'd seen for days, and none of them had been able to understand her. Aimee had been right.

"How fast do you think we can get this warrant through?" Elise asked.

"I don't know. You take it. I need to call Aimee."

"Can I get you some water? Or a soda?" Sarah asked as they walked into the living room.

"No, thank you. I'm fine." Aimee sat on the couch as Sarah sat across from her in one of the easy chairs. "Is Thomas home?"

Sarah blinked. "He's in his room playing. Did you need to talk to him?"

"Not just yet." The most important thing was to warn Sarah to keep Sean as far away from her little boy as possible. She heard her cell phone ring in her purse. Without looking at the caller ID, she reached into her bag and turned it off. "I need to talk to you about Thomas. Are he and Sean close?"

Sarah smiled. "They are. Sean's been amazing. He and Thomas have developed a really special bond, and I'm so grateful. I didn't know how Sean would feel about me, or about his dad having a new family. But he's been so nice to us. He plays with Thomas and takes him to movies and all kinds of stuff."

It was typical for a molester to work on getting a child's trust first, especially a child who might be in a new or precarious position. Thomas would undoubtedly have some anxiety about his new living situation and his mother's new relationship. It was a typical pedophile move to target a child in a vulnerable situation like this, gain his trust, then separate him from other adults that he might trust or confide in. "I see. Does Thomas seem happy to go with Sean?"

"Oh, yes. I think he hero worships him a little. Thomas's biological dad left us when Thomas was just a baby. He wasn't much interested in him then, and he hasn't gotten more interested as time has gone by. Thomas was starved for male attention. Now, with Carl and Sean spending so much time with him, he's on cloud nine."

"Sarah, what I have to say to you is difficult. I don't have proof of what I'm going to tell you, though I expect I will soon. I think it's possible that Sean may have molested Thomas, or may be planning on molesting him."

Sarah sat straight up. "What?"

Aimee began to repeat herself, but Sarah interrupted her. "No. Don't say that again. I heard what you said; it's simply not possible. I don't know why you would come here and say something horrible like that."

"Believe me, I don't *want* to tell you something like this, but I couldn't rest until I'd warned you. I think that Sean raped Taylor Dawkin years ago. I think it's quite possible that he is a sexual predator, and that the time he spends with Thomas is being used to gain your son's confidence and forge a bond that Thomas will be too frightened to break."

"No. That's not true. We can call Thomas in here right this second; he'll tell you himself. I'm *sure* Sean has never touched him inappropriately or anything like that. Thomas would have told me. I would have known. I would have seen it! What kind of a mother do you think I am?" Sarah stood up, her whole body shaking.

Both women froze as they heard the sound of the garage door opening and a car pulling in.

"That's Carl now. He's home for lunch. He'll tell you you're wrong, too. And then you're going to have to leave." Sarah headed for the kitchen.

Aimee hadn't expected Carl to show up in the middle of the afternoon. Maybe she *should* have waited until they had everything set with search warrants—but that could take days. If there was any chance that she could make sure Thomas didn't become a victim, or put a stop to his victimization, it was worth it.

Carl strode in ahead of Sarah, a concerned look on his face. "Dr. Gannon, what kind of accusations are you making against my son?"

And then Sean walked in.

CHAPTER
27

J osh called Aimee's office number. After four rings, it went to voice mail and he hung up. Then he tried her home number, which also went to voice mail. When her cell phone did the same, he slammed the phone down with a curse.

"No luck reaching Aimee?" Elise asked.

"None." He drummed his fingers on the desk. Where the hell was she? She needed to know about the car, that she'd been right. It was all tied together. "How long do you thing that search warrant is going to take?"

"I have no idea."

"I'm going to talk to the captain. Maybe he can turn some screws." Josh headed up to the administrative offices on the upper floor.

How could she salvage this situation? She could leave and let the police handle it the rest of the way. But how could she leave Thomas here? How could she walk away, knowing what kind of danger he was in?

She couldn't.

"I'm sorry, Mr. Walter. I know this kind of information is hard to hear, but I don't feel I can keep quiet knowing there's a young boy in this house who, if he hasn't been victimized yet, probably will be soon. I suspect that your son, Sean, is a pedophile."

Sean's face went a ghastly white. Carl's went beet red. "You think Sean is *what*?" he thundered, crossing the room to loom over Aimee.

"I think he might be a pedophile. I'm reasonably certain he raped Taylor Dawkin when she was about eight years old." Aimee refused to cringe from Carl. She was done cringing. It was what he wanted, but it was not going to work for him today. *Not ever.*

Sean pushed forward. "Did Taylor tell you that? Has she started speaking?"

"Sean, be quiet." Carl kept his eyes on Aimee.

Aimee held his gaze. "No. Not yet. She will soon, though—now that I know what to protect her from."

Sean sank down into the chair behind his father and buried his head in his hands. "It's almost a relief."

"I told you to be quiet, Sean," Carl said from between clenched teeth. "This woman doesn't know anything. She's just throwing around a bunch of psychological mumbo jumbo to get a rise out of us."

"No, Dad," Sean said, sitting up and looking at his father. "It's not mumbo jumbo. I should know—I've been seeing a therapist for close to seven years now."

"You what?" Carl glanced back over his shoulder at Sean.

Aimee started to edge toward the door. Sarah now had enough information to watch out for her son, and the moment of confrontation was often a violent one. She needed to get out of here now.

"I've been seeing a psychologist, Dad. I had to do something. I wasn't going to live to see twenty-one if I kept on the way I was." Sean looked up at his father.

"What the hell did you need to see a psychologist for?" Carl demanded, now looming over Sean.

Aimee moved closer to the door.

"Dad, don't you think it's a little late to pretend that everything's okay? I'm twenty-two years old. I'm an alcoholic and a reformed drug addict. And Dr. Gannon's right: I raped Taylor Dawkin when I was thirteen years old and she was eight. I did it in our garage—practically under your nose."

"It's ridiculous to haul us up here and drag us over the coals for not making progress on this case, and then refuse to help us get a goddamn search warrant." Josh was on his feet, hands braced on the captain's desk, leaning forward to get right in his face.

Captain Gonzalez ignored him. He'd been on the force too many years to be intimidated by anyone yelling at him. "Sit down, Josh. I'll make some calls."

Josh sat down and looked at his watch. It was already after noon. "This thing is coming to a head, and I'm sure I'll find some answers in that house. *If* I can get there before Sean Walter destroys whatever evidence might still be there."

"I'm calling, all right? Sit tight for a second, will you?" Gonzalez started dialing.

Josh sat down.

―――

"I told you to shut up, Sean." Carl backhanded Sean across the face.

Sarah screamed.

Aimee made a break for the door. She didn't make it two steps before Carl grabbed her by her hair. She tried to twist away from him, but he grabbed her arm and twisted it up behind her back.

With her head yanked backward, Aimee could see the vein pulsing in Carl's forehead. His breath sounded harsh in her ears. "Where do you think you're going?"

A small voice from the doorway said, "What's going on?" Thomas had come down the hall and stood now in the entry into the living room.

Sarah started toward him, but Carl whirled and glared at her. "Stay right where you are," he said, his voice quiet but full of menace.

She cowered back toward the kitchen and dropped her gaze to the floor.

"Dad, don't do this," Sean said. "You don't have to do this."

"Will you shut up?" Carl screamed. "How many times do I have to tell you to shut your trap?"

Sean stood, blood dripping from his nose. "I'm done keeping quiet, Dad. I have been trying and trying to keep the lid on all this, but it's too big. It's going to come out, and you might as well accept it. I can't protect you. No one can protect you."

"Accept it? Are you insane? Do you have any idea what I've done to keep your little secret about Taylor? Do you have any idea the lengths I've gone to? And you just blurt it out to little Miss Fancy Pants?" Carl gave Aimee's arm a vicious jerk.

Aimee cried out. Thomas still stood in the doorway, tears welling in his eyes. She mouthed the word "run" to him, but he took a step toward her instead.

"I know exactly what you did, Dad. You killed them, didn't you? You killed Orrin and Stacey." Sean buried his head in his hands.

Carl's grip on her arm loosened. "You knew?" he whispered. "You figured it out?"

"It didn't take a rocket scientist, Dad."

"Do you know why?" Carl hissed.

"I'm guessing it had to do with Orrin's embezzling." Sean shut his eyes. "I should never have told you. I should have gone to Orrin and let him straighten it out himself. I had no idea you'd do something like that. Not to Orrin."

"I had no choice," Carl screamed, yanking Aimee's arm up again and bringing tears to her eyes. "You left me with no choice."

"And how did I do that, Dad? You didn't have to murder him. You could have called in the authorities."

"Not when he knew that you raped his daughter."

Sean stepped backward as if shoved. "Orrin knew?" he whispered. "He knew?"

"He'd figured it out. Thanks to this bitch." Carl shoved Aimee away and she fell to the floor, landing hard on her left arm. She felt a snap and screamed as pain shot up her arm.

Thomas dashed past her and into his mother's arms at the other side of the room. Sarah crouched and grabbed her son to her, pressing his face into her chest as if to shield him from seeing any more.

Carl glared over at Aimee. "Orrin said the doctor here had started asking questions. When did Taylor's personality change? Did she seem afraid of someone or something in particular? What might have happened to make her change again? Once he had someone showing him how to put it all together, it didn't take him long to figure it out.

"Orrin told me that if I went to the authorities about the embezzling, he'd tell them about you. I couldn't let him do that. You were just a kid. The stupid girl was probably asking for it anyway, following you around like a puppy dog all the time. She should have expected to get kicked.

"I couldn't let Orrin keep bleeding the company dry of all our cash, either. So like always, I did what I had to. I do what needs to be done, and I don't look back."

Aimee's mind reeled. She had been right, and terribly wrong. All of this had its roots back in Taylor's past. She looked over at Sarah, whose horror was clear on her face.

Sean stared at Carl. "He was your business partner and your friend for over a decade, Dad. And that's all you have to say? You did what needed to be done?"

"Do you want me to cry? What difference would it make? It's done. I wish it hadn't come to that. Orrin and I were . . . uniquely suited to each other. It's going to be extremely difficult for me to find someone to replace him."

"That's *it*? You regret that you'll need a new business

partner?" Sean shook his head. "I think my shrink was right, Dad. I think you're a fucking psychopath."

Carl's face turned purple. "Watch it with the name-calling, sonny boy. It won't be hard to tar you with the same brush. Who lured Taylor Dawkin into the garage?"

Sean braced his shoulders and confronted his father. "And who taught me to be the way I am?"

"What the hell does that mean?" Carl demanded.

Sean's Adam's apple went up and down. "That was the real issue, wasn't it, Dad? You were afraid that if people found out about what I'd done to Taylor, then they'd find out about the years you spent raping me."

The phone rang on the captain's desk. "Gonzalez here," he said, then listened a few seconds.

Josh was up and out of his chair.

"How long?" he asked and waited again. "He'll be right over." He hung up and looked at Josh. "You've got a search warrant. Judge Leal's assistant has it waiting for you."

Josh took off at a run. The first stop was downstairs to pick up Elise.

She took one look at him barreling down the narrow hallways, grabbed her jacket off her chair, and was right behind him by the time they hit the parking lot.

"It's signed?" she asked as she buckled herself into the passenger seat.

"Yep, and we're on our way."

"Have you been able to reach Aimee?"

He shook his head as he squealed out of the parking space. "Still no answer."

"She'll just have to find out about all the fun and games later." Elise braced her hand on the dashboard as Josh took a corner fast. "It would be nice if we actually arrived ourselves, though, don't you think?"

Josh tried to calm down. Elise was right. Five minutes one way or another wouldn't make a difference—he hoped. "Call crime scene, will you? We're going to want them there fast."

Elise was already pulling her cell phone off her belt. "What's our ETA?" she asked after she hung up.

"Five minutes," Josh said.

"Rape you? Is that what your mother told you? Is that why she said she left? Because I raped you?" Carl snarled at Sean.

Aimee tried to get up, but pain flashed through her like lightning as she put weight on her left arm.

"Mom didn't tell me anything." Sean faced his father squarely. "I'm not sure she even knows. She did know there was something seriously wrong with me, and sent me to one therapist after another until we found one who could help. I'm pretty sure he saved my life. At least what's left of it."

"And he's the one who told you that you'd been raped?" Carl stepped closer to Sean, attempting to intimidate as he had with Aimee.

Sean cowered for a second, and then gritted his teeth and stood straight. Aimee's heart clenched. She should have seen it before—old habits die hard. Sean was frightened of his father. He might be older and stronger now, but the memory of being a small child completely at this man's mercy would never die.

"No one had to tell me I'd been raped, Dad. No one had to tell me who raped me. You stopped doing it by the time I turned nine, but that doesn't mean I don't remember it."

"The memories of a child are unreliable. Any lawyer or judge will tell you that. I don't know what you think you remember, but you're wrong."

"I'm *not* wrong, Dad. Where do you think I got the idea to rape Taylor? Normal kids don't rape other kids. I don't know how much worse it would have gotten if Mom hadn't wised up and taken us as far away from you as she could."

"And yet here you are, crawling back for more," Carl sneered. "How bad could it have been if you wanted to come live with me again?"

"I only came back for one reason: to stop you from doing to Thomas what you did to me."

Josh dug his cell phone out of his pants pocket and tossed it to Elise. "Call Aimee again, will you? Her numbers are all in my contact list."

Elise took the phone, but didn't start dialing. "She's probably in the shower or something. You know she got home safe and sound."

Josh took a turn at ten miles more per hour than he should have. "I have a bad feeling. Call Aimee."

Elise's eyebrows rose, then she flipped open the phone and started dialing.

"To Thomas?" Sarah Barlow finally spoke. "You were going to . . . do those things to Thomas? My Thomas?"

Thomas whimpered and buried himself deeper in his mother's arms.

Aimee finally made it into a sitting position, her left arm useless, nausea and pain rolling over her in deep, throbbing waves. She fought back the urge to vomit.

"I would never hurt Thomas," Carl said, his tone suddenly syrupy smooth, the rage gone from his face.

Chills went up Aimee's spine. The man was a chameleon, switching from one emotion to another in the blink of an eye. Aimee suspected he didn't feel any of them. He'd just learned how to show them to the outside world. Sean was right; Carl was a psychopath, a man without a conscience.

"I love Thomas. You know that. I want us to be a family. Don't listen to what Sean is saying; he's jealous. If I'm such a monster, why didn't he report me to the authorities?" Carl smiled at Sarah.

"Fifteen years after the fact? Who would have listened, Dad? What authorities would have done anything with that? Besides . . ." Sean's eyes filled with tears.

"What?" Carl asked. "Besides *what*?"

Tears rolled down Sean's cheeks. "I still love you. Despite everything, you're still my father. I couldn't do that to you. I couldn't expose you like that to the whole world."

Aimee saw the anguish on Sean's face and also the shame. She knew all too well the paralysis shame caused. She knew the anguish it left in its wake as it boiled through one's system.

"You accuse me of raping you, and then you say you're here because you love me? You are one sorry excuse for a person." Carl practically spat as he spoke.

"You think I don't know that? I see the contempt on your face when you look at me, but it's not even a tenth of the contempt I feel for myself. Why do you think I started drinking when I was fifteen? What did you think those suicide attempts when I was nineteen and twenty were about? That's the *real* reason I came back. The idea of you doing that to another boy, making him feel the way I do, was too unbearable."

"You are such a pussy, Sean. So I had a little fun with you when you were a kid. It's nothing more than my father and his brother did to me, and you don't see me whining about how they ruined my life. They made me strong. I took it like a man then, and I take it like a man now that it's my turn."

"Not anymore, you won't." Sean started toward his father.

"That's Aimee's car," Josh said as they pulled up to the Walter home.

Elise turned to him. "Why would she be here?"

Josh gritted his teeth. "She's here warning Sarah Barlow about Sean. I'd put money on it."

"Why the hell would she do that? You explained why she needed to stay away."

"Because she's convinced he's going to rape his step-brother, the one whose puppy he buried." Josh got out of the car.

"And you *let* her?" Elise got out of her side.

"Have you noticed that there's not a lot of permission being asked on her part? Ever?" Josh started up the driveway.

"I'd tell you you're a lucky son of a bitch if I wasn't so worried about her right now." Elise fell in step with him.

Carl grabbed a heavy crystal vase of cut flowers, heaved it up, and cracked Sean across the skull hard enough to shatter the vase. The connection made a sickening sound, like a ripe melon being dropped on the ground, and Sean sank to the floor.

Sarah screamed again.

Aimee again tried to scramble for the door, but Carl's voice stopped her. "Don't move a muscle."

She looked back. Carl had grabbed Thomas and held the little boy against him, a piece of jagged glass pressed against the boy's jugular.

"If I cut him, he'll bleed out before you even get to your car." Carl's voice was even, but his chest was heaving.

"He's just a child," Aimee pleaded.

"True. He is only a child," Carl crooned, swaying back and forth a little bit. "A beautiful child, isn't he?"

"Please, Carl," Sarah begged. "Please don't hurt him."

"Shut up," Carl snarled over his shoulder. "Shut your stupid mouth, Sarah."

Thomas began to cry, and Carl leaned down and kissed the top of his head. "Hush, Thomas," he said in honeyed tones. "Hush now. You know I love you. I adore boys this age. Just ask your big brother. We're going to have so much fun together. You'll see."

"I don't want to," Thomas cried. "I want to go be with Mom."

Carl pressed the piece of glass against the boy's throat, and Thomas screamed as a bright red dribble of blood ran down his neck.

Then the front door burst open, and Josh and Elise charged in with guns drawn.

Josh took in the scene in an instant. Aimee was on the floor, her arm cradled to herself. Sean was on the floor, blood flowing from his head, but his chest rose and fell. He was still breathing.

Carl stood with a jagged piece of glass pressed against the little boy's neck.

"Let the boy go, Carl," Josh said. "It's over. Let him go."

He had a good, clean shot to Carl's head. He could easily take him out.

"I don't think so, Detective Wolf." Carl's voice shook a little and his eyes didn't leave the gun.

Josh took another step into the room, and Carl shifted toward Sean's body. "There's no way out of this for you, Carl. You might as well let the boy go." From the corner of his eye, Josh thought he saw Sean twitch.

Carl shook his head and laughed, hysterical and high-pitched. "You might as well shoot me, Detective. I'm not going to give up."

"Come on, Mr. Walter." Elise walked forward, too, boxing Carl in with Sean at his feet and Aimee just a few yards away. "Nobody needs to get hurt here. Let's end this now before it gets any worse for you."

"Worse for me? How much worse can it get?" Carl was panting now; sweat had sprung up on his forehead.

Sean Walter had twitched again; Josh was sure of it.

"Killing a child in cold blood? No jury would ever let you go. But Orrin and Stacey? It wasn't premeditated. You might be able to convince a jury of that," Aimee said, her voice strained.

"Shut up!" Carl screamed. "This would have all gone away if it wasn't for you. You couldn't just leave it alone! You had to keep asking questions, sticking your nose in where it didn't belong. This is all *your* fault." He stepped toward Aimee but Thomas didn't move, and for just one fraction of a second, Carl was off balance.

That was all Sean needed. He straightened his legs, entangling them with Carl's, and scissored them hard. Carl Walter came down with a crash.

As Carl fell, Sean grabbed Thomas and swept him out of harm's way. Elise leaped forward, planted a knee in Carl's back, and cuffed him practically before his face hit the floor.

And Josh scooped Aimee off the floor, held her in his arms, and prayed he would never ever have to let her go.

———

Aimee clung to Josh. She was safe. Thomas and Sean and Sarah were safe. She repeated it to herself until she could accept that it was true.

"How did you get here?" she asked, still not letting go.

"When we ran the ANI to see what vehicles were registered to the house, I found out that Carl owned a Mercury Cougar. It has a very distinctive set of taillights. It's the pattern that Taylor's been drawing."

It all clicked into place. "Taylor must have seen Carl driving away from the house in the Cougar. She saw the taillights. Then she went in the house and found her parents dead on the floor. It all crashed down on her. Sean raped her in the garage behind that same car. The taillights must have seemed like a symbol of destruction, of death and pain and humiliation. That's why she painted them on the wall. That's what she was trying to tell us."

"I still thought it was all Sean. Everything pointed to him." Josh shook his head.

"For good reason. He figured out that his father had killed Orrin and Stacey, and was trying to protect him." It was amazing what the parent/child bond could withstand.

"That part I still don't get. Why would he do that?"

"Do you love your father, Josh?"

"Of course."

She shrugged. "There you have it."

"My father didn't rape me or kill anyone. His biggest fault is pulling his pants up too high."

Aimee shook her head. "It doesn't matter. He's still

your father." She looked over at Sean with new eyes. Another little boy who might still be saved. He'd certainly worked hard to save himself. Her heart broke for him, even knowing the monstrous thing he'd done to Taylor more than a decade before. Then he'd been a victim, creating more victims in his wake, yet somehow he'd found the strength to change himself, and try to change the horrible path his stepbrother had been on.

Sean had chosen not to be a victim anymore. He'd bear the scars of what had happened to him forever, but he'd chosen not to be defined by those scars.

She could make the same choice.

She pushed herself away from Josh's broad chest and looked up into his eyes. "I was so scared."

"It's over now," he assured her.

But he was wrong, in a way. Events like this were never over. What had happened in that living room had changed her, just as what had happened with Kyle had changed her. This time, though, she wouldn't let it put her life on hold. She had so much to live for, so much to open herself to.

"No," she said. "It's just beginning."

And she pulled him to her for a kiss.

CHAPTER
28

Three months later

S ean slammed the trunk of the BMW closed and dusted his hands off on his jeans. "Thanks for coming to see me off."

"I wanted to say good-bye," Aimee said. "And to wish you well."

Josh slid an arm around her waist and she leaned into him. It wasn't easy to see Sean again. It would have been easy to let all the anger and fear wash over her again, but she held it at bay.

Sean scratched his head. "I appreciate it. There are lots of people who are glad to see me leave, but not too many wish me well. I'd sort of hoped that Sarah would understand and let me say good-bye to Thomas, but I can see her side of it."

"Maybe she'll come around," she said. Aimee didn't think so, but it was possible. She placed her hand over Josh's. Anything was possible.

"Yeah," he said, the pain evident in his eyes. "Maybe someday."

He opened the car door.

Josh came forward and stuck out his hand. "Good luck, man."

"Thanks." Sean shook his hand, then turned to Aimee. "You'll tell Taylor that I said good-bye, right?"

She nodded.

"Make sure she knows that I'll never bother her again. But if she . . . if she ever needs to talk to me, to yell at me . . . I don't know. If she ever needs to kick me in the balls as hard as she can, all she has to do is call."

Aimee nodded. "I'll tell her."

Taylor was living in Redding now with Marian's family. She had a long road ahead of her, but she was making progress. Remembering what Sean had done to her all those years ago had been the first step. The anger that was buried so deep for so long was now very much on the surface. She understood in an intellectual sense that Sean had been as much or even more of a victim than she had been, but she wasn't ready to forgive him yet. She might never be. In the end, that would be Taylor's decision to make. Sean seemed to understand that.

He got in the BMW, shut the door, and rolled down the window. "Thanks again, Aimee. For everything." He put the car in reverse and backed down the driveway.

"He's a very sad young man, isn't he?" Josh murmured.

She leaned against the warm breadth of his chest. "He is. He's come a very long way. He may not have gone about things in exactly the right way, but what he tried to do was very brave."

Josh kissed the spot on her neck that always made her shiver. "He's not the only brave one."

She turned and kissed him, still amazed at how good and how right that felt, then rested her head against his chest.

"Are you okay?" he asked, his voice a low rumble.

She smiled. "Never better."

Sexy suspense that sizzles

FROM POCKET BOOKS!

Laura Griffin
THREAD OF FEAR
She says this will be her last case.
A killer plans to make sure it is.

**Don't miss the electrifying trilogy from
New York Times bestselling author Cindy Gerard!**

SHOW NO MERCY
The sultry heat hides the deadliest threats—
and exposes the deepest desires.

TAKE NO PRISONERS
A dangerous attraction—spurred by revenge—
reveals a savage threat that can't be ignored.

WHISPER NO LIES
An indecent proposal reveals a simmering desire—
with deadly consequences.

Available wherever books are sold or at www.simonandschuster.com